Lewinson

PRAISE FOR *WE WERE MOTHERS*

"A close-knit community in a seemingly idyllic town is torn apart when a pretty college student goes missing and the first of many dark secrets is uncovered. *We Were Mothers* is a twisting tale of small-town complicity and deceit with some astute insights into marriage and motherhood. The escalating tension and the many surprises will keep readers urgently turning pages. An engrossing read!"

—Mary McCluskey, author of *Intrusion* and *The Long Deception*

WE WERE MOTHERS

KATIE SISE

This is a work of fiction. Names, characters, organizations, places, events, and incidents are either products of the author's imagination or are used fictitiously.

Published by Little A, New York

www.apub.com

ISBN-13 (hardcover): 9781503903623
ISBN-10 (hardcover): 1503903621
ISBN-13 (paperback): 9781503903616
ISBN-10 (paperback): 1503903613

Cover design by Kimberly Glyder

Printed in the United States of America

To Dan Mandel, for believing.
To Luke, William, Isabel, and Eloise, the children who made me a mother, the best thing I've ever been.

We were women who wanted more than they could give us.
Dangerous women? No, of course not!
We were mothers. Shouldn't that count for something?

PART I

THE DAY MIRA MADSEN DISAPPEARED

CORA

3:39 p.m.

Swooning over a man who wasn't her husband made Cora feel terribly guilty, but how could anyone not swoon over Jeremy? His lashes were thick and dark, his tanned skin glowed, and his built frame towered just the right number of inches over six feet. It made things hard. Not hard like fighting in a war or raising toddlers, more like a deep ache in Cora's belly that never let up, no matter how many times she'd stood next to Jeremy at summer barbecues she hosted like this one, praying he wouldn't see the beads of sweat trailing between her legs. Cora tried to tell herself it wasn't entirely her fault, but she knew deep down that it was. She should be stronger, or more in love with her own husband. Or maybe she should volunteer at the nursing home or the women's prison to gain perspective. Yes, *perspective*: she would try that.

But today, on the second birthday of her beloved twins, George and Lucy, Cora took in the dark ghost of stubble along Jeremy's jaw and forgot all about perspective.

"So I usually nap them from one to three," she heard herself say, "but George always wakes up forty-five minutes into the nap, and then there's this whole soothing process I have to do with 'Wheels on the Bus,' and I sing the verses in Spanish, because George actually seems to find the language soothing." Why couldn't she think of anything more interesting to talk about? "Anyway," she went on, racking her brain for something fascinating to say. What did she used to talk about before having children? Sex? No, that would be inappropriate. Drugs? She'd never done them. Rock 'n' roll was out of the question; she'd spent most of her life avoiding the topic of music because she loved top 40 songs so much. Maybe she'd never actually been interesting?

"Being a mother sounds like hard work," Jeremy said kindly.

Warm air gusted between them, carrying the scent of barbecued chicken, and Cora felt herself blush. It was such a ridiculous conversation. If she'd ever overheard it before she'd had kids, she would have felt so sorry for the woman saying it. And sometimes she did feel sorry for herself! Life had gotten sort of small lately. "So is Jade adjusting to life in Ravendale?" Cora asked before she could think about it too much more.

"I think so," Jeremy said.

He thought so? Hadn't they talked about it?

Cora battled the urge to gaze into Jeremy's hazel eyes. She asked herself the very same question she'd been asking since his and Jade's wedding, when she stood by Jade's side as her maid of honor on that bright white beach in Turks and Caicos:

Who in God's name marries someone this hot?

Cora couldn't imagine sipping coffee in her bathrobe across from someone who looked like a famous actor. But maybe that was it; Jade had majored in theater at Vanderbilt. Maybe she liked waking up and feeling like she was in a movie.

Before Jeremy could answer, fingers lighted on Cora's arm, and she turned to see Jade staring with big green eyes flecked with gold. Behind her, the parents Cora had met at Ravendale Moms and Tots scrambled after their toddlers on George and Lucy's new swing set and miniature rock wall.

"I miss Maggie," Jade said.

"Me, too," Cora said, because she did miss her little sister, but also because it was what Jade and Cora always said to each other. It was like a secret handshake.

"Do you need anything from the kitchen?" Jade asked.

Cora shook her head. She waited a beat, thinking Jade would ask Jeremy if he wanted anything, too, but she didn't.

Cora glanced at Jeremy, who watched his wife saunter across the patio. Were they all right? No matter how close Cora and Jade were, Jade had always saved her real secrets for Maggie.

"Mama! Juice!"

A sticky hand slipped beneath the hem of Cora's khaki skirt. She'd kept the skirt since college, even though she was pretty sure khaki skirts were out of fashion. Really, she probably should have worn skinny jeans like everyone else. She was still technically in her early thirties (did her next birthday, thirty-three, count as midthirties?), and even though she wasn't beautiful like Jade, her ass was definitely still high enough for skinny jeans, no matter what that salesgirl at The Bumble Bee had said when she'd begrudgingly let Cora purchase them. Ravendale was filled with statuesque women, and sometimes the shopgirls just didn't know how to dress someone who was five one.

Cora glanced down to her son's hand against her freckled thigh, its chubby, starfish shape clammy and perfect. "George," she said, the sight of him making her even warmer. There was something both calming and terrifying about her babies, a soupy mix of feelings that had changed her in unimaginable ways, not so unlike Maggie's death. Maggie died six years ago in Ravendale, just after her graduation from Vanderbilt, and now Cora wondered if leaving New York City to move back to Ravendale had been a mistake. She saw Maggie everywhere: on the elementary school playground's swings, her skinny legs pumping furiously; trying on feather boas in the costume shop for her eighth-grade play; and scouring the library on Main Street for any books she hadn't already read twice. Cora saw Maggie flipping through design magazines in their mom's sunroom and painting her toenails on the lawn; she saw Maggie seated across from her at Buzzed, sipping lattes sprinkled with cinnamon. And then there was the evidence of Maggie on Cora's children: her son, George, had Maggie's bow-shaped lips; her daughter, Lucy, had her dark eyes. Every image and memory of Maggie clawed at Cora's insides like broken glass.

"Juice," George said, and his hand climbed so high Cora had to do a squirmy dance to avoid exposing the mesh postpartum underwear she got at the hospital and still sometimes wore. They were so comfortable!

"Careful," Jeremy murmured. He reached to catch Cora's arm, but he was too late. The squirming sent Cora off-balance, and she spilled white wine all over George's blond curls.

"Oh, sweetie, sorry," she said, trying to balance her glass while wiping the wine from George's hair. It was getting in his eyes, and his mouth maybe, too. Could he get drunk this way? Where was her husband? Why was George just wandering around the party by himself? So many times in public with the twins, Cora wanted to pull her hair out and scream *Sam!* at the top of her lungs, but she always worried the other mothers would call her deranged behind her back. Or maybe right to her face? Just last week one of the mothers had commented on her *tendency to hover*, which was confusing, because the twins were only two. Wasn't hovering still the correct strategy?

Jeremy leaned closer to help brush the wine off George's head. Cora smelled his minty breath. Of course he had fresh breath.

"Mama was having a conversation, so next time you'll have to say *excuse me*," she said slowly to George, trying to get back to okay. Guilt flashed through her like it always did—the wine, Jeremy—it always felt like she wasn't getting something right.

"You good, buddy?" Jeremy asked George. He seemed to really enjoy being George's godfather, but he was the kind of man you couldn't leave alone with small children. Once Cora had asked him to watch George at an outdoor party like this one so she could run to the bathroom, and she returned to find Jeremy immersed in a conversation while George toddled unchaperoned toward the stream. Cora never said anything to him, because that wasn't her way, but it struck her as odd. Terrible accidents happened all the time. Wasn't Jeremy concerned about that?

"Juice!" George said for the third time, his eyes squinting against the sunlight. Cora usually made her twins wear floppy hats, but the hats were so dorky looking she knew the birthday photos would come out better without them.

"He's getting tall," Jeremy said to Cora, and she smiled. Compliments about her children made her so happy! She opened her mouth to attribute George's healthy size to the twenty-one months of breastfeeding she'd done, but then snapped it shut. It was the kind of thing she'd caught herself saying to other mothers, and she was trying to stop because she had a feeling it made people hate her a little. Plus, she didn't want Jeremy thinking of her boobs like udders, like Sam did. (It wasn't a secret. The last time she'd tried to get Sam to touch them, he'd balked. *Just never know what might come out of those things!* he'd said.)

Here came Sam now, carrying their daughter, Lucy, and clutching two juice boxes. Cora fell in love with him all over again at moments like these. He was so capable, such a natural father. Of course he had juice!

"Jeremy," said Sam, clapping him on the back in that meaty way husbands who used to be college athletes do.

"Congratulations," Jeremy said.

"Kept them alive for two years," Sam said, grinning.

Dad jokes. Cora fidgeted, itching a mosquito bite on her elbow. She wanted Jeremy back to herself—it was something about the way he actually looked at her and listened, even if she was just talking about nap schedules—and then she hated herself for wanting it, especially in the presence of her daughter. What if Lucy sensed something? She was so perceptive. All Cora wanted was for George and Lucy to feel safe in the world, to know there was nothing that could compromise their family. Not even Jeremy.

"Where's Jade?" Sam asked Jeremy, stabbing a straw into the juice box. He seemed entirely unaware of Lucy rubbing her crotch against his chest.

"Lucy has to go to the bathroom," Cora said. She pulled Lucy from Sam's arms and turned to Jeremy. "Excuse us. We're potty training."

"Up!" George said. "Juice! Up!"

Cora took off with Lucy, heat rising to her cheeks as she maneuvered over the patio. Why did Jeremy have to work out so much and look like a soap star? He spent an hour each day at that little gym in town with its neat rows of free weights. He always tried to get Sam to go with him on Saturday mornings, but Cora gently reminded Sam that he was a father and that weekends with the twins were precious. And besides, Sam escaped to hike Castle Point for long enough stretches to count as a workout, so it wasn't like she was being irresponsible by keeping him from cardiovascular health. Jeremy used to invite Sam to play golf at the country club before the twins came, but Sam couldn't stand how Jeremy lied about his score. Cora wanted to point out that Sam lied about unimportant things, too, like his height (he was five nine but said five ten), and once, his cholesterol. Cora noticed adults telling white lies all the time, but if you were going to lie, shouldn't you wait until it was absolutely necessary?

Cora checked over her shoulder to make sure George was fine with Sam—her twins didn't hide their preference for her—and Jeremy caught her eye. Cora quickly turned away and kept moving, trying to shrug off his gaze. He often looked like he was on the precipice of telling her something important, and it made Cora think back to the night her little sister died. Both Jeremy and Sam had been with Maggie when she died, and Maggie and Jeremy had history: they'd slept together a few times when she first got to Vanderbilt. So what if Maggie had told

Jeremy something—a secret, or a final thought? Would he ever tell Cora?

Cora would never flat-out ask Jeremy, because she mostly had those kinds of conversations in her own head. She desperately missed the safe space math took up inside her brain while she was working toward her still-unfinished PhD. Math wasn't life or death: it was art; it was beautiful. And now all this, with her sister dying and her becoming a wife and mother; everything felt weighty and exhausting.

Anyway, Cora didn't think Jeremy would tell her anything of value about Maggie's death even if he knew something. Jade said Jeremy was more private than any man she'd ever met, and that she saw secrets behind his eyes, even when they were in bed. It made Cora thank God for Sam, who was simpler. Sam might get red and sweaty during sex—and there was that dumb look that passed over his face right before he finished—but at least he wasn't complicated. Who could ever manage a man's feelings and raise children at the same time?

Cora clutched Lucy tighter, trying to forget about Jeremy as she forced a smile at her party guests, her *best* smile, the one that said: *Aren't we having so much fun!*

"Are you having fun, sweetheart?" Cora murmured into Lucy's ear, smelling her lavender shampoo, kissing the smooth skin of her earlobe. Holding her close made Cora feel grounded, like her arms were meant to do this, to be a mother.

"Mama, more juice?" Lucy asked.

Those Goddamn juice boxes. Cora had insisted on a water-only party, but Sam forgot (or never listened in the first place) and returned with an economy case of juice.

No high-fructose corn syrup, he'd said, pointing to the label when she protested.

"You can have more juice in a little—" Cora started, but then something needle-sharp crashed into her leg. She looked down to see a little boy holding a plastic dinosaur with blood on its teeth. Fake blood? Her blood?

"He's a plane! A dino-plane!" the little boy said, and as much as her leg hurt, she couldn't help but think about how verbal the boy was. *A dino-plane?* That was clever. Were her twins clever enough? She'd drunk Crystal Light during pregnancy, and now she found herself really regretting the artificial sweeteners. Cora squeezed Lucy tighter and walked past Asher Finch, the freckled college boy who lifeguarded at the pool. She'd invited him and his family because they lived directly behind her, and because wouldn't it be awkward if they were all barbecuing and partying while Asher Finch was lying dejectedly on his hammock?

"Cora!" called a woman's voice.

Cora turned to see her next-door neighbor Laurel Madsen standing on the patio. Laurel's round sunglasses glinted, and Cora smiled at the sight of her immaculately put-together new friend. Cora had lived next door to Laurel for nearly two years, but only just lately had she felt they were developing a real friendship, and today, at the party, it was nice to see a new friend like Laurel mixing with an old friend like Jade. Jade was as close to a sister as Cora would ever have again, not that anyone could ever take Maggie's place, and now that they were all back in Ravendale, Cora wanted to make sure Jade felt included in her group of friends. Jade and Jeremy had only recently moved back, and even though Ravendale was only an hour north of New York City, it was a different world, and it could be isolating. Especially when their husbands worked such long hours. And not that Cora even had that many friends here, but she was trying. Tomorrow she was co-chairing a fundraiser with Laurel (at Laurel's request), and the whole thing made her feel exceptionally good, like she belonged here in Ravendale, and like she wasn't just some impostor returning to her hometown to raise children. The fundraiser was all Laurel's idea, taking place at the local gym where a guest instructor was teaching a self-defense class. Fees from the class were being donated to a nonprofit that raised awareness about sexual harassment and assault, and planning the fundraiser felt so *important* and *adult*, even if Cora had no desire to take a self-defense class first thing on a Monday morning. A few weeks ago, when Laurel had asked Cora to co-plan the event, Cora had immediately said, *I'd love to!* And then she'd headed straight to the Lululemon outlet store to buy an outfit that almost made her look like a person who worked out.

"Hi, Laurel!" Cora said, sashaying across the patio. She'd been pleased when the entire Madsen family had RSVP'd yes to the Paperless Post invite she'd spent way too much time making. Laurel's daughters, Anna and Mira, had come, along with Laurel's husband, Dash, a gorgeous, brooding surgeon. *What is it about surgeons?* Cora wondered, recalling the image of Dr. Madsen driving up the street in his Range Rover wearing scrubs. It was so cliché, and yet . . .

Both Anna and Mira babysat for Cora's twins, but Anna was Cora's favorite. It wasn't even that she was so naturally good with kids, but she seemed so overprotective and safe with them, and that counted for more as far as Cora was concerned. Plus, Anna always said yes to babysitting, no matter how last-minute Cora called, unlike Mira. And Mira was so stunningly beautiful it was a little off-putting; she acted like babysitting was a chore, and it made Cora nervous, actually. She found herself trying to say things that might impress Mira.

"What a beautiful home you and Sam have," Laurel said with a big smile. "I've never been inside before today."

Cora shifted Lucy onto her other hip. "That can't be true, can it?" she asked, knowing it was. Every time Cora had invited her, Laurel turned her down, citing already-made plans. Cora didn't take it personally. She figured it was an older-mom thing; she'd noticed the way nearly all the Ravendale moms with older children already had their tight group of friends. They weren't desperately looking for companionship, like Cora and the other new moms. Even the mothers who had third or fourth children the same age as George and Lucy seemed totally uninterested in making playdates with Cora. They shuffled their children in and out of story times and Musical Mother Goose classes without making eye contact; instead, they stared down at their phones like they had somewhere far better to be. Cora looked forward to the time when her children were older and she no longer reeked of desperation. She didn't want to wish away these years when the twins were little, but, God, the sheer loneliness.

Still, tomorrow: the fundraiser! She'd meet all of Laurel's friends!

"Thank you so much for coming," Cora said as Lucy squirmed in her arms. Cora really needed to get her daughter to the bathroom, but there was an all-consuming tug toward Laurel. It reminded Cora of college, when Maggie and Jade had pledged Cora's sorority, and there was a sorority sister who enthralled all three of them, somehow keeping them hanging on her every word. Years later they still couldn't make sense of what it was that girl had about her. Maggie said it was her ice-blue eyes and white-blond hair, and that only children and angels were meant to have that coloring.

It was typical Maggie. She always spoke like a writer, which was what she'd wanted to be when she was younger, ever since she was eight and holed up in her bedroom writing short stories and plays. She wrote the plays with two parts—one for herself and one for Cora—and they performed them for their parents, who smiled and clapped freely. At Vanderbilt, Maggie changed her mind and decided she wanted to be a neo-traditional interior designer, and she was good at that, too. She was good at lots of things, actually, but the things Cora and Maggie knew how to do were so different that it seemed pointless to be competitive.

Cora shivered. It was agonizing when she thought of Maggie. Every image of her sister brought a crushing feeling to her chest, like fists were pounding and letting up only when she was sorry enough. It was tolerable when she was alone at night in her bed, but a bit trickier in the daylight with Laurel Madsen scrutinizing her face.

"Are you having fun?" Cora asked Laurel, unable to come up with anything profound to say.

Lucy whacked Cora's cheek with her strand of bubble-gum-pink birthday beads. Cora tried to brush it off like an accident. "Silly!" she said, even though it stung. Why were her children always hurting her? A smack to the face, a heel in the rib, or the corner of a book to her eyeball—she was always bracing herself around them.

"Such a fun party," Laurel said.

Cora tried to form a sentence that sounded worthy of her Ivy League postgraduate degree, but she couldn't, so she smiled instead. This kept happening since she'd had the twins; it was like two-thirds of her brain was occupied by iron-fortified baby cereal and vaccine schedules, and the rest was trying to make up for the sudden deficit.

"I'm so glad you're having a good time," Cora said.

Laurel's nose twitched and she frowned a little, making Cora wonder if that wasn't what she'd meant by calling the party fun. Maybe Laurel was just objectively observing the party as a fun experience, but she herself wasn't actually having a good time?

"I'm headed inside to the bathroom for Lucy, can I get you anything to drink?" Cora asked.

"Actually, I'd love a—uh-*oh*," Laurel said, tsk-tsking.

Sudden warmth made Cora's midsection tingle. Sometimes the area around her Cesarean scar went numb. Maybe it was just that? She looked down and saw her soaked top.

"Oh! Lucy. It's okay!" Cora said.

Lucy's face crumbled as she kept peeing. So much pee! The damn juice! "Mama?" Lucy said, like she couldn't believe it was happening, either, and at her own birthday party.

"Excuse us," Cora said to Laurel, who looked sad for them both, which Cora found mildly stupid. It was just a shirt: Madewell, sale rack. A dozen more like them in her closet. Fixable, unlike so many other things.

"Lucy," Cora said, "it's really okay. Just a mistake. What do we say about mistakes?"

"Okay to make a mistake!" Lucy chanted as they moved toward the screen door. Cora kissed her daughter square on the lips. Kissing her children's mouths was one of her favorite things to do. She wondered how many more years she could do it before one of the other mothers called social services.

Inside the house, the air-conditioning was blasting (Sam hated being hot; he was uncharacteristically angry as soon as the house hit seventy degrees), and as Cora moved past the kitchen, she saw her mother, Sarah, talking to Jade. Jade was using a butcher's knife to cut more carrots, and Cora was glad for the help, but the knife was really too sharp to be using with so many children around. Cora didn't even like owning that knife. She watched the blade crush through the center of an unwieldy carrot, ran the odds of something *really* bad happening with the knife today, and decided they were too low to say anything to Jade. She didn't want to make her think she was being careless in front of children. Jade didn't have her own kids yet, and there was no way to make that comment without it being mildly hurtful.

"Lucy!" Sarah cooed. Ever since Lucy and George had been born, Cora's mother had had a proper place to rest her eyes. The gap years without Maggie meant Sarah had to focus her attention on Cora, and Cora felt sure it wasn't comfortable for her. Not that she'd ever say so to her mother, because that wasn't their relationship, and Cora would rather simmer. When Cora and Maggie were growing up, Maggie and Sarah had fit like puzzle pieces, while Cora sat outside the box of her mother's adoration with her math equations (fractals!) and her inability to sit still and sip coffee with Maggie and Sarah and talk and talk and *talk* like they used to.

"We'll be right back after a quick change!" Cora said to her mom and Jade, whisking Lucy toward the back staircase. Jade raised her long fingers in a wave. Besides celebrities, Jade was the only person Cora knew who could make two cocktail rings on one hand look exactly right.

Sarah merely smiled, which wasn't really enough for Cora, if she was being honest. Cora wanted her mom to jump to attention and come help with Lucy; she wanted her mom to be more hands-on, period, but she also knew it was her own doing. Cora had always thought her way was best, whether it was math homework or raising babies. Once when Cora was drowning in postpartum hormones—and she still regretted this—she'd warned Sarah that if she kept bouncing a newborn Lucy so aggressively she might get shaken baby syndrome. After that low moment, Sarah backed off and let Cora do more of it herself. Cora would take that night back if she could and ask for help again, but she didn't really know how.

Cora fumbled with the baby gate. It was so hard to do with just one free arm! She looked helplessly over her shoulder at Jade and her mom, but they were already tucked neatly back inside their conversation. And where was her dad? He had promised he'd come today, and the party was nearly over. They'd already done the cake!

Cora hoisted Lucy over the gate and onto the steps, which started Lucy shrieking while she unlatched the gate.

"Sweet girl, shhh," Cora said, a sweat breaking out on her neck at the first sound of Lucy's cry. Her love for her twins was so visceral; her entire body reacted to whatever they needed in any precise moment. Her boobs still felt like they'd caught fire when one of the twins cried out in the night, for God's sake. Would those milk ducts ever shrivel up, or give up? Would it be like this when they were teenagers? It was exhilarating, but so exhausting.

"We get to go the *secret way*," she said to Lucy, and the trick worked: Lucy stopped crying and smiled with tiny lips made pinker from the fruit juice. Both Cora and Lucy loved the back staircase. It made the old farmhouse feel like an adventure, like there were passageways and trick paths you could choose to alter your course.

"Shhhhh," Lucy said, bringing a tiny finger to her mouth. Lucy had just started becoming a more active participant in their games, and every time, it gave Cora a small thrill. Cora brought her finger to her lips, too, so Lucy would know her mother understood exactly what she meant: *This secret staircase is more fun when we creep together like ghosts.* Cora picked up Lucy and arched onto her tiptoes; they both fell silent.

Up they went, and even the step that sometimes creaked didn't make a sound as they ascended the staircase. On the landing, Cora was about to laugh and tickle Lucy when she heard a voice coming from Lucy's room. *Strange.* Why would party guests go upstairs to the bedrooms? She opened her mouth to call out, when she felt a sweep of cold along her neck, the chill that had started a few weeks after Maggie died. The first few times it had happened, Cora was sure Maggie was actually somehow present, hovering just outside her reach, even though Cora didn't know if she believed that was possible. She had always believed in things like *math*: in truth and order.

"Hello?" Cora called out. A burst of laughter—maybe Laurel Madsen's?—sounded from below in the kitchen. "Hello?" Cora tried again, louder this time. The upstairs voice stopped, and suddenly all she could hear was the thin hum of the air-conditioning.

"Mama?" Lucy asked, her tiny fingers tightening on Cora's shoulders.

Cora steeled herself. "Come on, sweetheart, it's all right," she said, and they started together toward the shadows in Lucy's room.

SARAH

3:51 p.m.

Sarah eyed the crudités in her daughter's kitchen while that pompous woman Laurel Madsen laughed at her own joke. Sarah forced a smile at Laurel and her teenage daughter—Anne? Annie? Sarah was forgetting names so easily these days. The girl blinked with big, round brown eyes as Sarah picked up a watery celery stick and held it between her fingers like a cigarette (weren't those the days!). Smoking was one of the things Sarah missed most about the seventies, how her hands could be entirely occupied while her mind obsessed over whatever felt wildly important back then. She was still obsessive, but now her hands had nothing to do, and often her mind raced so quickly, she found herself power walking on the treadmill in the middle of the night trying to catch up.

Sarah watched Laurel's sleek, professionally blown-out blond hair fall like a curtain as she leaned toward the mother next to her. "I told her that Anna couldn't possibly teach her son to swim, when he won't even put his mouth in the water to blow bubbles," Laurel told the mother. It was teenage hair, Sarah decided, even though Laurel had to be somewhere in her late forties. (Sarah herself was faring fine in the hair department, thank you very much, but not without weekly deep-conditioning treatments and tasteful blond highlights from Athena at the salon.)

Laurel's deep-brown eyes blinked as she waved a piece of paper, obstructing her teenage daughter's face. To everyone standing around the kitchen island, she said, "I'm just saying there should be at least one gluten-free option at the snack bar. So many adults and children have gluten sensitivities!"

Sarah chomped her celery. Imagine if she lit up a cigarette right now? *It's gluten-free, ladies! The cigarette is gluten-free!* She stifled a laugh just thinking about what Cora's sensible friends would do. They might even be *bitchy* about it, God forbid! (Cora prided herself on not being a bitch; being *nice* seemed to be more of a thing, now.) Sarah glanced around the kitchen at her daughter's mom-friends, suddenly exhausted. *Mom-friends*: because they weren't purely friends, except for Jade, of course. They were women Cora wouldn't have befriended if their children weren't in each other's orbits, and Sarah understood perfectly. She used to have plenty of mom-friends.

"What about a grain-free option, too, while we're at it?" asked a mother so petite she looked like she might fall over from the strain of holding a gigantic toddler.

When had it become so socially unacceptable to smoke or be bitchy? Was Diet Coke next?

"Paleo?" asked the mother next to her. She held a baby with a shock of red hair who sucked away on a packet labeled *Organic Bananas and Blueberries!* "Grain-free is a Paleo thing, right?"

"Here we go again," whispered Jade to Sarah.

"Indeed," Sarah said. Jade's perfect features were bathed in a square of sun from the skylight Cora and Sam had installed last year. The kitchen was lovely, just like the rest of the house. Cora had known enough to know she needed a decorator—she didn't have impeccable taste like her sister, Maggie—and Sam made enough for them to hire one, so good for them. Of Sarah's two daughters, Cora cared far less for material things, and her decision to hire a decorator was likely the result of feeling overwhelmed with decorating such a large home. Sarah recalled the links Cora had sent to listings for relatively small but charming homes. It was Sam who insisted on the grand six-bedroom in which they currently lived.

The tiny mother blurted, "Grain-free is only just a part of Paleo; it's not the same thing." Her gigantic toddler held out a Cheerio and dropped it on the floor, and the tiny mom either didn't notice or pretended not to.

"Grain-free is too restrictive," Laurel said, shaking her head as she waved around her petition. "We need to start smaller. A wholesome, gluten-free option should just be a given these days, and I'm not talking about potato chips. The pool has to realize that children need access to healthy snacks to make good choices. It's a life lesson, really."

Sarah swallowed down the celery and reached for a carrot. Laurel Madsen's voice was grating. It seemed like because her daughters were older than those of the other moms of the toddler set, she was the giver of important advice. *My daughters are actually older than yours, Laurel, so take that!* Or maybe, Sarah thought, because one of her daughters was dead, and the death was considered her daughter's own fault, she wasn't actually equipped to give advice?

It's not just Maggie's fault, it's your fault, too, Sarah Ramsey, for having raised a child who would do such a thing!

It was probably exactly what these women were thinking.

There was so much blame with mothering, even if your daughter didn't cause her own accidental death. Sarah had noticed it when the girls were toddlers—especially for the poor mothers of boys—just how cruel the other mothers could be when little Patrick threw sand in the face of dear little Mary! *Christ.* Weren't they meant to throw sand? Did it really reflect on some inner sociopathic desire the mother was meant to immediately quash by reading scores of parenting books?

Mothers took their children's behavior so personally, and Sarah thought it was a waste of energy, because when you were a mother you had zero control, and having a child was a tremendous act of optimism bordering on magical thinking. It was the biggest chance you could ever take. Sarah used to think she was protecting herself by having only two children, because the odds were better that something wouldn't go terribly wrong. How shortsighted was she? How foolish?

So incredibly foolish.

"I'm not feeling well, all of a sudden," Sarah whispered to Jade. "The party's almost over, anyway, isn't it? You'll say goodbye to Cora and my grandbabies for me?"

Jade nodded, giving Sarah a sweet, empathetic look. Sarah loved Jade for more reasons than she could count. "I'll walk you to your car," Jade said.

Sarah didn't argue. "Goodbye, everyone," she said loudly and suddenly. Now that she was sixty, she felt it was more okay to seem slightly off, eccentric even. *It's possible the world is going to pieces while you're worried about gluten-free options at the snack bar!* she wanted to add, but she didn't.

Laurel's eyes widened the tiniest bit as she waved a polite goodbye. Her teenage daughter checked her phone. The mom of the red-haired baby asked no one in particular, "Are there any more banana-blueberry packets?"

Jade's hand went to the small of Sarah's back.

"You look so pretty today, dear," Sarah said as Jade guided her out of the kitchen. Jade's hair was the color of espresso and tied into a low ponytail. Her coppery skin was courtesy of her father, a genius Indian scientist, and her sparkling green eyes matched those of her mother, an equally brilliant Dutch biologist. Jade's dark hair and green eyes were such a striking combination, and Sarah loved telling her how beautiful she was, because Jade's own mother hadn't. (Jade had told Sarah it wasn't out of meanness; it was just that her mom didn't seem to think to comment on it.) Maybe that was the better way, to not focus on looks, but everyone Sarah loved became beautiful in her eyes, and she said so out loud and often.

In the foyer, Laurel Madsen's husband, Dash, was staring down at his phone. Sarah had an appointment with Dr. Madsen tomorrow, actually, so now it felt official that he was her doctor, and what was it about doctors that made her so uneasy? It was something about the way they looked right through her. She always felt rejected before she even opened her mouth.

"Good afternoon, Dr. Madsen," Sarah blurted. "I'm seeing you tomorrow for my appointment." *Oh God.* Was that okay to say at a party? Was it violating HIPAA or something to mention the appointment in public? Sarah held up her right hand and gave it a gentle twist. Her hand had been aching along the line from her wrist to her thumb for months. She was hoping to avoid surgery, but just last week her neighbor was going on about some miracle surgery that allowed her to text again.

Dr. Madsen glanced up from his screen. He was so handsome—six foot four or five with Icelandic coloring: pale skin, baby-blue eyes, and blond hair peppered with gray. "I'll look forward to that," he said, smiling.

Sarah suddenly couldn't move with Dr. Madsen standing right there. What was wrong with her? There was an uncomfortable moment as Dr. Madsen pocketed his phone and then gave Sarah a small wave as he passed on his way into the kitchen.

Jade cleared her throat. "Ready?" she asked Sarah, kind enough not to mention the awkwardness.

Sarah nodded, and Jade opened the front door and stepped onto the lawn. The fresh, warm air wrapped around Sarah like a much-needed blanket. How could Cora live in such a freezing home?

"Hot," Jade said.

"Thank God for it," Sarah said, feeling the tiny bones in her hands and feet tingle as they thawed. She was just starting to feel better walking along the brown-green grass—all the young mothers had decided fertilizer was akin to cyanide—when she saw a silver Mercedes pull into Cora's driveway.

Dammit.

Clark and Abby: Sarah's ex-husband and his new wife. (Abby wasn't so new anymore—it had been over a decade since Clark's affair, and seven years since Abby and Clark got married—but to Sarah, she'd always be *his new wife.*)

Which made Sarah the old wife.

Tragically, Abby wasn't any younger than Sarah. She was a year older, in fact. Clark had committed the ultimate betrayal by falling in love with one of Sarah's mom-friends. Sarah had served Abby lamb at a dinner party the night before Clark told her about the affair, and Abby had looked up at Sarah as she refilled Abby's wineglass (like a maid, Sarah couldn't help but think when she looked back on it), and complimented the citrine earrings Sarah wore. "Clark gave them to me," Sarah had purred. And had Abby reacted to that? Had she seemed bothered by the fact that Clark still bought Sarah romantic gifts while he was busy fucking her? Sarah couldn't remember. She'd certainly heard of that phenomenon—women whose husbands went overboard with gifts to assuage their guilt during an affair—but Clark had also been avidly sleeping with Sarah every single night. It was what Sarah reminded herself of every time she wanted to bury her head in the sand. *He was still attracted to me, Abby! He was maybe even still a little in love with me!* This thought process meant she frequently thought of sex with Clark. She hadn't had sex with anyone since then, so there was no one else to think about, really.

Clark flung open his car door and raised his big hand in a wave like everything was hunky-dory. *Here we are, at our only living daughter's home for a birthday party for our grandchildren! Except, look! I've brought a date.*

Sarah swallowed. It still stung so badly. "You're late," she said, instantly hating herself for saying it.

Clark ignored her. He glanced over the top of his Mercedes at Abby, who was carefully getting out of the car like she was the Queen of England. Abby was not only a year older than Sarah, but she also had curly red hair that she wore braided down her back like roadkill. (Sarah's hair was cut into an immaculate bob.) Abby was also a little chubby compared to Sarah, who was stick thin on account of her tendency toward anxiety and a general disinterest in food. It just would have been so much easier if Clark had left Sarah for a thirtysomething Pilates instructor. Abby was an accountant, for Christ's sake.

Sarah and Jade stood still as statues, watching Abby round the car to stand next to Clark like a red-haired Barbie doll. She even waved like one, with her arm bent at an odd angle. Sarah forced a tight smile. *Chubby* wasn't the right word for Abby, she knew. *Curvy* was more like it. Especially compared to Sarah, whose boobs had been shrunken and droopy for the three decades since she'd breastfed the girls. Maybe Abby hadn't breastfed. Maybe that was her flaw?

"Hello, Sarah," Abby said diplomatically as she did her Barbie-wave. Jade shifted her weight beside Sarah.

Sarah didn't say hello back. It was the only perk of being a slighted wife whose daughter was killed a year after her husband married another woman: she could pretty much do whatever she wanted.

"Didn't you bring a gift?" Sarah asked Clark. He was standing there with his tan, smiling face and his shiny Ray-Bans, wearing the gray shorts Sarah had bought him years ago. (They may have been the last thing she'd ever bought him, come to think of it.) He was also wearing a pink polo shirt Sarah never, *ever* would have bought him, and it made him look old and boringly rich, versus excitingly rich, which was how

Sarah had always preferred him. He stood there completely and utterly empty-handed.

"I had the gift sent," Clark said.

Sarah looked at him like she had no idea what he was talking about.

"Amazon," Clark said.

"You get two-day shipping if you join Prime," Abby said.

"Duh," Sarah said, but then she felt a little guilty when Abby's mouth dropped a half inch. "Let's go," Sarah said to Jade, her voice hushed. "And drop your hand from my arm. I don't want it to look like you're helping me walk. I'm not dead yet, dammit."

Jade did as she was told. Sarah picked up the pace, practically skipping to her car. She turned to see them still staring at her, and she could just make out Jeremy and Sam on the side of the lawn where the grill was, watching the scene unfold as they drank beers.

Just get to your car; one foot in front of the other.

Sarah made it to her Lexus and placed a shaky hand on the hot metal handle. She slid inside, starting the car after giving Jade a wave. She was able to keep her tears at bay until she saw Clark curl his hand around Abby's.

JADE

4:00 p.m.

It was humid, even for July. Warm air stuck to Jade's exposed arms as she sat on Cora's lawn and watched Sarah zoom down the street and out of sight. The pressure in her chest let up a bit with Sarah safely on her way.

Grass tickled Jade's bare legs. Clark and Abby had already disappeared inside, and Jade leaned back on her elbows, happy to be alone. Her gaze settled on the familiar homes in Cora's bucolic neighborhood. Houses worth over a million dollars still managed to keep their country aesthetic with sky-blue front doors and gracefully aging shutters. Jade lived just two streets over in the same rambling, shingled Cape Cod–style house she'd grown up in. She and Jeremy had purchased it from her parents, who'd already been retired in Florida for a few years, and it made her nervous to have Jeremy own half of it, for him to have so much control over something that felt solely hers. Jade knew that wasn't the right way to look at it; Jeremy was her husband, her partner. He was supposed to be her best friend, though it had never really felt like that, even when things were good.

Jade stuck her hand into the pocket of her jeans and took out a crumpled piece of paper. She stared down at the seven numbers scrawled in loopy handwriting. She hadn't even bothered writing the

914 area code because it was just one town over in Mount Pleasant. Mount Pleasant was more free-spirited with its yoga studios and stores filled with wind chimes and crystals, whereas Ravendale was libraries, coffee shops, and a brick playhouse that screened independent films. The differences were small but marked enough that the kind of help Jade was looking for meant she had to stray from the meandering stone walls of Ravendale.

Jade took out her phone and dialed the number. She counted the rings: *One, two, three, four.* They sounded like warning bells.

Ring.

Ring.

Ring.

She was about to hang up after the seventh ring when a small voice on the other end said, "Mount Pleasant Hypnotherapy and Wellness. How may I help you today?"

"Hi," Jade said quickly before she could chicken out. "This is Jade Moore. I'd like to make an appointment, please." She felt breathless as the woman took down her information. Was she talking to the actual hypnotherapist? Or a receptionist? She hoped it was a receptionist. It would make the whole operation seem more legit.

"Would you like to share anything about the nature of your visit?" the maybe-receptionist asked.

Jade wasn't expecting that. "Um, actually, I guess I . . ."

Just then Jeremy rounded the side of the house and strode across the front lawn, clutching a Corona. Through his thin T-shirt, Jade could make out the stomach muscles that all the mothers at the pool found so sexy. (Did they really think she didn't know?) "What are you still doing out here?" Jeremy asked, his voice low. Why was he always so suspicious of her?

Because he's smart, Jade, a little voice answered. *Dangerously smarter than you.*

"Making an appointment," Jade whispered to him, trying to sound annoyed instead of nervous. She turned and said into her phone, "I'd like to talk to the hypnotherapist about some problems I'm having with infertility."

The woman on the other end of the line said "Ah-ha" like a revelation. "I had a cancellation for tomorrow at eleven a.m. Are you available then? Let's see, after that, the next availability is Friday morning."

"Tomorrow at eleven is great," Jade said, mentally timing the trip from Cora's fundraiser, the self-defense class at the gym that started at nine. It couldn't possibly run more than an hour and a half? And then, the open house at twelve thirty . . . "I have another appointment at twelve thirty in White Plains, should I expect to be done with the hypnotherapist by twelve?" She felt Jeremy's eyes on her. *Shit.* Why had she mentioned the second appointment?

"Absolutely, we'll just need an hour," the woman said kindly.

Jade got off the phone and onto her feet. She was so much smaller than her husband. They stood together on Cora's front step, staring into each other's eyes, and for just a breath, Jade had the desire to both kiss and hurt him. Her knees went weak with the startling confusion of it. He was so steely and handsome standing there, so tall, his hazel eyes hooked on hers. She was sure he was thinking about things he wanted to do to her, too.

"A hypnotherapist? Really?" Jeremy asked.

"Why not?" Jade said, and for a moment she wanted to open up to him about everything, but of course she couldn't. "Maybe she'll help me unlock some deep, dark secret that's keeping us from getting pregnant."

Jeremy laughed, and Jade felt chilled even with the hot sun blasting. "Do you have a deep, dark secret?" he asked, like he couldn't imagine anything more hilarious.

Several, actually, Jade thought. "Do *you*?" she asked.

Jeremy didn't break. The corners of his lips twisted into a smile. "Let's go back to the party, darling," he said.

LAUREL

4:11 p.m.

Laurel's anxiety rose with each breath. Her hands gripped the edge of her neighbor Cora's marble kitchen island, and she spoke faster and faster, trying to escape the feeling. She could hear herself prattling away to Isabella Gonzalez, Sam and Cora's successful banking friend, who'd been kind enough to give Laurel's older daughter, Mira, an internship this summer. It was like an out-of-body experience: Laurel knew she was talking too much, but she couldn't stop wildly steering the conversation in whatever direction her words took it. "We try not to label experiences for the girls," she said to Isabella, who popped a tomato in her mouth. Laurel watched Isabella's perfectly painted dark-purple lips purse as she chewed the tomato. Her sleek cream cocktail dress was quite formal for a birthday party, but it showed off an adorable baby bump. Laurel always felt a pinch of sadness when she saw a pregnant woman. It reminded her of how hopeful she'd once been. "Good day versus bad day, that kind of thing," Laurel said. "We let the girls just *be*, so they can learn to exist in a moment without constantly judging it."

Was that really her voice? It was like listening to a scratchy record. Laurel couldn't understand how or why Isabella was still listening to her so intently. Why hadn't she politely excused herself?

"You'd be amazed at how often adults judge nearly every experience," Laurel went on.

Isabella nodded as she dipped a carrot into hummus, and Laurel sighed. The nervous overtalking was simply what happened now at parties when Dash and their girls were present. Laurel was fine when she was by herself: *solo* was her preferred modus operandi. Because that way, she could run the show, and she often did. She was wealthy and empathetic, fashionable and smart, a quartet of adjectives that often drew others into an orbit. Her social life was a carefully controlled rhythm, and when she was alone, Laurel Madsen was the conductor.

But as it was, her girls ran around Cora's lawn and home with their ethereal beauty on display in short-shorts and sundresses for anyone who wanted to view. And the men did want to view, particularly where Mira was concerned. Anna was still young enough that nonperverted men mostly looked away, but still, what if something happened to her, too? Based on what Laurel had found that morning hidden inside a drawer in Mira's bathroom, Laurel knew that one of the things she'd been scared would happen to her older daughter already had, and it made having to pretend everything was okay so much harder.

Laurel turned away from Isabella to see Cora's father and stepmother standing just outside the kitchen on the patio. Laurel was a decade younger than Clark and Abby, but she'd known Abby since she was a child. Abby had grown up in Ravendale just like Laurel, and Laurel remembered when Abby used to lifeguard at the town pool during her summers off from college. When Laurel was nine years old, she idolized Abby, dreaming of having hair just like hers: long, braided, and strawberry blond. All of the boys fawned over Abby and her large chest crammed into the lifeguard uniform: a red bathing suit with a white cross that marked her breasts like a target. Laurel used to wonder about what all that attention would feel like, and years later, when she knew the feeling firsthand, she found it both thrilling and sickening. The power of her body to make men feel a certain way made her high, but it was nearly canceled out by an intense vulnerability that descended moments later.

Laurel watched through the screen door as Clark rested a hand on the curve of Abby's back. For all the things Laurel's husband was, and for all the things he'd done to her, at least Dash hadn't done what Clark Ramsey had. Laurel thought of Abby's four grown boys, two of whom barely spoke to her after she'd left their father for Clark. What could ever be worth losing your children?

Laurel checked her watch. Only thirty more minutes until her and Dash's session with Rachel, and Laurel was dreading it. The sessions weren't helping their marriage as they had when they'd first started last year. Everything felt colder and more clinical lately.

Isabella was saying something, and it entered Laurel's awareness like a shrill buzz. Laurel turned her attention back to Isabella, having no idea what she'd just said. If Laurel was going to carry on the way she'd been, the least she could do was listen when another woman said something, but this, too, had been happening: it was like the sound of her own voice kept the world anchored, and when she stopped talking, she felt as if she were floating adrift on a flimsy life preserver.

Laurel needed to leave this party before she unraveled completely.

"Excuse me," Laurel said to Isabella, who smiled and then checked her phone. Laurel slipped past two women drinking mimosas and found her younger daughter, Anna, sitting alone at Cora's kitchen table. Laurel followed her daughter's gaze out the window to see their neighbor Asher Finch playing catch with a toddler. "Go find your sister," Laurel whispered into Anna's ear. "Tell Mira it's time to go home. *Now.*"

CORA

4:23 p.m.

I hope you don't mind me being upstairs, Mrs. O'Connell. I just needed to make a private call.

That's what Mira had said when Cora found her standing in the middle of Lucy's room by herself, clutching her phone and staring at the doorway like she'd been waiting for someone. It was weird. And Cora had sworn she'd heard voices, but apparently she'd just heard Mira talking on her phone. It was also a little strange that Mira was upstairs in Lucy's room while the rest of the party was downstairs, but she'd spent plenty of time in Lucy's room while babysitting, so maybe she felt comfortable leaving the party and coming upstairs. Millennials were all a little bizarre, anyway.

"We're just so glad you and Anna and your parents could join us today, aren't we, Lucy?" Cora said.

Lucy was flat on her back on her pink changing pad. Her little legs squirmed. Cora loved every fold of skin on the twins' chubby thighs, and she wanted to kiss them now, but she worried Mira would think kissing a child's legs was further evidence of how lame she was.

Mira gave Lucy a smile that looked forced. She was *twenty-one now,* as she'd told Cora, which meant, according to her, that she really should be spending the summer in New York like the rest of her friends instead of stuck in Ravendale and forced to commute. And she said she would be, if her father weren't so *ridiculously strict.*

"So how's the internship going with Isabella?" Cora asked as she fumbled through Lucy's drawer for her favorite pair of purple underwear featuring Olaf on the butt.

"It's fine," Mira said, not meeting Cora's eyes.

Cora glanced out the window to the yard, where Asher Finch was tossing a foam baseball to the little boy holding his dino-plane. It hit the boy's head, and his mother, Antoinette Campbell, one of Cora's friends from Ravendale Moms and Tots, came running. Cora's hands froze in midair. Hopefully Antoinette realized Cora wouldn't have a real baseball right there by the play set? They were so heavy! Cora watched as Antoinette scooped her little boy up and made a fuss over examining his skull. *It's foam!* Cora wanted to shout out the window, but she didn't. She forced herself to turn her attention back to Mira. "Very nice of Asher to come, too," she managed.

Mira followed Cora's gaze out the window but frowned when she saw Asher standing there looking mortified as the little boy tried to extricate himself from his mother's arms. Asher was Mira's boyfriend, at least according to Laurel, but did mothers really know anything at all about what their teenage and twentysomething daughters did? When Lucy was older, would Cora?

"So are you enjoying college?" she asked Mira, running her hand over the part of Lucy's stomach that curved beneath her belly button.

Mira gave a one-shoulder shrug. "College is fine," she said. It gave Cora some relief that Mira sounded bored about even college. Maybe it wasn't Cora, Lucy, and George, after all; maybe it was just Mira's personality.

"The guys are just so dull," Mira went on, and Cora was taken by surprise. They didn't really have that kind of relationship.

"Well," Cora said, "there's a lot of drinking in college, and that can make almost anyone dull." She knew it wasn't a cool thing to say, but it was true. She'd felt that way even in college.

"I guess," Mira said. She looked so much younger than her twenty-one years, standing there and clutching her phone like a lifeline, only a year younger than Maggie had been when she died. Mira was beautiful, no doubt. And the shorts she wore showed off her mile-long, tanned legs. But she looked tired, too.

"You're young," Cora said. "You're so young." She turned back to Lucy, a little embarrassed. She hadn't meant for it to come out like that. Her daughter had found a yellow crayon on the changing table and was holding it between two tiny fingers. "Just not in your mouth," Cora told her.

"I'm not that young," Mira said, and Cora started at the dark note in her voice.

"No, of course, I didn't mean it like that," Cora said. "Could you grab me another dress from Lucy's closet?"

Mira rolled her eyes on her way to the closet, but Cora was too tired to let it bother her. Parties were exhausting.

"I'm actually dating an older guy," Mira said, coming back across the bedroom with a navy dress spotted with gold stars.

"Are you?" Cora asked, reaching for the dress. Was this even an appropriate conversation to be having with your babysitter? What if Mira meant she was seeing a *way* older man, not just some twenty-three-year-old? Cora gently stretched the dress over Lucy's head. She didn't like it as much as Lucy's other dresses, but she didn't say anything, of course, because it wasn't like Mira was on the clock babysitting, and Cora didn't want to treat her like a servant.

"Yeah," Mira said. "I am. And he's really sexy."

Cora's heart sped up a bit. This was starting to feel not quite right. "That's nice," she said, letting out a nervous laugh.

"You know how older guys are," Mira said. Cora lifted her eyes. Was Mira challenging her? Was she wondering how long Cora would go along with this line of conversation? "They know what they're doing," Mira said with a wink.

And that was enough.

"Would you pass me those shoes?" Cora asked sternly, pointing to the sparkly silver ballet flats on the edge of Lucy's changing table. "So are you . . ." *studying anything interesting at school* was what she'd been about to say, but Mira interrupted with a wave of her hand.

"Just don't tell my mom," Mira said.

Cora's chest tightened. Had she seriously just said that?

"Mira, I'm not comfortable with that. I think . . ." Cora started, but right then Mira's little sister, Anna, burst into the room.

"Hi, Mrs. O'Connell," Anna said to Cora, and then, to the baby, "Hi, Lucy! Happy birthday!"

"Hello, Anna," Cora said, flustered and uneasy. Lucy said a jumbled version of "Happy birthday!" back to Anna.

Anna smiled. Then she turned to her sister, her expression changing. "Mom says we need to go," she said.

Mira gave the same small shrug. This time, a spaghetti strap made its way off her shoulder and onto her toned arm. A glittery silver heart charm on her necklace caught the light.

"It was nice talking to you, Mrs. O'Connell," Mira said. Both girls gave Cora waves that felt distinctly teenaged, fluttery in their excitement, and then they turned and walked away.

Cora scooped up Lucy from her changing table and sat her in a plush rocking chair. She sorted through a freshly folded stack of laundry on the floor, and then changed her own top before joining her daughter, snuggling back against the cushions. A chandelier from Pottery Barn cast sparkly light across her daughter's chalky pink walls, and Cora let her eyes glaze over. Lucy grabbed a board book stuck in the cushion and opened it, pointing at the pictures and proudly naming them. Cora let go of a breath as Lucy snuggled closer, and stared at the empty doorway through which Mira and Anna had just passed. She knew she should go back to the party, but she needed a minute. Should she say something to Laurel about Mira dating an older man? Maybe Mira had just been making it up to impress Cora, or maybe just for the sake of drama? Sometimes Maggie had been that way. She'd exaggerate a small thing for no other reason than being a little bored.

Lucy closed her book, and Cora rose from the chair. "Let's do Mama's lipstick, okay? And then we'll go back to your party."

"Lip-tick," Lucy said, and Cora nuzzled her cheek. Lucy still smelled like Chanel No. 5 from when Cora's mom had held her while they cut the birthday cake.

Cora felt the scratchy sisal carpet runner beneath her feet as she walked down the hall and into her bedroom. She headed toward the bathroom, but a package on her pillow stopped her. She moved closer and saw it was a manila envelope, and written right on the front in block handwriting was her name. Cora set Lucy carefully on the bed. She turned over the envelope—there was no mailing label affixed to it—and carefully tore it open. Inside was a green notebook. In the same neat, careful lettering on a pink Post-it note attached to the cover was written: *I'm sorry, but you should know.*

Cora's heart picked up speed. She glanced down at Lucy, who stared up with bright brown eyes. "You sit here for one second, okay?" she said, setting Lucy carefully on the bed.

Cora started to flip open the notebook just as footsteps sounded behind her. She spun around to see her husband holding George. "What are you doing up here?" he asked.

"Nothing," Cora said, her fingers gripping the notebook. "Lucy had an accident, so we came upstairs to change."

"Mama!" George called out.

"Hi, George," Cora cooed.

"Let's go back downstairs, okay? I'm fielding everyone by myself," Sam said, irritated. He couldn't handle outdoor parties when the sun was blaring; Cora should have timed her pregnancy for a winter birthday. "Your dad and Abby are here," he said.

"Are they?" Cora asked, her voice shrill.

"Are you okay?" Sam asked.

"I'm fine," Cora said. She turned casually to her bedside table and slipped the notebook inside. "Ready?" she asked Lucy, scooping her into her arms.

Cora's legs felt shaky as she followed Sam back down the hall. What could that thing possibly be? "Careful," she barked as Sam started down the secret stairs. It was a reflex—an annoying one—but she couldn't help it, no matter how many times Sam reminded her he'd had loads of practice walking down stairs. *But now you're carrying one of the two most important people in the world to me,* she wanted to say, but she worried she'd hurt his feelings. He was such a great husband—even if lately he had been more distracted than usual, forgetting the obvious parenting things she reminded him about—and she didn't need to point out that she loved the twins more than him.

Cora followed Sam through the kitchen and waved to one of her friends from Ravendale Moms and Tots. Cora really hoped she'd provided the right kind of lunch—the woman was on some diet that featured prehistoric food. It was nearly impossible to cook for these mothers.

"Cora?" said a raspy voice.

Cora turned to see Isabella Gonzalez, radiant with purple lipstick and a dusting of shimmery shadow over her lids and cheekbones. "Isabella!" Cora said, and then Isabella's husband, Terrence Washington, rounded the corner. He broke into the wide grin he always wore, exposing the charming dimple in his clear black skin. Sam and Terrence shook hands, and Cora found herself smiling at the sight of them. Sam had met Isabella and Terrence at Columbia Business School, and they reminded Cora of life as a twentysomething in the city with Sam, when things weren't perfect but definitely simpler, and when sex was way more fun. "It's so good to see you," Cora said as she embraced them. "It's been so long. Can you say hi, Lucy and George?"

Lucy waved an enthusiastic hello. George frowned. He was so constipated lately.

"They're darling," Isabella said softly. Cora noticed a tiny bump at Isabella's waist.

"Thanks," said Cora, "I can't believe they're already two!"

"How are you feeling, Terrence?" Sam asked, and Cora kicked herself. She hated how having children had made her so much less considerate of other people! She should have asked Terrence right away how his back was doing—he'd broken it, for God's sake.

"The rehab has given me excellent quad muscles," Terrence said. "Isabella can hardly resist my new buff legs, right, Isabella?"

Isabella laughed, but it didn't sound quite right.

"I heard you were at Hospital for Special Surgery," Sam said. He was the one who had invited Terrence and Isabella to the twins' party, and Cora had agreed it was a wonderful idea to reconnect with them. "Jeremy said you were getting the best treatment."

"Did he now?" Isabella said, her voice razor-sharp.

Cora flinched. Even Lucy seemed to notice Isabella's tone. (See, *perceptive*!)

"I'm doing much better, thank you," Terrence said, a little too formally.

Six months ago, after Terrence had been laid off, Sam helped him get a job working for Jeremy's hedge fund. (Isabella never seemed to need anyone's help: J.P. Morgan made her an offer during her final year at Columbia, and she'd already worked her way up to managing director.) But then two months ago, Terrence fell down a flight of stairs late one night at work and shattered three vertebrae. Jeremy told Sam and Cora there were drugs found in Terrence's system at the hospital, which shocked

Cora. Though how could you ever know something a person was desperate to keep hidden?

All four of them stared at each other. Even the children were quiet. Cora's thoughts drifted back to the envelope on her bed, but she forced the image out of her mind. "So how long are you in town for?" Cora asked Isabella. Not *in town*, exactly: Isabella and Terrence owned a weekend home twenty minutes away in Greenwich, Connecticut.

"Until tomorrow night," Isabella said. She still seemed upset about something as she put a hand on Terrence's arm and said, "Let's get you something to eat." Then she waved at George and Lucy before heading toward the kitchen.

Cora turned to Sam, but he wasn't looking at her. He was watching Isabella and Terrence round a corner and disappear into the kitchen. Wasn't it a little odd to walk away from the hosts at a party? Weren't the hosts the ones who usually excused themselves first? It was one of those small social nuances Cora usually found exhausting, but she noticed it now, and it felt slightly off.

"Let's go find your dad," Sam said, still not looking at her. There used to be a time when Cora could send Sam a glance, and he'd return it with one of his own, and it was as though they could communicate anything to each other that way.

Sam opened the screen door, and they carried the twins onto the patio. Cora glanced around and realized the Madsens must have already left. How strange that Laurel hadn't said goodbye. Or maybe Cora was just being too sensitive today, and anyway, they'd see each other tomorrow morning at the fundraiser. Cora had the sitter coming at eight so she could make it to the gym by eight thirty to help Laurel set up. Where had she put that Lululemon workout outfit?

Sam raised a hand when he saw Clark and Abby standing near the grill. Cora dutifully followed him toward her dad and stepmother, but the last thing she wanted was to make small talk. Her thoughts felt disjointed—she needed to get back upstairs to the notebook. It might be some kind of joke. *You should know.* Maybe some invite to a mystery theme party, or something silly like that. People in Ravendale had extra time and money on their hands; they threw theme parties all the time. The last one Cora attended had her and Sam wearing all black and engaging in a murder-mystery whodunit. Sam had been designated the murderer, and he'd kept it a secret from Cora the entire night! It was sort of off-putting, actually. Cora had found herself mildly irritated when she realized he'd lied so successfully.

Sam and Cora made their way across the patio toward Clark and Abby. Sometime after the affair, when her mom would constantly talk about Clark and Abby—*I just ran into Clark and Abby at Accardi's! Is nowhere safe?*—Cora had started thinking of her father as *Clark* instead of *Dad*, and then soon after, her mom as *Sarah*. It was sad but sort of freeing. In many ways, Sam and the twins were her family now.

A few mothers from Ravendale Moms and Tots were still out on the lawn, looking slightly stressed as they managed their children on George and Lucy's play set. Abby held a pink paper plate and ate watermelon as Clark talked to Jade and Jeremy. For the first few years they were together, Abby was never comfortable enough to eat around Cora and Maggie. Maggie always thought it was funny: adultery as a diet plan. Cora found the whole thing so unsettling and awkward that she wanted to hide and emerge years later when everyone was okay with the situation, but that never really happened. Nearly a decade after Clark moved out, Sarah could still barely be in the same room with him and Abby.

"Lucy! George!" Clark said when he saw them. "Happy birthday!"

Cora leaned in to kiss her dad's cheek. Lucy squirmed and laughed as Clark tickled her bare leg.

"Did you get the gifts?" Abby asked. Rubies dangled from her chandelier earrings. She'd started dressing more bohemian in the last few years, and she'd actually managed to look prettier and younger.

Sam leaned in to peck Abby on the cheek. Cora never knew whether to hug Abby or shake her hand or just run in the opposite direction, which is what she mostly wanted to do. "The kids loved your presents, right, guys?" Cora said to her twins. Actually, George had thrown the puzzle at Sam and caught him square on the kneecap. George hated puzzles; he couldn't figure them out. *Ugh*—the Crystal Light. Had it really been worth it?

"I'm sorry we missed the cake," Clark said, "but I wanted to avoid your mother."

"Clark," Abby said sharply. Jade's eyes widened, and Jeremy took a swig of his beer. Abby looked at Cora. "I'm sorry," she said.

"I meant I wanted to avoid a scene," Clark said to Abby. He turned to Cora. "You knew what I meant, right, darling?"

"It's fine, Dad," Cora said. "We missed you."

What the hell was in that notebook?

"Will you excuse me for a minute?" Cora asked. She put Lucy into Sam's free arm, trying to ignore her protests. "I'll be right back. I forgot something upstairs."

SARAH

4:51 p.m.

Sarah pulled into her long, winding driveway. Sometimes, especially on days like today, she fantasized about what it had been like only a dozen years before: the feeling of approaching her beautiful home and family with a trunk full of groceries or the odd school supply from Target for one of the girls' projects. There would be salmon for Cora, who liked *brain food*, as she called it, and tons of fruit and vegetables for Maggie. For Clark, there'd be chicken or lamb from Accardi's, the butcher shop on Ravendale's Main Street. Sarah loved cooking for Clark and the girls, especially when Cora and Maggie floated around the kitchen while she chopped vegetables and stirred sauces, telling her this and that, the rhythm of their voices like a warm blanket or a soak in the tub. Clark and the girls were all Sarah had ever wanted. She knew it was more PC to want a career, too, but she didn't: she wanted only her family. She had friends, of course, but she wasn't able to keep up those friendships after Maggie died—it was far too exhausting, and what could they ever have in common after that fateful night? Many of Sarah's old mom-friends still tried reaching out, and sometimes, when she was feeling up to it, she met them for lunch at the club. But everything had changed, and Sarah wouldn't pretend otherwise.

Now when Sarah pulled into her three-car garage, there were no groceries and no more school supplies: her trunk was empty except for the wool blanket that Cora insisted she drive with for safety purposes. Sarah refused to stop cooking fancy meals just because she was alone, but now she ordered from FreshDirect and Blue Apron so she could avoid the grocery stores and the *feel-so-sorry-for-you* stares from the other mothers. Grocery stores equaled families and motherhood, and it was hard for other women to forget what had happened to Sarah as they watched her sort through avocados to find the freshest ones.

Sarah slipped her key into the lock and opened the back door into a spacious mudroom lined with cubbies. She knew she should get rid of the cubbies because all she could see when she looked at them were tiny pink jackets and backpacks, but she couldn't bring herself to. She'd kept Maggie's room the same, too, with posters of Brad Pitt and Helena Bonham Carter from that late-nineties movie *Fight Club* Maggie had loved.

One year ago, Sarah had turned Cora's oversize room into a guest room. She had a contractor build bunk beds with a slide so that George and Lucy would—fingers crossed—start having sleepovers as soon as possible.

In the kitchen, Sarah opened a bottle of Syrah and poured a glass. She puttered around, wiping already-clean countertops, and then drank another glass filled almost to the brim. Her computer was open on the granite countertop, and it drew her like a magnet: Google and all its possibilities.

What are the chances of . . . she started typing, but her search history popped up, momentarily stunning her. Was she really so morbid?

Sarah shut her laptop and moved into the sunroom with its cheery blue patterns. She slumped into a wicker chair and looked out at her manicured lawn, careful not to spill the wine. After Clark left her, he kept paying for the weekly landscapers, housekeepers, and every other service that cost a fortune to maintain the house. He never asked Sarah to sell it, maybe because he felt guilty, or maybe because he was still making a killing at the hedge fund he'd started in the late eighties. Probably both. No matter what anyone said about hedge funds being a dying breed—*The market always outperforms hedge funds!* Hadn't Warren Buffett said something like that?—Clark perpetually maintained a long list of clients waiting to hand over their millions. Clark looked like money, and maybe more importantly, like the good life. It was what had attracted Sarah to him in the first place. She'd wanted to build something good, and they had, and she'd never taken their life for granted. Even on the most challenging days of motherhood, Sarah knew that what they had was absolutely everything.

So how could he leave them?

Sarah traced a fingertip over the twining wicker chair. Yes, the girls had been already away at college when it happened. Clark had waited until Maggie was a freshman and Cora was a senior, both of them at Vanderbilt. It infuriated Sarah how proud Clark seemed of this fact. He came up behind her one morning at her desk, just as she was perusing real estate listings in Palm Beach. (Clark had always wanted to buy a Florida place for them to retire to, and Sarah realized only in retrospect that he'd stopped talking that way for six months prior to his announcement.) *I need to talk with you,* he'd said, and Sarah immediately bristled. Clark wasn't formal; she couldn't remember any time during their marriage when he'd declared the need for a conversation. Sarah had let her eyes rest on her computer for a beat longer, taking in a photo of a property's screened-in lanai, sensing it would be the last time she saw it and knowing implicitly that she and Clark wouldn't make it to Palm Beach. She turned to face him. *What is it?* she asked, fear in her voice. Was he sick? Dying?

For the longest time Clark couldn't get the words out, and Sarah looked deep into his eyes, trying to gauge just how off-kilter her world was about to go. Finally, he said: *I've been with Abby. It happened, and I'm sorry, but I love her, too.*

Sarah didn't understand at first. *He'd been with Abby? Where?* She watched the deep lines in Clark's forehead crease, and then he asked, *Are you okay?* And that's when she knew he meant he'd been *sleeping* with Abby, and a breath later she connected that fact to the next part of what he'd told her: he *loved* Abby. Sarah stood on shaking legs and lifted a hand to slap him, but it wasn't in her nature to hurt anyone, really, and so she just lowered it pathetically to her side. *So tell her it's over,* she managed to say, and as she stepped toward Clark, her chenille robe came loose, exposing the bare skin beneath. Clark looked at her: at her breasts, her stomach, and her pale-blue lace underwear. His deep voice had an uncharacteristic waver when he said, *It's not over, Sarah. I love her. I wanted the girls to have us together while they lived in this house, but I can't keep carrying on like this; I don't want to lie to you anymore.*

So you're leaving me? Sarah asked, and she immediately felt embarrassed, as though a terrible joke had been played on her, and everyone knew and felt sorry.

Clark nodded, and Sarah clutched her robe over her breasts and spat, *I don't understand, Clark. You've just been pretending to be my husband, to love me?* But even as the words escaped her mouth, she knew they weren't true. There was still so much good between them—she could feel that, even if anyone else would have called her delusional. Was it possible to fall in love with someone new while still truly loving your wife? Or *was* she delusional?

It was the crux of the problem, and it was the reason Maggie was dead. The rug had been pulled from beneath Sarah. The wound was so fresh one year after Clark and Abby married, and suddenly Cora's engagement was upon them, and the engagement party Sarah was throwing their eldest daughter became this huge, intangible thing: it became the very way she was going to show Clark what he was missing. Because Sarah, if she were honest, still believed she was rightfully Clark's wife. Abby was merely a distraction, a woman who would run her course. Clark, eventually, would realize what he'd done, and then he'd come home.

Sarah grabbed a white fur blanket from the back of the chair and covered her bare legs. She stared onto the lawn, where a fat-bellied robin perched on her stone birdbath and dipped its head.

The truth was that right up until the night Maggie died, Sarah would have taken her husband back. She would have made him grovel and beg; she would have expected him to cry; but she absolutely would have taken him back. And that's the scenario she had been thinking about the night of Cora and Sam's party, when she slipped into a cocktail dress and greeted her guests. That's what she was imagining for nearly the entire evening, right up until the moment she found out Maggie had been killed.

After that night, no matter how much it still hurt to see Clark and Abby, Sarah never once wanted him back in her home. Because if Maggie's death was Sarah's fault, then it most certainly was Clark's, too.

Little girls, big house, handsome husband.

How had she lost so much?

LAUREL

4:57 p.m.

Laurel put a hand on Dash's arm as they walked the incline of their gravel driveway with their daughters. He shrugged her off. She knew he would—he hated any display of public affection, even and especially in front of the girls—but she felt so unsteady she had to try.

"You okay, Mom?" Anna asked. Her younger daughter was always sensitive to her moods. Sometimes Laurel wondered if Mira thought of anyone besides herself. Laurel tried to tell herself it was what college girls were supposed to be like, but was that true? When they visited Mira at Colgate, Laurel noticed other female students with their hopeful faces as they gathered signatures for children's rights overseas, or some other equally noble cause; or the students who threw Frisbees and tacked up flyers for upcoming theater productions; or even the girls who huddled together, laughing and smoking cigarettes. Mira didn't seem to be passionate about much at all, except the normal drama about clothes, fights with Anna, and wanting to spend her summer in the city. Mira blamed her parents, but she was the one who didn't apply in time for an internship in New York. When Sam O'Connell mentioned he could get her an internship with Isabella, Mira agreed because she had no other options, but it wasn't paid, and Dash used that as his reason to keep her living at home.

Mira worked Saturdays, Sunday mornings, and Mondays at Buzzed, and then took the train into New York Tuesday through Friday to work for Isabella. So maybe she was just exhausted, and that's why she clammed up whenever Laurel asked her what she thought about working as an intern. (Laurel had felt badly about how much Mira was working until she remembered she had never had a day off when she was saving for college spending money, either.) Mira's grades were perfectly respectable, and Dash thought she was on track for medical school, but Laurel suspected otherwise. Mira barely mentioned wanting to be a doctor. At Mira's age, it had been all Laurel could talk about.

"I'm fine, sweetie," Laurel said, giving Anna's hand a squeeze. Instead of letting go when Laurel did, her daughter held on tighter as they neared the house. It was a beautiful blue-gray contemporary. When Dash and Laurel had moved from their New York apartment to Ravendale, Laurel had wanted to buy one of the restored historical homes that sat proudly on the hills surrounding the small town's Main Street. She'd grown up here under very different circumstances, and she wanted something beautiful, something that telegraphed: *I belong here now, in this rambling farmhouse with history, the kind of home and moneyed family this town treasures.* But Dash insisted on contemporary, and Laurel acquiesced because it was his money—money made from cutting and slicing, from precision and skill; money made in a way Laurel had always hoped to make it herself. Dash was the brooding med student she'd fantasized about more than two decades ago, and now he'd fulfilled his every goal while Laurel had his children.

Laurel was from a middle-class Italian family, of which there were very few in Ravendale. With her stick-thin limbs and blond hair, she looked nothing like the rest of the Marinos. Laurel was sure her family secretly thought she and her blondness had finally moved where they belonged: away from the tiny houses lining the train tracks and into the bigger, beautiful homes near Main Street. Still, they'd been so proud of her for studying to become a doctor, helping wherever they could until she got pregnant with Mira and withdrew from med school. Laurel and Dash were already engaged when she got pregnant, so it was only a scandal to their parents (both Catholic). During the pregnancy, Laurel was sure she'd return to finish her final year of medical school, but the moment the doctor passed Mira into her arms, she knew that wasn't true.

"You'll need to hurry to make tutoring on time," Dash said to the girls as they stepped onto their front porch. The Ravendale Community Center provided free tutoring to small groups from five to eight most evenings, and Dash thought it was worthwhile for the girls to volunteer as tutors for younger students. (Dash thought a lot of things, most of which revolved around what would look good on the girls' resumes. It was one of his ways of caring for them, and Laurel had to admit he'd been right: both girls had gotten into schools they were proud to go to.)

Mira and Anna didn't say anything, and Dash barely waited a second before asking, "Did you hear me?" He hated when they didn't answer him right away.

"Maybe we could skip tutoring today?" Anna asked meekly, and Laurel flushed with nerves. Rachel was due soon for their session. Normally Laurel and Dash went to Greenwich to meet with Rachel, but every month or two, she came to them. The girls had never crossed paths with her, though Laurel had manufactured a lie just in case: *Meet Rachel, our new decorator!* Rachel sort of looked like a decorator with her stylish clothes, thick-framed gray glasses, and chic, straightened black hair.

"We could go to the gym instead," Mira said. She was obsessed with working out this summer at the local gym, which was a first. Laurel glanced down to the Fitbit circling Mira's wrist and made a mental note to call the gym's manager and double-check that everything was ready for the fundraiser tomorrow.

"Tutoring first," Dash said. "Then go to the gym if you'd like."

Laurel relaxed a bit, even as the girls exchanged a glance. They almost never contradicted Dash.

"Sure, Dad," Mira grumbled as her father unlocked the front door. Laurel saw their neighbor Asher Finch on his lawn, watching them.

The heavy wooden door opened to a stone foyer, and the Madsens stepped inside. Their house had an open floor plan, with the kitchen and living room visible from the entrance. Years before, Laurel had read that it was bad feng shui to open the door and see straight through to the back of the home, and she told this to Dash when the realtor first showed them the house. Dash had stared at her like she couldn't possibly be as bright as he'd once thought, and he made the offer on the home that night.

Mira and Anna took off their shoes and ran upstairs to get their books.

In their absence, Dash stared at Laurel. She shivered as his eyes traveled over her skin.

"Mom?" Anna called from upstairs. "Have you seen my . . . never mind!" Mira lost things, but Anna only misplaced them in her messy room. It was a subtle difference, but it meant something to Laurel. Mira had become so indifferent and careless this year, and there was a coldness about her that reminded Laurel of Dash. Mira wasn't calculating like he was, at least not yet, but something in her was changing, and Laurel felt powerless to stop it. Laurel purposely didn't make too many close friends in Ravendale, but when she casually brought up her concerns about Mira to other mothers, they said their teenage daughters were unrecognizable, too, so it was nearly impossible to know whether to be truly concerned.

Still, Laurel was.

The girls flew down the steps with the matching leather satchels Laurel had found at Saks. Mira and Anna were far past the age when Laurel could buy them the same thing, but they'd both seen the bag online and wanted it, and Laurel had said, *I'm buying two. If anyone argues, I'll cancel the order immediately!* It was such a Ravendale thing to do, to threaten your children with your remarkable buying power. What percentage of mothers in America bought their daughters bags from Saks? Less than 1 percent, Laurel knew, and yet here she was, in that 1 percent, where she'd always thought she wanted to be. She'd gotten to that place in a very different way than she'd planned—by marrying a surgeon instead of becoming one—but she was here, nonetheless, far away from everything that had happened in that tiny house near the train station.

At least, that's what she tried to tell herself.

JADE

5:08 p.m.

Jade stood on the patio with Jeremy, Sam, Clark, and Abby. She was starting to think the twins' birthday party would never actually end, and that she'd be eternally stuck in purgatory with her husband and other people's toddlers.

So many things would be different if Maggie were alive, and social gatherings were one of them. Maggie had that rare gift of being funny without ever being mean, and she would have kept Jade laughing with running commentary on the party without actually having made fun of anyone. Jade sometimes thought about how much easier high school would have been if they'd been friends then, but they hadn't run in the same circles. Jade was busy being artistic and vegan, while Maggie was the golden girl. It wasn't until they went to Vanderbilt that they sought each other out, because they were the only other kids from Ravendale in their class there.

Maggie had made Jade so much less self-conscious, and now that she was dead, Jade was back to square one: wondering if she'd said the right thing, or if she'd said anything at all. Her mind was running elsewhere nearly all the time, trying to figure out how to get things back on track with Jeremy and wondering how much of the chasm in their marriage was caused by her secret feelings, the ones she'd tried so hard to bury. Was it common to feel such distance from your husband after only a few years of marriage? Was that what other women were talking about when they complained about their husbands, or were Jade and Jeremy way off the chart of what was normal?

Jade glanced in the direction Cora had gone after announcing she'd forgotten something upstairs. It seemed like Cora always wanted to run away during conversations with Clark and Abby, so good for her for finally doing it.

Sam and Cora's old friends Isabella and Terrence were at the party, too, and Jade kept meaning to go over and say hello and check on Terrence, but something held her back. Terrence had gotten hurt badly at Jeremy's work, and Jade had called Terrence and Isabella so many times since. But they never returned her calls, and she had the odd feeling it was on purpose, though she couldn't imagine what she'd done to upset them.

Cora's friends with children were standing just outside the sandbox and talking over each other. Jade had noticed that moms of young children often interrupted each other, and so many had verbal diarrhea, which was a shame, because what they had to say wasn't really that interesting. And no offense to them, because Jade thought they were actually very good mothers. *Doting, careful, involved . . .*

Qualities Jade wasn't sure she possessed, so could she really do this? Was wanting a baby enough?

The toddlers inside the sandbox were taking turns throwing and eating sand. One boy peed on a plastic windmill, which didn't bother the mothers enough to stop their conversation.

Jade took a swig of pink lemonade. Cora had really stepped up her game for this birthday party. The picnic tables were full of treats like nut-free, egg-free, gluten-free, dairy-free apple tarts. One of the tables was covered with a pink gingham tablecloth, the other with a blue one. On the pink table were two glass jugs of pink lemonade labeled with a chalkboard tag: *PRINCESS PUNCH!* On the blue table were the same jugs filled with a minty green lemonade tagged: *DINOSAUR DELIGHT!* Would Cora have done a party like this if it were just for family? Jade didn't think so. This seemed to be somewhat for the other mothers, which Jade totally understood, because that was life as a woman, and not even her artistic, supposedly free-spirited self was immune to it. And Cora seemed to be doing better this year, which made Jade happy. (Last year, at a restaurant for the twins' first birthday party, Cora needed to leave at least twice to cry in the bathroom—presumably because of the stress of the party, or of motherhood itself, Jade wasn't sure—and when she came back, everyone acted like they hadn't noticed.)

Jade turned back to her group and tried to smile at her husband, but his eyes were elsewhere. She followed his glance and saw it land on Terrence and Isabella.

"How's the jewelry coming?" Abby asked her.

"It's been good, thanks," Jade said. She took another sip of lemonade. "I just finished an order for a new boutique in Chicago, and I have a trunk show at Barneys at the end of the month."

Abby beamed with delight at this news. "That's just wonderful," she enthused, absentmindedly touching her own jewelry, a multistrand gold necklace with rubies that matched her chandelier earrings. Jade didn't make chandelier earrings. Her jewelry line was more *rock 'n' roll*, as she was sure Abby would describe it. Jade used jagged quartz and other dark stones and trinkets attached to vintage-looking chains; the most delicate piece in her collection was a pair of mother-of-pearl earrings shaped like daggers. She used to make more conservative pieces when she was younger, but her aesthetic changed after a few summers in Africa working with her mom, who was there on government funding to study malaria.

Sam avoided Jade's eyes. It was so much easier for adults with little kids to do that. It was like they only half looked at you, half listened.

Jade knew she should offer to help Sam, who was trying to manage his twins and his beer, but she didn't. She liked other people's children—she really did—but she liked them from afar. It made her feel guilty, because Cora had chosen her to be the twins' godmother. Jade reassured herself she'd do a better job when they were older.

God. So then what was she *doing*? How would she feel when and if her own child arrived? Everyone said it was different when the child was yours. But did that apply in her situation? What if she just wasn't meant to be a mother? Weren't you supposed to know before you tried to welcome a baby into your arms?

"Lucy, sweetie," Abby cooed, reaching for Lucy.

"No!" Lucy screamed at Abby, clutching Sam's red neck with her fingers.

Sam was visibly sweating. Clark let out a nervous laugh, and Abby flushed. Cora had told Jade that only two of Abby's four sons still spoke to her, and one of them had children, but he also had a rule that Abby could come over only once per month. It made Jade feel ill. Certainly a woman shouldn't be punished like that for falling in love with someone else, right? Clark was allowed to visit Cora's kids whenever he wanted. Maybe the repercussions for a woman having an affair were much worse?

"Let's get something to eat," Clark said to Abby. They both looked mildly embarrassed as they excused themselves and headed inside.

Jeremy waited until Clark and Abby were out of view before reaching for George, who went easily into his arms. Jeremy was godfather to the twins, a job he took seriously by purchasing expensive gifts. A playhouse called The Tudor Mansion, for just under six hundred dollars, was his most recent display of affection. One of the reasons Jade was so nervous about becoming a parent with Jeremy was that he loved playing the hero and soaring above and beyond the call of duty, but he seemed to have a distaste for actual *duty*. Day-to-day chores bored the shit out of him, so what would he be like with the daily grind of raising his own child? Jade shuddered at the thought of Jeremy taking even longer work days and showing up only for the parent-child photo ops: weekend baseball games, school plays, or swims in front of his adoring fans at the country club. As far as Jade could tell, those magical moments were a very small percentage of actual parenting.

"Georgie-boy," Jeremy said once the little boy was snuggled in his arms. It made Jade cringe. It was painful to think about how much he wanted her pregnant.

The phone in the pocket of Jade's shorts buzzed, and she took it out to see a text.

> Thank you for booking an appointment with Mount Pleasant Hypnotherapy and Wellness! Your appointment for tomorrow is confirmed for 11 a.m. Please call the office with any changes. Have a great day!

Maggie had always been in favor of anything and everything outside of the mainstream. Hypnotherapy wouldn't even register as alternative therapy, just one that made sense given the situation. When Jade and Maggie were at Vanderbilt, Maggie regularly visited a palm reader in downtown Nashville who told her she would live a long, happy life as long as she lived with an honest heart. At the time, Maggie and Jade had taken that advice as though it meant *everything*, and they vowed to follow it as they carried on living their lives as early twentysomethings.

An honest heart. And look where Jade and Maggie were now.

"Excuse me," Jade said to Sam and Jeremy, leaving them standing there. Guys were so strange, the way they could just stand silently together. Sam and Jeremy had been best friends since college, too. They'd all met at Vanderbilt, when Cora, Sam, and Jeremy were seniors, and Maggie and Jade were freshmen. Jeremy had paid so much attention to Maggie, and everything had felt so muddled and convoluted, so much so that when Cora, Sam, and Jeremy graduated, it felt like freedom.

Jade slipped into the house, passing the four or five mothers in the kitchen and keeping her head down to avoid getting swept into a conversation she didn't want to have. She felt hot even though the house was freezing. She cut a sharp right into a closet-size bathroom and locked the door behind her, then dug a hand into her pocket and removed a pill: so small and yet so powerful. Holding it between her fingers, Jade marveled at its ability to keep her in control. Then she turned on the faucet, cupped a hand beneath it, and used a palm full of tepid water to swallow it down.

CORA

5:16 p.m.

Cora was upstairs in her bedroom having her first panic attack. She knew it was a panic attack because Jade had described one to her. Free-loving Earth-mama Jade had had at least a dozen panic attacks in the year after Maggie died, and she'd downloaded them to Cora in detail.

Like I'm actually dying, like there are hands around my throat, squeezing tight.

That's what she'd said to Cora six years ago, and now the words trailed through Cora's mind like smoke.

Breathe, Cora. You're not actually dying. You're just not. You may, however, be married to a lying psychopath. But, congratulations, you're not dead yet!

Cora pulled her knees to her chest and dropped her head. She wanted to read the notebook pages again, and to do that she needed the squiggly spots in front of her eyes to fade away, and she needed a clear head, the kind of head she'd used in graduate school to solve the complicated equations barely anyone else could, the kind of head she'd used to consider Sam's marriage proposal.

Could she have been so wrong?

In. Out. In. Out. Those were the words Jade had said to herself over and over to get herself out of the panic attacks, and they were the words Cora used now. *Just breathe, girlfriend.* That's what Maggie would have said.

Cora let go of a long breath. She could feel her heart thudding against her chest. Her hands were so hot and sweaty it was hard to hold the notebook. She watched her fingers shaking as she flipped it open and started rereading.

That First Night with Sam O'Connell

by Mira Madsen

It started with just one glance. That's the way people always say it starts, like in love songs, and they're right.

I was babysitting at the O'Connells'. It was time for me to go home, but Sam was always so funny about paying me, like he thought I'd feel like a hooker or something if he passed me thirty dollars. "It's just babysitting!" I wanted to say. Anyway, he always let Mrs. O'Connell pay me, and she's always all harried trying to find the right change while the babies cry for her. (I still call them the babies, because they still act like babies, pretty much always whining and clinging to their mom.) And Mrs. O'Connell would always freak out about not having change, and she couldn't take the sound of those babies crying for more than three seconds, so she'd just fork over twenty-dollar bills, so I'd always make out with about five to fifteen dollars more than I'd actually earned. Which was obviously just fine by me. Anyway, so that night, as usual, she couldn't take the trauma of her children fussing. They were right in Sam's arms, and you'd think it would be enough if you were a baby and your dad was holding you, but nope, had to be the mom holding them! I mean, babies are starving everywhere with flies on their eyelids, but, hey, got to make sure these ones are totally comforted in every second of every day. Mrs. O'Connell actually once told me she believes that "a child gains their self-worth by having all their cries attended to as babies." Are you freaking kidding me?

So she's going through her wallet and Sam's standing there with the babies and she literally rips them from his arms, and of course they go from crying to whimpering, so that's a little better for her. So then she's all flustered and says, "Good night, Mira! I'm going to put the twins to bed!" And I'm like, "Good night, Mrs. O'Connell!" And in my head I really mean it, it's not like I'm thinking, "Good night you unbelievably huge loser," because I'm not that cruel and mostly I feel sorry for her. So there she goes up the back staircase. Sam and I are in the kitchen, and he managed to catch the wallet Mrs. O'Connell threw at him. But he doesn't get the money right away. He sort of looks down at the wallet and looks up at me, and we're standing there alone for the first time ever. He's got a good body. And he's got that hot-dad look that I'd never even noticed before this year as an actual thing. Like Matt Damon. But there he is just staring at me in the kitchen, and I swear I could feel it everywhere in my body. I thought I could melt. I mean there's Asher, who's a little younger than me actually, he's still only twenty, and I'm not saying I don't feel anything when he looks at me, because I do. But it was nothing like this. Sam looked at me, and I felt the whole room shift. I know it sounds crazy. But I also know he felt it, too, because then he takes this giant step forward and he's just right there and I can reach out and touch him and I want to but I'm feeling frozen and way more nervous than I want to admit. So I just stand there staring. And then he puts his hand right on my hip. I was wearing my jeans, the low-rise ones, so his hand touches my skin and it feels like a shock. And I do mean down there. Ah! I know that sounds cheesy! But it's probably the first time I felt something like that because with Asher

I've known him forever, for my whole life, and it's all so the same thing every time. It's Asher saying something like, "Do you want to?" and me pretending like I really want to, and Asher taking off my clothes in the most unsexy way, mostly just fast, and Asher not being able to do the buttons and me finally having to just do it, which feels about as sexy as taking off my clothes in a dressing room. But this was nothing like that. There was still space between us, but when Sam's hand was on my hip like that it might as well have been everywhere. His fingers curled right over the top of my jeans and he tugged me a little forward and I was shaking with how hot it was to have him doing something to me that he was very much not supposed to be doing. Then he leaned in and kissed me and it was so incredibly urgent, like he had to kiss me because if he didn't he would die. I swear I would have done anything with him right then. I didn't care that Mrs. O'Connell was upstairs, I really just did not care. But then one of the twins cried, I think Lucy. She screamed out once. And at the sound of that obnoxious little scream, Sam stopped kissing me and looked like he'd gotten slapped across the face. I knew it was over the second he heard that baby's cry. It was like a switch flipped and he couldn't be near me. He backed up so fast he crashed into the kitchen table. I swear to God I saw tears in his eyes but maybe I'm just imagining it wrong, and then he saw the wallet and he looked like he was really going to freak out. But he didn't. He put his hand clumsily into the wallet and got out eighty bucks, which was way too much, and paid me. He didn't say anything. Not even goodbye. He ran up the back stairs toward Mrs. O'Connell and I had to walk myself out. It was so crazy. And now I just keep replaying it over and over again. I can't wait for it to happen again! Hopefully it will, and hopefully it will be soon.

LAUREL

5:21 p.m.

The girls were gone.

Dash waited until he could hear the roar of the engine fade before looking at Laurel, and when he did, she saw on his face everything he wanted from her. Was this how sexual desire played out in other marriages? Could women sense exactly what their husbands needed, or did it catch them off guard—and were they scared, too?

It was just so frightening not to know what he was going to do, or when he was going to do it. It was the only benefit of using Rachel this past year—Laurel could finally breathe a little with some kind of warning, unlike before, when she had to brace herself every time the girls weren't home.

I can do this. For the girls. I can stay to raise my girls.

Laurel was constantly reminding herself how short it was—the act itself lasted only ten minutes. She tried to smile at her husband, tried to pretend like everything was okay, as though they were two normal people standing in their living room, considering each other.

Dash stepped closer.

"You promised you'd wait for Rachel," Laurel said carefully, trying to keep her voice calm. Guilt flickered over Dash's face, the way it always did before everything began. With a trembling hand, Laurel reached inside her bag and retrieved her phone.

How far away are you? she texted. Please hurry.

SARAH

5:24 p.m.

Sarah had accidentally drunk the entire bottle of wine. Nothing good ever came of that, she reminded herself, but it had just gone down so easily.

She was in her living room now, curled up on one of the gorgeous cream Lillian August couches she'd purchased with Maggie in New Canaan. Two months after Maggie's graduation and two weeks before her death, she'd scored a full-time position at an interior design firm in downtown New York City. She'd chattered nonstop with Sarah about everything and anything having to do with design, and she'd encouraged Sarah to update her living room, and asked, *Please, Mom, can I do it?*

Of course Sarah had let her.

Maggie's plan had been to move in with Jade, who already had an apartment on the Lower East Side and was bartending and auditioning. Sarah had believed that if any unknown girl in New York City was going to make it as an actress, it was Jade. Sarah had seen her perform at Vanderbilt, and the girl was not only stunning, but talented, too. Not that Sarah was an expert, but it didn't take an expert to know when someone was special, and Jade was exactly that.

But after Maggie's death, Jade unraveled. She barely auditioned; she barely ate or got out of bed. Sarah took to riding the train into New York and visiting Jade once a week, and the visits helped them both as far as Sarah could tell. Jade had been Maggie's best friend for the four years since they were freshmen, and being with her felt as close to being with Maggie as Sarah could imagine.

Jeremy also frequently checked on Jade during that time, showing up after work in suits that looked almost as expensive as the ones Clark wore. He was Sam's best friend, three years older than Maggie and Jade, and had been friends with both girls during the year they overlapped at Vanderbilt. Sarah knew that Maggie had been romantically involved with Jeremy at some point, and the fact that Maggie had been with Jeremy when she died made it unsettling to see him so often, but Sarah had tried to accept whatever was happening between him and Jade. And of course now they were married, though Sarah had never entirely warmed up to him. There was something she couldn't quite name—a distance about him, maybe? Not that it mattered; Jeremy mostly seemed to avoid her.

Sarah opened her laptop. She alternated between the photos and videos of Maggie on her phone and computer (she continually swapped out and sent new videos of her daughter to her phone), and now she scrolled until she got to the photos of Cora and Sam's engagement party.

Maggie.

In the photo, Maggie was staring at the camera, her blond hair just cut into a chic style she'd described to Sarah as a *lob*, which, according to Maggie, if only you read *Us Weekly* you would know meant *long bob*. The front pieces were longer than the back and angled perfectly around her delicate features. Maggie's dark-brown eyes held the camera just as Jade turned to look at her and smile.

Sarah knew it was crazy to study the pictures from the night Maggie died, but she was seized with the desire to memorize every detail from the party right up until the moment her daughter disappeared. She couldn't bear to talk to anyone about it, but she could study the evidence, and she often did just that: she pored over photographs and videos. To Sarah, it felt as though, if only she looked hard enough, then maybe she could understand why the hell her daughter did what she did that night.

CORA

5:32 p.m.

Cora needed to stand. *You do it all the time, Cora, just get to your feet.* Surely she could still stand even now that she knew her husband had kissed the babysitter.

Up she went. She wasn't exactly standing; it was more like trying to balance on two tingling bare feet while holding a notebook filled with poison. She opened the top drawer of her bedside table, slipped the notebook beneath a library book about how to set loving boundaries for children, and then took three steps toward her window. She looked out onto the lawn. She needed the guests gone, and then she could deal with Sam.

She checked her watch. Even her wrist appeared to be shaking. Would these mothers ever leave? The party had started at two. Why hadn't Cora put an end time on the invitation? How was she supposed to face her guests? *Thanks so much for coming to our children's party! Did you have a chance to meet Mira, our gorgeous twenty-one-year-old babysitter? My children and I adore her. And Sam made out with her last month!*

Cora glanced down at Sam holding Lucy on the patio like nothing had happened, like everything hadn't just changed. She counted the mothers—*one, two, three*—so only three left, with one husband each and about seven children between them. Where were Isabella and

Terrence? Had they left? Cora would just say a quick goodbye to the mothers, and that would be that.

Let's get this show on the road, dammit!

It was what her father used to say when he attempted to usher Cora, Maggie, and their mother out of the house to go somewhere: church, a school function, a birthday party like this one.

Oh God. Was her dad still here?

Cora smoothed away a blond hair that had fallen over her face. Did it matter? Clark would never pick up on something being really, truly wrong with Cora. He had always been a doting father, but even when they were all living at home together, he often missed the subtle clues that Sarah picked up implicitly. (Thank God Sarah had already gone home.) Still, Cora's dad's inability to discern her every mood growing up had never bothered her. He'd been there for everything—science fairs, swim meets, and nightly dinners around the kitchen island. He was one of the only men at the country club who routinely played golf with his wife and daughters instead of his friends. He seemed to truly enjoy his family, and that had meant the world to Cora, and she knew Maggie had felt the same way. And then he'd done this thing with Abby, and even though it hurt Cora deeply, it didn't take away the love he'd given her for the first two decades of her life. Even now Clark was still able to be there for Cora, in his own way, with surprise visits to play with the twins, or with the Mother's Day and birthday cards he never forgot.

Jade was the only liability, the one with whom Cora might not be able to fake being okay. And telling Jade right now wasn't an option because it would make it way too real, and there was a chance that nothing Mira wrote had actually even happened. The way she'd written that byline: *by Mira Madsen* . . . was that normal for a diary entry? Maybe it was some kind of fictional short story?

But so much of it was true: Cora's behavior, and Sam's inability to pay their female babysitters. And worse, Cora was pretty sure she knew what night Mira was talking about. A little over a month ago they'd gone out for sushi. At the restaurant, Sam had worried maybe Cora shouldn't be eating so much tuna, because he wanted a third baby. *Tuna has a lot of mercury that builds up in your body, in your bones,* he'd said. And Cora had snapped, *Don't you think I hear enough about dietary choices from the other mothers? Honestly, Sam, please be a man,* and she knew she'd hurt him. He was quiet for the twenty minutes that followed, drinking his wine way too quickly. He didn't perk up until she switched the topic to when he'd like to start trying for another baby. Sam was the only person with whom Cora could manipulate a conversation. She could easily influence his moods, mostly by talking about the children, both the ones they had now and the future ones they might make. Was that a warning sign? Was it only their children who made him happy, not Cora, or even his work? He'd always hated banking. Sometimes Cora swore he did it only as some kind of messed-up competition with Jeremy, who so clearly loved the insane pace of the finance world. Cora didn't care about money or status; she could live in this house or a two-bedroom shack, and Sam knew that. If Sam kept working in finance, it wasn't because of what Cora wanted or needed, it was because of something *in* him, and she couldn't help but think it somehow had something to do with Jeremy.

That night after the mercury-sushi, Cora had driven them home in silence. She was exhausted, and all she could think about was how much she hoped Sam wouldn't try to have sex with her. In the house, it was exactly as Mira had written: it was nearly half past eight when they walked in the door, and the twins weren't asleep, even though Cora had told Mira to start reading the new Peppa Pig books at seven and to have them in their cribs by eight. So yes, Cora had obviously seemed flustered, because she was passive-aggressively trying to translate to Mira that she was *displeased with the situation*. Cora had swept the twins upstairs, exactly as Mira had written, and left Sam and Mira alone in the kitchen.

That night, when Sam finally came upstairs, Cora was so busy going on about how tired she was—so that she could avoid sex—that she hadn't really paid attention to how Sam was behaving. She just remembered he was still drunk (and didn't that make him so much more likely to do what Mira said he did?) and that he didn't push back when she started her familiar routine of feigning exhaustion. And then the light was off and she was happily sexless, and then, in fact, Cora had thought about the fact that Sam hadn't approached her for sex in some time. She was pretty sure it'd been a few months since he'd nuzzled up against her while she was reading in bed, and she wondered if that was normal for a married couple to go that long. But she hadn't given it much more thought. She'd fallen asleep easily that night and woken up again around two in the morning to Lucy's first nightmare.

Cora stared out her bedroom window down to the birthday party. One of the gingham tablecloths had come loose from its corner. Only the Dinosaur Delight green lemonade concoction weighed it down, and it whipped around like a flag. Cora watched as Sam shifted Lucy to his other hip. Jeremy was holding George, laughing at something Sam said. Could Sam really have done this? Cora didn't think he had it in him; she really didn't. But could she be certain? Could *anyone* be entirely certain about their spouse?

In the yard next door, Asher Finch was on his beloved hammock with his hands folded behind his neck, looking in the direction of Dash and Laurel's house, as usual.

Three mothers. Just say goodbye to the mothers, and they'll see it on your face that it's time to leave.

Cora walked out of her bedroom on shaking legs. Down the hall, down the stairs, through the foyer she went, right as Jade emerged from the bathroom.

"Jade?" Cora said, hating the way her voice sounded like a question. *Act normal, dammit!*

"Hi! We had so much fun," Jade said. "I think we need to get going, though, and get back home to walk Nelson. Hope that's okay?"

More than okay! "Of course," Cora said. "I'm so glad you came. Kisses to Nelson!" *Kisses to Nelson?* Cora didn't even like dogs, which she never admitted to anyone, because it was like saying you didn't like children. *Say something else; talk about George and Lucy.* "And the kids are going to love those Magna-Tiles."

"They got great reviews online," Jade said.

Cora smiled. She could do this.

Jade opened the screen door to the patio, and Cora put one foot in front of the other and walked toward her husband, who was likely a liar and a creep, and possibly a sex addict. Wasn't that what they were calling the celebrities who did this kind of thing? Jade split off and headed toward Jeremy. Sam spotted Cora and gave her a funny look, and she suddenly felt enraged.

Really? You're *giving* me *a funny look?*

How could he?

She felt tears start. Even when she got the mothers to leave, there were still her sweet, precious babies to take care of. How was she supposed to do that without collapsing, without screaming and crying and accusing Sam of what he may or may not have done?

"Cora!" called Antoinette Campbell. She was carrying her two-year-old and trailed by her bald husband. Behind Antoinette's approaching figure, Cora saw the familiar white car with Connecticut plates pull into the Madsens' driveway, and then out of the car stepped the dark-haired woman who visited them every month or two. Laurel had mentioned she was the only blond in her family, and Cora had never met the woman but figured she was a relative of Laurel: a sister, maybe?

"Thanks so much for having us!" Antoinette said to Cora. Antoinette was the unspoken leader of the mothers, and her leaving seemed to start a fire beneath the other two.

Soon Cora was double kissing her mom-friends, cooing baby talk to their toddlers, thanking everyone for coming in her most gracious tone of voice. "Aren't we so lucky to have met you all this year!" she overheard herself saying. God, she was laying it on thick. Was she hoping to have them on her side if she decided to divorce Sam? If he'd really done this, if he'd made a move on their twenty-one-year-old babysitter exactly like Mira had written it, was she supposed to leave him? And what about the way Mira had called her little entry *That First Night with Sam O'Connell*? The rest of the notebook was empty, but the title hadn't escaped Cora: it implied there was another night. Mira had certainly wanted there to be more.

Oh God.

Tiny dots sparkled in Cora's vision. She staggered toward Sam, but just then Isabella emerged from the side of the house and approached her, saying, "Terrence is in the car already, so sorry, we looked for you to say goodbye, and then . . ."

Cora nodded. If she could just sit down.

"Cora," Isabella said, leaning closer. She touched Cora's forearm. "I need to talk with you about something important. Do you think we could arrange a time to get together, tomorrow maybe? I'm working from home. I could easily come to you."

"Tomorrow?" Cora asked. Her voice sounded slurred. She needed these people gone.

"At Buzzed, maybe," Isabella suggested. "We could grab a coffee? How about at eleven?"

Cora nodded. *Just leave, Isabella, please.*

"I'll see you then," Isabella said, smoothing a lock of shiny black hair. "Thanks so much for having us. I left the receipt with the gift in case George and Lucy already have something like it," Isabella said, and then she took off and disappeared behind the side of the house.

Cora's stomach rumbled like it had during the first trimester with the twins, and she moved toward Sam out of instinct, but he didn't see her. He was leaning in to hug Antoinette. Cora watched his palm land on the curved side of Antoinette's stomach. An innocent gesture, but it sent Cora spinning, and then everything in her stomach was coming up. Oh, dear God, she was vomiting! And it was so green. The Dinosaur Delight!

"Cora!" Sam shouted, horrified as he turned to see Cora hunched over.

"Darling?" she heard her father say. He must have been flustered—Cora had only ever heard him call Sarah *darling*. The other mothers said things like, "Oh no!" and "Is it a stomach bug? Get the children off the patio!"

Jade squatted beside Cora and pulled back her hair while Sam tried to assure George and Lucy that "Mommy's okay, she's just eaten something funny."

"Are you all right?" Jade asked when Cora was done heaving. Clark was at her back, his hand between her shoulders.

Cora lifted her gaze and locked on to Jade's green eyes. "No," she said. "I'm really not."

LAUREL

5:36 p.m.

How much longer?" Dash asked Laurel.

Laurel glanced at her phone. There was no answer from Rachel. "Any minute," she said. "Can you wait? Please?"

Laurel wondered if other men with a penchant for rough sex tried to figure out a way to make it safer for their wives, because maybe Dash caring about her in that way was something they had that other couples like them didn't; maybe Dash finding Rachel to keep Laurel safe meant a part of him didn't want to hurt her.

But he did—and often.

It started when the girls were in elementary school. Laurel knew some people would call it S&M, and for years she thought of it as just that because she had to, to survive. She told herself she was any normal wife confronted with the emergence of a husband's midlife sexual fetish. But slowly she admitted that to term it S&M had to require some kind of desire and consent from both parties, and Laurel didn't want it—not at all. She'd tried to make it stop—they'd gone to multiple therapists—but it didn't work, and she was faced with the decision to leave him or comply. She was terrified of both options, which meant she was terrified nearly all the time. Sometimes there were quiet periods when Dash wouldn't approach her for sex for months—or if he did, it was a milder version and he barely hurt her—and during those months and years, their marriage almost felt normal. But as the girls got older, the frequency and roughness escalated like a freight train, and Laurel faced the reality of her situation. She didn't want to be hurt during sex ever. As of the last year, per Rachel, there were safe words and ways to get Dash to stop when he was going too far, but working with Rachel to come to a safer compromise didn't make Laurel love Dash more—it made her hate him. And now she counted down the days until Anna left for college, because leaving him then wouldn't even draw suspicion. It was the natural time marriages dissolved. Laurel had been paying very close attention: when the houses in Ravendale became empty of children seemed to be the precise time people who had been wanting to leave picked up and *left*. She would be one of them.

Laurel was Catholic and from a devout family. She didn't blame her inability to leave Dash right away entirely on her religion, because it was so much more than that, but she wondered: Would she otherwise have stayed this long? It was a dangerous cocktail of reasons that made her stay: her history growing up with an abusive father, her religion, plus her desperate need to create and maintain the life she wanted for the girls and herself, and to show her family she was nothing like them. She still pretended that was true by holding on to all the ways she was different; for starters, Laurel's father had hurt her mother in front of his children. *That's how I'm nothing like them. My girls don't have to suffer like I did.*

Stubbornly staying in Ravendale—and she knew it was desperately stubborn to stay after all the ways her father had embarrassed her—was a way to prove herself. Living on the right side of Ravendale in a beautiful house was what she'd always wanted, and she got it.

So how could Dash have turned on her like this after all he knew?

In the fall of 1986, during the homecoming football game Laurel's freshman year at Ravendale High School, in front of nearly the entire student body, Laurel's father had had too much to drink. Laurel's eldest brother was playing wide receiver, and the team was losing badly. Her father was getting drunker and more enraged until he started screaming from his seat in the stands, embarrassing Laurel beyond anything she thought possible. When her mother tried to get him to leave the game, he hit her square across the face. Dozens of people saw it. The incident passed over the stands like a wave of whispers until it reached Laurel, shivering on the first row of bleachers with her newest high school girlfriends. Someone called the police, and they arrested Laurel's father while her mother, with a bloody face, pleaded with the cops to *Please just let us go home*. Laurel watched the whole thing like she was floating outside herself, unable to speak. It felt similar to the way she left her body behind now, with Dash.

That night at the football game exposed Laurel and her family's secrets, and then everything changed. None of the mothers allowed their children to go to Laurel's house for the rest of high school. Worse, they looked at Laurel with both disgust and fear in their eyes, like they were watching her every movement, sure she was destined for catastrophe. Besides a few kind teachers and the counselor she was forced to see at school, only Laurel's boyfriend stuck by her side, a serious and principled boy named Mark DeFosse. Laurel could sense how much Mark wanted to shield her from her father's violence, but he was so young, what could he have done?

Meanwhile, Laurel set about proving Ravendale wrong.

She got straight As and went to Princeton on scholarship. Mark and Laurel couldn't make it work during college, and Laurel was devastated, but at least the rush she felt meeting new, brilliant young people who didn't know about her past made it a little easier to forget him. Mark had stayed in Ravendale and attended the police academy, and the couple of times Laurel had gotten pulled over in Ravendale—once for speeding, once for a broken taillight—her heart pounded until the cop got out of the car and she saw it wasn't him.

Having to drop out of med school at Columbia when she was pregnant with Mira was Laurel's first and only setback on her course toward proving to every one of those mothers that she belonged here in Ravendale, but she easily circumvented that: if she couldn't be a doctor, then she'd be the best mother she could possibly be. And it was easy! She genuinely loved and adored the girls. Of course she missed the challenge of medical school, but the girls soon became her everything, and she worked hard to forget the future she'd imagined.

The worst betrayal, the thing for which she couldn't forgive Dash, was that she'd told him everything that had happened within her family. She and Dash had stayed up late in med school, studying, talking, bound by some kind of code of pain they'd both grown up with. Dash had been raised in a cold home where no one physically hurt him, but no one physically touched him, either, let alone embraced him. He barely spoke to his parents now, and when Laurel and the girls endured a trip to Wisconsin a few years back to visit Dash's family in their low-ceilinged ranch, no one looked anyone in the eye.

So had Dash singled her out? Did some part of him sense she'd stay because anger and unhappiness were what she'd known, too?

Laurel's parents were dead now. And it wasn't like her four brothers ever wanted to talk about what had actually happened in their house all those years ago. Laurel was sure that if she'd had a sister, they'd have the kind of relationship where they would talk through everything. They'd try to make sense of what had happened to them. Growing up, she thought of domestic abuse as the ultimate lowbrow behavior. She didn't think it could also be happening in her affluent friends' homes across town. But now she knew it happened across the classes; now she knew it happened to her. It felt like a hulking thing she couldn't escape, like it had always been a part of her, passed down from her mother in her DNA somehow.

The doorbell rang and Laurel exhaled. Dash moved quickly, and then the door was open and Rachel was inside, kicking off her chic sandals and exchanging a glance with Laurel.

"Help us," Dash said, his voice low.

"Shut up, Dash," Rachel said. "You need to get yourself under control. I shouldn't be getting texts like these." She held up her phone and showed Dash the text Laurel had sent asking her to hurry. Laurel's stomach dropped. *Please don't make him angry with me!* Sometimes Rachel was so cavalier, so sure in her professional ability, but it was Laurel who had to endure Dash.

Dash's eyes cut from the phone to Laurel. She prayed the start of sex would be enough to calm him down. "The bedroom?" Laurel asked carefully. The bedroom was so much softer. There were fewer things he could hurt her with.

"Here," Dash said, and then he reached for her arm. No matter how many times he grabbed her to start sex, it always took her breath away. He was so animalistic, so teeming with whatever pent-up feelings lay beneath his skin. (At her? For her? Or did it have nothing to do with her?) He took her wrist and curved it behind her back. His mouth went to her neck.

"Dash, the bedroom," Laurel whispered, "let's go to the bedroom."

Dash let out a low moan. He never spoke actual words during it, and Laurel was grateful for that, because she was certain she didn't want him to vocalize what he was thinking.

"Please, the bedroom?" Laurel tried again, this time turning to Rachel.

Dash turned to look at Rachel, too, the referee for disagreements like this.

"Here," Rachel said simply, and Laurel whimpered.

"We need to close the blinds at least," Laurel said, and silently all three of them went to work. Laurel caught sight of Rachel bending to clear a stack of magazines so she could close the drapes over a sliding glass door. Was this par for her course? Did an S&M expert routinely tidy up a home before her clients got to work, or before she got to work on *them*? (And was *S&M expert* even the right term? Laurel wasn't sure how Dash had found Rachel. Had he googled local dominatrices? Extreme sex therapists?) Rachel adjusted the drapes so there were no openings, Dash turned off the lights, and Laurel bolted the front door. When they were finished, they all stared at each other, and for a moment, it felt like things could be normal, like Rachel could be here simply as a visitor, just like all the other women Laurel had ever entertained in her living room. But then Dash stepped toward Laurel and pushed her against the stone fireplace. She managed to arch her neck forward so that only her back hit the stones, not her head. She cried out as loudly as she could, because maybe that would be it—enough to satisfy him. Sometimes he hurt her only once, but usually it was twice: once when he initiated sex and again right before he finished. She shivered when she spotted the fire pokers so close.

Dash gripped Laurel's neck. Rachel watched carefully from her position a few feet away. Laurel's hands shook as she lifted her skirt, and her gaze fell on the stack of bumper stickers Anna had left on the console, the ones with *NYU* etched in purple letters, proudly showing off the university where she was going in the fall.

Just one more summer, Dash. One more summer, and then I leave you.

JADE

5:49 p.m.

After tucking Cora into bed with a cold washcloth against her forehead, Jade and Jeremy left the O'Connell house and stopped off at the tailor. Everything in Ravendale was overpriced. It was something everyone who lived here begrudgingly accepted, because mostly they could all afford to. Still, two hundred dollars for alterations on a jacket?

"It's a three-thousand-dollar suit, Jade," Jeremy said as they stepped inside the tailor's shop. "There's no point wearing it if it doesn't fit."

The shop was wood-paneled and blessedly air-conditioned. Jade recalled a dozen years ago, when she'd glimpsed a seventeen-year-old Maggie getting alterations on her prom dress and noticed how alluring Maggie looked in her silver beaded gown. Maggie was short like Cora but stood taller, and she was so incredibly magnetic.

The tailor ushered Jeremy and Jade into a dressing room. Jeremy undid the button of his shorts and let them fall to the floor. He stared at himself in the mirror.

Jade stared, too. Her husband stepped onto the raised block in the tailor's dressing room, surrounded by mirrors that broadcast his image eternally. It was like staring at a sea of Jeremys, all a few inches over six feet, well built, with a close-cut beard that bordered on being stubble. It was sexy; he was sexy. Even after all this time together, Jade saw how incredibly attractive he was. She saw him, and now she just wanted him to see her, all of her, including the things he didn't want to accept, like how she wanted to adopt children, for starters. She wished more than anything that he wanted to sleep with her for reasons other than making a baby; some primal part of her needed him to desire her. But the problem was that Jeremy, for all of his hotness, liked being adored more than he liked actually having sex. Jade didn't realize it until they were engaged. Once the ring was on her finger, Jeremy stopped performing as much in quite a few areas of their life together. He stayed at the office longer and didn't return with flowers; he slept on the couch or in an upstairs bedroom for weeks on end. Jade had never cared about flowers, but she did care about being intimate. There was so much she'd never told him, so many secrets between them, and the sex felt like one way they were truly a couple. Jade was always amazed that even in her saddest moments, the ones where she dreamed of Maggie being alive, her body was still able to respond to a man's touch. Bodies were funny like that. The automatic nervous system at work; no matter how she felt about losing Maggie, Jeremy could still make her feel good and forget, and those were the moments she craved. It was something about the heaviness of his body; when he climbed on top of her and pressed her to the bed, she felt everything inside of her quiet, as though the sheer weight of him could temporarily crush all the pain and loss she still carried after Maggie's death.

As soon as they were married, Jade felt like a nymphomaniac for all the times she asked and got turned down. Surely this couldn't be normal, she bemoaned to Cora, who looked at Jade like she'd won the lottery for marrying a man so disinterested in sex.

But things changed two and a half years ago when Sam and Cora announced they were pregnant: Jeremy immediately wanted to get Jade pregnant, as if children weren't something he'd even thought about until he saw Sam's two little ones swimming on a sonogram. What was it that bound Sam and Jeremy so tightly? It was bizarre. Or maybe it wasn't; maybe it was just typical competition fueled by machismo.

The problem was that Jade had always told Jeremy she didn't want her own biological children. Before they were married, she made it clear to him that she'd wanted to adopt since the day she'd learned what the word meant. She was her parents' only biological child, but as soon as she turned ten, they started taking in foster children, mostly babies and toddlers. What would have happened to those children if Jade's parents had been so bogged down in raising three or four biological children that they didn't feel they could take on any more? When Jade explained these sentiments to Jeremy, he'd acted as though he understood and even agreed, but they were both still in their twenties, and maybe he didn't really care back then, or maybe he thought she would change her mind when some sort of biological clock started ticking. Now Jade just prayed that her not getting pregnant would be a sign to Jeremy that she was meant to become a mother the way she'd always known she was. If she had her own child, that would be taking away the child she was meant to adopt! She knew what she was destined for, but now Jeremy had changed his mind, or maybe he'd never planned to go along with her desire in the first place. So what was she supposed to do?

The tailor whipped open the curtain and stared at them. Jeremy's hazel eyes didn't fall away from the middle-aged woman like most men's would if they were standing there in underwear. Jeremy wore his favorite light-gray boxers and a button-down shirt, and Jade saw him watch the tailor, waiting for her reaction.

"Let's see how it looks on," the tailor said, unmoved. She passed Jeremy the navy jacket she'd made alterations to and then disappeared again.

"Did something happen with Isabella and Terrence that you want to tell me?" Jade asked. "They were weird at the party. Isabella kept glaring at me."

Jeremy slid his arms into the jacket and smoothed the fabric.

"He's pissed and embarrassed," Jeremy said.

"Why would he be embarrassed about falling down the stairs?" Jade asked.

"Most people would be," Jeremy said.

"I don't think so," Jade said.

Jeremy shrugged. "I think it's more the drug thing I told you about. And he's leaving the fund. There are hard feelings all around."

Jade was sure there was more, but she was also sure she wouldn't be able to get it out of him, because when had that ever worked?

Jeremy cleared his throat. "I saw the paperwork you left for me," he said, considering himself in the mirror.

"What paperwork?" Jade asked. She hadn't left him any paperwork.

"The stuff you printed out about adoption."

Jade swallowed. She'd kept those papers in the top drawer of her desk, and she'd been planning to save them for when she'd carefully prepared something to say to Jeremy, maybe a new angle to appeal to his needs, too. "It's supposed to be the best adoption agency around here," she blurted. Her heart picked up speed as she stared at his reflection, his face calm as he considered her in the mirror. Even after all this time, he could still make her nervous. The way he reacted to everything was so completely unpredictable. Her therapist said that was typical for narcissistic personality disorder, with which she'd diagnosed Jeremy after Jade detailed his behaviors. Jade wasn't sure if it was fair for her to diagnose Jeremy without actually meeting him, but he did fit a lot of the boxes, like how anything he decided was bound to be decided in relation to him, or how he was unable to separate himself from any equation or to see people in any way other than in relation to or as an extension of himself.

"You know I've always wanted to adopt," Jade said for what felt like the thousandth time in the last few years. She ran the toe of her sandal over a patch of carpet, careful to avoid a dropped pin. What if Jeremy had been thinking about it lately, too, now that it had been so long that she hadn't gotten pregnant? What if he, like Jade, was imagining the phone call announcing that a child, the one who was meant for them, had been found and was ready to come home?

Jeremy returned his gaze to himself. "And I said I didn't think adoption was for me," he said. "And I still don't."

"You mean it's not for you right now, or ever?" Jade asked.

"Yeah, it's just not for me, Jade, sorry," he said. He lifted his cocky chin and stared at his reflection from a different angle. "I've always wanted my own kid."

"But I'm sure you could get past needing a little clone trailing at your legs," Jade snapped, and then instantly regretted it.

Jeremy turned on the tailor's block to face her. "Are you fucking kidding me, Jade?"

"I'm sorry, but couldn't you please just think about it some more? Or we could see a couples therapist and talk about it. I want to adopt, please, I—"

"And I said no." He suddenly looked ridiculous standing there in his suit jacket and underwear. "It takes two, doesn't it?"

"Actually, no, not with adoption," Jade said carefully. This wasn't exactly how she had envisioned this conversation going, but that part was true.

"Let's get out of here," Jeremy said, shrugging free from the jacket. He pulled his shorts on and then pushed open the curtain and nearly plowed into the tailor.

"There were a few more things I wanted to see," said the tailor, holding a pink-and-purple pincushion.

"It's perfect, thanks," Jeremy said. "I'll pay you now."

"I'll wait in the car," Jade said, forcing a smile at the tailor for God only knows what reason. She moved from the slick air-conditioning to the hot sidewalk, spotted her BMW SUV, and headed toward it. She could fit at least three kids in that car, even with diaper bags and hockey gear. Tears streamed down her face as she imagined herself looking in the rearview mirror at the three faces that looked nothing like hers, exactly as she'd always dreamed. It felt further away than ever.

LAUREL

6:14 p.m.

Laurel looked down at the positive pregnancy test in her hand. Two pink lines. One was very faint, but Laurel knew that didn't matter. There was no such thing as being only a little bit pregnant.

Dash had left right after Rachel did. He always left after sex, even for a short while, unless it was very late at night, in which he case he slept. Laurel always marveled at how deeply he slept; it was a little scary, actually. Twice during their twenty-year marriage, the fire alarm had gone off, and both times, Laurel had to shake Dash awake so he could turn the thing off while she soothed the girls back to bed. They weren't actual fires, only false alarms, but if there were ever a real one, could Laurel leave him there, sleeping like that, to die that way?

No one would blame her. She could say she'd fallen asleep in the family room watching TV, and that upon hearing the alarm, she ran to the girls' bedrooms to save them, having assumed Dash was already safe outside, but by the time she realized he wasn't at their designated meeting place, it was too late, and she couldn't risk going back inside to save him. She was a mother; she had little girls who depended on her.

Laurel shifted her skinny butt on the floor of Mira's pink-tiled bathroom. She couldn't take her eyes off the pregnancy test. Early that morning, she'd found three positive tests hidden inside a plastic Rite

Aid bag in the very back of Mira's bottom drawer, behind the organic Tom's of Maine deodorant that Laurel insisted the girls use. The regular deodorant brands used such terrible chemicals to block sweat glands. It was the kind of thing her own parents never thought about—chemicals, clean food, even bike helmets—and that made Laurel even more determined to make things as healthy as possible for the girls. She'd been trying so hard to protect her daughters; she was always trying to protect them. And now this.

Laurel had to assume it was Asher Finch. Maybe she'd been too lax letting Mira hang out with him so much this summer. But the girls had known the Finch boys forever; they'd played together since they were small, romping between backyards and swing sets like the land belonged equally to all of them. The older Finch boy, Ethan, was interning in the city this summer, and Asher was between his freshman and sophomore year at Boston College, two years younger than Mira and one older than Anna. And Asher had always seemed so totally harmless and lazy with his chronic hammock swinging. Laurel thought it was good for Mira to have a boyfriend. Mira and Anna barely had any experience dating, unless Mira was keeping secrets about whatever happened in college. But Anna was still home—she didn't leave for NYU until August 28—and Laurel was sure she'd never had a boyfriend, and she was eighteen! When Asher had started showing an interest in Mira, Laurel was thrilled. Asher was from a perfectly nice family; Robert and Dorothy Finch were the most vanilla, community-minded people on the face of the planet. Dorothy baked cakes from scratch and ran the Sunday school program at the Catholic church in town.

Had Mira told Asher? If yes, had Asher told his parents? Did Asher and his parents want Mira to keep the baby because he was Catholic? Did Mira want to keep the baby?

The Finch parents weren't at the twins' birthday party today; only Asher had come. *Why* hadn't they come? Was it because they were reeling with the news of an impending grandchild?

Obviously Laurel would support Mira no matter what she wanted to do. She'd raise the baby herself if Mira asked, or she'd stand by Mira if she wanted to raise the baby, or give him or her up for adoption. But she'd also accompany her daughter to a clinic and hold her hand if Mira decided she couldn't do any of those things.

Laurel started to cry. Her shoulders heaved, and she wiped her tears with the back of her hand. She felt absolutely sure that if only she'd been another kind of mother, none of this would have ever happened. If she'd just done something differently, if she herself had been stronger or a better role model for the girls—because didn't they know something was wrong with their father? Didn't they know their mother should have left long ago? Couldn't they sense it?

SARAH

6:17 p.m.

Sarah was back in her kitchen, her hand aching as she scrolled through videos of Maggie on her laptop. It was something about the angle of her hand and the scrolling, and whenever she tried to switch hands, it just set off the same pain on her left wrist and thumb. What if Dr. Madsen told her she wasn't a candidate for surgery and that what she really needed was to take a break from her computer? Could she bear to part from Maggie like that? She could always invite Cora over and force her to do the scrolling and playing of videos, but that seemed unfair because Cora didn't even know about Sarah's behavior. It was sort of Sarah's secret, actually. She thanked God for technology the same way she'd noticed grandmothers thanking God for FaceTime with grandchildren who didn't live locally.

Sarah used to think she'd never have that problem—she'd always thought both her girls would end up in Ravendale. Ravendale was so beautiful, so idyllic with its rolling hills and stone walls. Except for the ticks—Sarah hated ticks. But other than ticks and cold winters, what would ever keep the girls away?

Death, apparently.

Maggie being a grown woman and a mother in Ravendale felt like just another thing Sarah had lost. Sometimes it felt almost unbelievable—like an entire life had been mapped out, and suddenly there was nothing except the impossible, imaginary scenes Sarah kept seeing in her mind's eye, mostly ones that involved her caring for Cora and Maggie's children. No matter how fantastical and improbable it was, ever since Cora and Maggie were small, Sarah had always imagined taking care of their children while they raced off to work. *Got to go, Mom! Just heat up the bottle—thirty seconds, okay? Not too hot!*

And Sarah could practically hear herself laughing and saying things like, *I remember, sweetie, I raised you, didn't I?* She and her daughters would exchange glances that all at once expressed their gratitude to Sarah for raising the kids so they could work and also the bond they shared with their mother, which was unbreakable and lasting. Sarah knew it was a lot to ask for, but she had seriously thought there was a possibility it could happen, enough so that she'd been mildly put out when Cora decided to stay home and raise her own children.

There it was! Sarah stopped scrolling and clicked on the image of Maggie with her hands up to the sides of her face as she feigned surprise at something Cora said. Sarah pressed play, and Maggie's sweet voice filled the kitchen. *"Mom! Do you know that Cora has no idea she's actually in the witness protection program? She thinks she's your biological child!"*

The sound of Sarah's laughter from behind the camera sounded unfamiliar to her ears. Surely she hadn't laughed like that since her daughter died. It sounded almost giddy.

The video was taken at sunset during Cora and Sam's engagement party. Guests flitted across the patio in dresses, skirts, and blazers. It was a proper party, and Sarah loved proper parties. Hadn't she and Clark loved getting ready together for parties in that massive walk-in closet? Every time Sarah asked Clark to zip her into a dress, he couldn't help but kiss her bare skin before he did.

In the background of the video, guests laughed and drank near the rosebushes, but the three magnificent faces in front of Sarah's camera upstaged all that background beauty: Maggie, Cora, and Jade.

"Maggie," Cora said to her sister and then turned back to her mother behind the camera. *"Mom, Maggie says she has to tell us something very important after the party's over."*

"And I just did!" Maggie said. *"You're not my real sister! Mom and Dad are hiding you. I think from the mob."*

"Oh my God, Maggie," Jade said. She laughed, but it was a nervous one. Jade hated being on camera, which made no sense given she wanted to be an actress. She once explained the phenomenon to Sarah: when she embodied a character, it was entirely different because she wasn't herself. *Myself is harder,* she'd said.

"I'm just saying," Cora said in the video, her sweet face made up so nicely by the woman Sarah had hired to do their makeup: rouge on her cheekbones, just the right amount of brown-black mascara on her barely there lashes.

"You're just saying what, darling?" Sarah asked from behind the camera. She remembered being vaguely aware that Clark and Abby had entered the background of her shot right then, and yes, there they were, six years younger. Abby was heavier then, actually. She wore a floral caftan and held white wine, and Clark was devastatingly handsome in his gray suit. He turned and looked away from the party guests to where all four of them stood alone on Sarah's deck. Was he looking at his daughters? Or at Sarah?

Sarah rewound the video and watched again, but she couldn't be sure. He'd turned back to Abby so quickly.

"I'm just saying it's a lot of suspense, whatever it is," Cora said to the camera. Behind her, Terrence and Isabella crossed the patio with matching glasses of white wine. Sarah had loved when Cora and Isabella became friends because they were both so incredibly intelligent. Cora could have gone into finance, too, with her numbers brain, but she was drawn instead to the *theory of mathematics*, as she put it. Still, it seemed like a perfect match, though Cora and Isabella had lost touch when the twins were born and Sam and Cora moved out of New York

to Ravendale. *Hold on to your friends,* Sarah had told Cora when George and Lucy were little, but Cora seemed too tired to hear her.

Sarah pressed stop on the video. The smell of ginger wafted through the kitchen. She'd ordered sushi to sober up—all that rice always did the trick.

Sarah looked at Cora's questioning face paused on the screen. Sarah never told Cora what Maggie had been about to tell them that night, because she figured now that Maggie was gone, it wasn't her secret to tell. But Sarah knew, of course. She had her dead daughter's diary, after all.

CORA

6:19 p.m.

Cora was lying in her bed with a cold washcloth over her forehead in the exact same position Jade had left her in an hour ago. She thanked God for Jade, who had insisted she rest with a bucket beside her bed and gave her strict instructions not to move. Plus, Jade being there fluffing pillows and tucking her into bed meant Cora didn't have to look at Sam. *Let me take care of the kids,* Sam had said. *They ate enough at the party, anyway, and I'll do bath and bed, and then I'll come check on you.*

They actually didn't eat enough at the party, thank you very much, Cora thought, but she didn't have the energy to tell Sam. Let him figure it out himself when they started screaming for snacks in an hour.

Should we call Sarah? Jade had blurted out, which made Sam roll his eyes. *I don't need my mother-in-law here,* he'd said. *I'm actually quite capable of taking care of my children.*

I mean to take care of you, she'd said to Cora. *If you won't let me stay . . .*

You're two streets away, Cora had said. *I'll call you or my mom if I need someone.*

Jade had nodded while Jeremy mumbled *Feel better* to Cora. He was hot even when he was grossed out. And he had to be grossed out:

Cora had continued vomiting all over her patio and also on Antoinette Campbell's shoes, and she'd just kept on vomiting even when there was nothing left. Cora was sure two of the mothers had actually left before she was done getting sick, which felt strangely personal. Weren't they supposed to stay to make sure she was okay?

Cora shifted onto her side. She stared at her bedroom wall, where she'd used putty to affix four pictures the twins had painted. They looked so artistic, Cora had thought, with confident bright-blue streaks across the paper. Cora had helped George write *For Daddy* on his. She'd had to convince him on that. Both twins had wanted to dedicate their pictures to Cora, but Cora hadn't wanted Sam to feel left out. What had been the point?

None of it felt real. Of course there were things about Sam that felt unknowable, things Cora couldn't always put her finger on. Ever since the night Maggie died, they had both changed, certainly. But hadn't they all changed? Clark, Sarah, Sam, Cora, Jade, and Jeremy: Wasn't that inevitable?

In the wake of Maggie's death, Sam and Cora would retreat to separate rooms in their New York apartment. Cora had thought of it as Sam giving her space, but they'd never done that before, and then it never really stopped happening until the twins came. After George and Lucy were born, everything was full of bouncing, happy life. Cora burst into tears all the time that first year she had the twins, but even that felt like relief. She'd been bottled so tight since Maggie died, and her love for the twins was the only way she could release just the tiniest bit of pressure.

Cora had thought it was natural for Sam to retreat. Something remarkably tragic had happened during a time that was supposed to be magical. (Those were the kind of words the wedding magazines used: *magical, treasured, honored*. As though the newly engaged couple were embarking on something so sacred and rightfully theirs, something that wasn't meant to be spoiled by the maid of honor dying. There were certainly no advice columns in *Modern Bride* to help Cora after her engagement party.)

When Cora had suggested postponing the wedding, her mom and Sam turned to her like she'd slapped them. *Maggie wouldn't want that,* Sarah had said.

What about what I want? Cora had thought, but she kept quiet, and she and Sam dutifully resumed planning their wedding a few weeks after burying Maggie.

Maggie's death was so painful beyond anything Cora had ever known that she figured out how to turn off her emotions and pretend when she needed to. The wedding was taking place in Ravendale, and everyone knew what had happened to Maggie and that Sam had been with her when she died, so when Cora and Sam went to the Ravendale shops to choose their wedding cake, flowers, and the like, they were confronted with vendors who could barely meet their gaze as they made apologies. Cora didn't know how to behave at those meetings; should she seem happy at all about her wedding? Should she break down and cry when the vendors shared a story about Maggie from growing up? It was that kind of town—everyone knew everyone, and it was hard to be an adult with the *real adults* constantly reminding you of what you were like as a child. Cora had come up with a carefully crafted persona to present at those wedding meetings: tentative, sad, and grateful to be alive.

Because she really was those things. Cora was absolutely grateful to be alive, and it was what she told her sister when she talked to her throughout the day: *I won't waste this.* She knew it was dramatic, and she never thought she'd talk to a dead person or make promises about living life fully, because it was so not her way. But how else could she talk to Maggie? If Maggie could somehow hear her, shouldn't Cora respect the fact that Maggie would never get to have a wedding, or laugh with her and Jade again, or have kids, or do anything at all, ever again?

And now this with Sam. Maggie would also never have the experience of her husband kissing the babysitter. Would Maggie have seen this coming?

Those months during wedding planning, Sam had gone dark on Cora. She'd never said it out loud, and she never admitted it to anyone but herself, but Cora had been disappointed in the way Sam dealt with the aftermath of Maggie's death. Shouldn't he have been fully there for Cora? Shouldn't he have been able to help her with her grief? Maggie was her sister, her best friend, her everything. It surprised Cora, because Sam had been so good at helping her through the more manageable difficulties they'd faced so far, like navigating Clark, Sarah, and Abby. Clark and Abby had just gotten married the year before, and Sarah had been a raging mess, and it seemed like nothing Cora said was right or even modestly helpful, and Cora had felt so stressed and powerless during that time that she'd started seeing a therapist. She'd felt only lukewarm about the therapist and had stopped after a few sessions when Sam said, *I can help you with this, babe.* And he had.

But it was like a knife cut them when Maggie died, killing some vital part of their relationship, and Cora was so overwhelmed trying to survive that she didn't have the energy to fix what broke. And now here she was six years later, lying in bed, replaying another woman's—a *girl's*—words about her husband, wondering if everything was somehow connected.

The tinkling music from a children's show on the iPad filtered up the stairs. A few hours ago, Cora would have been furious that Sam couldn't take care of the twins for just one night without the iPad. Not now. Let him save his energy for tonight.

Tonight.

She'd do it as soon as the twins were sleeping. She opened the drawer of her bedside table, wondering how he'd react when she placed Mira's notebook in his hands.

LAUREL

6:31 p.m.

Laurel was reapplying mascara when Dash came home. She didn't want him to see her makeup smeared and realize she'd been crying. She was absolutely sure about one thing: if Mira decided to have an abortion, she certainly wasn't going to tell Dash. That was for Mira to tell him, when she was ready, if ever. But it wasn't going to stay a secret between Laurel and Mira; Laurel was going to talk to Mira tonight. Mira would be pissed that Laurel snooped in her drawers. (Really, Laurel hadn't been snooping: she was looking for the expensive dry shampoo she was sure her daughter had taken.) Mira could scream at Laurel all she wanted, but she was going to need her mother no matter what choice she made. Wasn't that what mothers were there for? You could rail against them, you could blame them, and you could hate them, but you still needed their love the way you needed water.

Laurel was a *good* mother. It was the singular fact that made her the happiest. She loved her daughters with a love she'd never even known she was capable of feeling. No matter how many things she wished she'd done differently, she knew the girls never doubted her feelings for them.

"Laurel?" Dash called up the stairs.

"Coming!" Laurel called back. She left their room and walked down a half flight of stairs to meet him in the foyer.

Dash gave her a tentative smile. He had a hard time looking her in the eye directly after sex. He never apologized, and he wasn't even particularly nice, but once he cooled down, he wanted her close.

"I picked up salmon," he said. He was an incredible cook. Laurel always thought of his surgeries when she saw him slicing through flesh.

"I ate so much at the birthday party," Laurel said, putting a hand to her stomach. She hadn't, actually, but sharing a meal with Dash right now wasn't at all what she wanted to do.

"Sit with me a minute," Dash said, and she followed him numbly toward the couch. There were so many things she wanted to say, like: *That hurt today, worse than usual.* Or: *We should see Dr. Berg again.* Or maybe: *What the fuck is wrong with us, Dash?*

She still deeply cared about him no matter how much she hated him. How was that even possible? There was so much life lived together, and when she looked at him separate from herself, as a man with demons and rage and pain, she felt overcome with tenderness for him. It felt almost spiritual, like she was outside both of them, like she wasn't Laurel (or Dash, either), but more like she was the space between them.

She still had to leave.

Anna was a strong girl; she'd be okay if they divorced. And Mira was so stubborn—she'd be furious at Laurel for divorcing her father, but she'd come around eventually. Laurel had been planning all of this since Anna entered high school, and the time since she'd decided had gone so fast—Anna was a sophomore the following year, then a junior getting good grades and doing plays, then a senior settling on *A big school in a big city: NYU's the right place for me, Mom, I know it!*

It had been nearly impossible to convince Dash to let Anna go to New York because he thought it was too dangerous for an eighteen-year-old to live there. Really, what got him on board was the reality that NYU was the best school to accept her. Mira had Laurel's and Dash's science brain, but Anna was creative, gorgeously so. To read her writing was like stepping into another world, like reading a real, published book. Laurel was sure her daughter could be a writer. Not to say she'd get published right away, but she'd figure it out. And Dash and Laurel could help with rent so that Anna could stay in New York after college and live in a safe neighborhood. Laurel would do all the things her parents financially couldn't.

But would Dash still be generous with the girls if Laurel left? She thought he would, out of love for them and pride, but could she be sure? He would punish Laurel some way; she just didn't know how.

Laurel shook her head to clear her thoughts. She was leaving, no matter what. That's what she'd been holding on to for years. Because of their appointments with Rachel, the sex now followed such a predictable map that she sometimes thought of the months and years in terms of how many times she had to endure it. *About half a dozen more to go,* she'd caught herself thinking earlier this year.

"I want to walk the gorge with Mira tonight," Laurel said slowly. "I just, I feel like we need a good chat."

Dash nodded, and a moment later, the door swung open and they turned to see Anna standing there with her hands on her slim hips. Anna was smaller than Mira, built like Laurel. Her blond hair was tied into a messy side ponytail, and mascara flecked beneath her eyelashes. "I have no idea where Mira went," she said, annoyed. "Literally I walked all around town trying to find her, and her phone is going straight to voice mail, and I texted her five hundred times, and she just doesn't respond. So I drove back!"

"Calm down, Anna," Dash said. He couldn't tolerate any overreaction from the girls.

"Did she say anything about going to Andrea's?" Laurel asked. Mira had told her earlier that day she wanted to sleep over at her friend Andrea's apartment. Andrea was in school at Westchester Community College, and she and Mira had met earlier this summer working together at Buzzed. "I told Mira she could sleep there tonight," Laurel said. Dash gave her a look. He wasn't a fan of Andrea, which Laurel thought was unfair and based on snobbish reasons, like her multiple tattoos.

"No, she didn't say that," Anna said. "She borrowed my keys and drove back to you guys because she forgot a book."

"She never came here, honey," Laurel said.

Anna shrugged. "She came back to the community center all upset and texting about something with someone, and she barely even worked with the kid she was supposed to be tutoring. She said she had to go and she'd be back soon, and then she didn't come back at all." Anna's voice was high and pinched, the way she always got when she was flustered by the indignity of her rude sister. "She's gone, Mom."

VOICE MAIL RETRIEVED BY THE RAVENDALE POLICE DEPARTMENT FROM ASHER FINCH'S PHONE, LEFT BY MIRA MADSEN AT 6:32 P.M.

Are you getting my texts? Are you home? Call me back, Asher, I mean it, we need to talk.

VOICE MAIL RETRIEVED BY THE RAVENDALE POLICE DEPARTMENT FROM MIRA MADSEN'S PHONE, LEFT BY DASH MADSEN AT 6:43 P.M.

Mira, honey, it's Dad. Anna's here, and she's concerned because you said you'd be back to the community center, and then you left and didn't return. Call home, Mira, as soon as you get this.

JADE

6:49 p.m.

Jade slipped her key into the green front door. "We should paint this door," she said to Jeremy. It was the first thing she'd said since the tailor's. "It's too dark against the shingles."

"Do what you want," Jeremy said, and Jade asked, "Do you care what color I paint it?" The old door creaked as she eased it open.

"As long as it's not something stupid, like yellow," Jeremy said.

"I wouldn't paint our front door yellow," Jade said, tension descending on her shoulders as she stepped onto the gray wooden planks of their foyer. A clear glass table sat in the entranceway, stacked with design books, a tiny gold box, and a seashell Maggie had found in Nantucket. Their beloved Nelson looked up from his spot on the rug nestled among his chew toys. "Hey, Nelson," Jade said, bending and scratching behind his ears. He was too old to get up to greet her, but he still smiled, his tongue lolling out as she patted his head.

"Want to go for a walk, boy?" Jeremy asked. He was always sweet with the dog.

"I'll get you his leash," Jade said, vaguely remembering taking it off this morning near the fireplace. She disappeared down the hall and tucked into the room she'd turned into a library, scanning the floor beside the fireplace and bending to retrieve the leash from where it lay atop a stack of magazines featuring her jewelry. This month, *Elle* magazine had featured one of Jade's pieces on Beyoncé, and even though her jewelry had been featured in magazines and she'd had celebrity clients for years, it still gave Jade such a thrill. She loved the anticipation of waiting the few months after her jewelry had been shot for the magazine to hit newsstands, and then there was the rush of racing out to buy it to see how the jewelry looked on the page. No matter how much the fashion world had changed with the immediacy of the internet, magazine press would always be her favorite. She loved holding it in her hand and imagining showing it to her children, or even her grandchildren.

Jade had become a jewelry designer by chance. She'd studied theater at Vanderbilt, and she'd liked auditioning in New York after graduation, but after Maggie died she couldn't bring herself to get out of bed. And when she went for her first audition nearly a year later (at Jeremy's insistence), she found she just didn't have it in her anymore. Putting on a happy face and trying to perform for casting directors no longer felt like something she wanted to do. The good-time-girl persona she'd always been able to summon to perform comedies seemed to have disappeared along with Maggie. Nothing felt quite so funny anymore. So Jade kept bartending at night, but instead of auditioning during the day, she stayed inside the safety of her apartment. To keep her hands busy, she picked up jewelry supplies at the craft stores in Midtown and started designing jewelry again, something she'd loved when she was younger. One day she was wearing one of her necklaces when the owner of a small shop on the Lower East Side spotted the piece and asked who'd designed it. When Jade told the boutique owner she'd made it herself, the woman placed an order for six necklaces to sell at her shop. That year, Jade showed her jewelry to a few more boutiques, some of which also placed orders. Over the next few years, it slowly became her full-time career, and even more than the thrill of the magazine press, she loved the way making jewelry never failed to quiet her restless mind.

Jade breathed in the musty smell of the library. She knew grander-scale rooms were more in fashion, but she preferred the coziness of the smaller rooms in her old house, and the library was her favorite. The walls and ceiling were painted charcoal, and an old painting of a distinguished-looking gentleman hung on the wall. She and Jeremy had no idea who he was—they'd found him at a yard sale—but during the first year they lived in the house, they often made up various ridiculous identities. Jeremy used to make Jade laugh. She'd been so intrigued by him when they first got together. It was his brain, and the way he was so wickedly smart and darkly funny.

Jade left the library and started back down the long hallway, two small chandeliers scattering light beneath her feet. In the kitchen, Jeremy opened a cupboard and sorted through a sea of healthy snacks: dried fruit, almonds, seaweed, sweet potato chips, and the protein powder he used to make his smoothies in the morning. He had been overweight as a child—he never mentioned it to Jade, but she'd seen pictures—and though Jade had never asked him about it, she knew it must have had something to do with the way he diligently counted calories now. Jeremy was the second of four boys raised in Darien, Connecticut, and his mother was a perfectionist and extremely hard on all of them except the youngest, whom she babied. (The other two brothers moved to California and came home only for Christmas.) Darien was only thirty minutes from Ravendale, but Jade and Jeremy barely saw his parents. Jeremy recognized now just how intensely unhappy his mom had been when he was growing up, though he hadn't understood that as a little boy. Jeremy's father was a functional alcoholic and wildly successful as a trader, but no matter how much Jeremy and his dad had in common with work, they still seemed to speak to each other only in two-word sentences. Jeremy clearly wanted his dad's approval, but Jade had never once heard his dad give it.

Jeremy's only brother still on the East Coast was twenty-four and lived at home, and they barely spoke. Jeremy was closer with the

California brothers, one an acupuncturist and the other a rep for a surfboard company. Jade often thought Jeremy would be much less tightly wound if he had those brothers living close, but that didn't seem to be in the cards.

"I wonder what happened to Cora," Jade said, watching him retrieve a package of raw almonds. "I can't believe how sick she got."

"She's probably pregnant," Jeremy said. He closed the cabinet and ran a finger over a knob that seemed to be coming loose. The house was falling apart in big and small ways, and Jeremy seemed to love reminding Jade how he'd suggested they buy something brand new instead of a home built in the 1940s. *But this home matters to me,* Jade had said, and he'd gone along with it. She reminded herself of that whenever he was being unkind.

"Ah," Jade said. "Pregnant. That makes sense."

"You didn't think of that?" Jeremy asked, turning to give her a look like he was somehow disgusted with her.

"I didn't," Jade said, crossing her arms over her chest.

Jeremy shrugged. "Most women would think of that first."

"I guess I'm not like most women," Jade said.

"I guess not," Jeremy said, ripping open the bag of almonds.

Sometimes Jade wondered if that was part of what bothered Jeremy about Jade in general, and especially about her not being pregnant yet. Jeremy had an ego, and he liked to maintain a certain image. Jade had fit in when they were in New York City, but now that they were in Ravendale, she already felt a little like an oddball. She was more bohemian than most of the women, and that plus not having any children was making it hard to find friends.

"I talked to that girl Mira at the party," Jeremy said, "and she asked about Nelson." He popped a handful of almonds in his mouth and talked while he chewed, which made Jade's skin crawl. "Maybe we should use her more. She could walk him when you go into the city so he doesn't have to hold it so long."

"Sure," Jade said. Mira had watched Nelson twice before, and it had gone fine. If Cora trusted Mira with her family, then that was enough of a reference for Jade. She handed the leash to Jeremy, and he took it. "Are we going to finish our conversation from the tailor's?" she asked.

"I thought we already did," Jeremy said. He bent and clipped the leash to Nelson's collar. The dog stood carefully, dutifully following Jeremy with his arthritic gait, leaving Jade standing all alone.

CORA

7:02 p.m.

When Sam finally came into their room, Cora was sitting in a lavender chair opposite the bed. Her legs were wrapped in a fuzzy white blanket, and she was staring out the window at an overgrown bridge that crossed a stream and connected the Finches' yard to the Madsens'.

"Finally got them sleeping," Sam said.

Cora turned slowly toward the sound of his voice.

"They really fought it," he said.

"They often do," Cora said. It was a snotty thing to say, but she actually hadn't said it snottily at all. She didn't have the energy for that. Who cared that she was the one who always did bedtime? Did all the petty injustices of being a stay-at-home mother while her husband took clients out for dinner and drank good wine and ate filet even matter anymore? To anyone?

"So what did Isabella have to say?" Sam asked. "I saw you talking with her at the end of the party."

Cora didn't speak. She just stared at him.

"Are you okay, honey?" Sam asked. His brown hair was rumpled on one side. He looked exhausted, actually.

Cora wanted to get up to retrieve Mira's notebook, but she suddenly felt like she couldn't move a muscle even if she wanted to. And the white fuzzy blanket felt so warm and protective, like Lands' End had personally made her a cocoon.

"In the top drawer of my dresser, Sam, there's something I want you to read."

His light-brown eyebrows shot up. God, he did look like Matt Damon. How had she never noticed it before?

He made his way across the carpet and opened the drawer.

"A green notebook," Cora said.

He pulled it out. "This?"

"Open it," Cora said.

Sam did. He started reading.

It happened slowly, his face flooding with color. Blood, Cora assumed. He looked like a pale-pink lobster, the kind she and Maggie had eaten on their family's yearly August trips to Cape Cod.

"Oh God," Sam said, still staring down at the pages. With shaking hands, he flipped through the book to see if there was more.

Cora didn't speak. Her tongue felt like chalk. "Sam," she finally said, and he glanced up. He stared at her with his mouth hanging slightly open. "Is it true?" Cora asked, her voice a whisper.

Sam dropped the notebook. He moved across the room like lightning, and then he was at her chair, kneeling at her feet.

"Sam," she said.

The fuzzy blanket suddenly felt hot and itchy, and Cora threw it off. Sam tried to touch her bare legs, but she pushed away his hands.

"Is it true?" she asked again, but this time there was venom in her words. "Fuck you," she spat. "Was there more? Did you do it again? Was there more of *this*?"

"No," he said. "Cora, it was so stupid, but I was drunk, remember? Remember that night? The sushi night? It was so fucking stupid, I just

did it, and it was so wrong, and I've been freaking out for weeks thinking she's going to tell someone."

"You've been freaking out she's going to tell someone? She did tell someone, Sam, she told *me.* Or someone did. Someone left this notebook on our bed packaged up like a present!"

Sam's eyebrows knit together. Cora could tell his mind was working, but she had no idea what he was thinking. "How *could* you?" she screamed, right into his face. "How could you do this to us? To the babies?"

"Cora, listen to me," he said. His body was in a tight crouch as he held on to her chair. He looked so pathetic sitting below her like that. "I know how bad it sounds, and it was bad, I'm not saying it wasn't. But it was like something came over me, like I was in college again and she was some chick at a party, I can't even explain it, and I have no idea what the fuck is wrong with me."

"You're not, like, sexting her or something, are you?" Cora asked. What if Mira's parents found out and told everyone? What if Mira told everyone? Cora would move. She'd move her family somewhere entirely different where no one knew them. And she wouldn't get babysitters.

"I'm not sexting her," Sam said. "I'm not in contact with her at all, okay?"

"Sam, God," Cora said, putting a hand to her forehead.

"I know. I'm so, so sorry, please, you have to—"

"What? I have to *what*? I can't forgive you," Cora said.

"It was so stupid, it was a mistake. Please, can't you just—"

"Just *what*? Forget it? No, I can't. Didn't you think of that when you did it?"

"I wasn't thinking when I did it!" Sam cried.

"And this was it? You swear to me?"

Sam nodded, but his eyes darted to the floor between them.

"Are you lying to me, Sam? Because I swear to God I'll leave you if I catch you lying ever again . . ."

"No! I'm not lying! Please, Cora, *please*."

"I need you to just go somewhere, okay? Get the fuck out of the house. *Go*, Sam," she said. Her voice broke, and he must have known she meant it, because he got up onto shaking legs and left.

LAUREL

7:13 p.m.

As Dash opened a bottle of Sancerre, Laurel mentally timed the trip she needed to make to White Plains by eight to meet the man she'd been talking to on the internet.

Dash had changed into navy J.Crew sweatpants and a gray T-shirt, and he was barefoot, which made Laurel think back to med school, when they'd padded around his tiny apartment in socks so they wouldn't wake the crazy older couple who lived below them. Dash and Laurel had practically been insomniacs back then, studying well into the night and retiring to Dash's bed around two. They always had sex, no matter how tired they were, because they were young and in love, but also because sex was a way to turn off their brains and use their bodies.

There were signs. Even in the early days, Dash often became wildly emotional during sex, either crying out or growing increasingly agitated until he finished, but Laurel mostly worried about the couple downstairs hearing them. She never worried for her safety. Dash was maniacal about achievement—he was at the very top of their med school class—and Laurel just assumed he was bottled up so tight and so carefully modulated during the day that sex was his release. If anything, she felt honored that he felt free enough to let go and behave that way with her. How could she have known what was to come?

Dash poured the chilled white wine and offered her a glass. "Thank you," she murmured as he kissed her cheek. His breath was warm on her ear.

"Want to sit on the patio?" he asked, and she nodded, following him onto the murky gray stones that needed power washing.

Dash sat in the love seat, his wide eyes begging her to sit beside him. She complied. Giving in to Dash now gave her a better chance of escaping on time to get to White Plains, and without questions.

Dash's cheekbones were still as chiseled as they were the day she'd met him over two decades ago. She took in his face—the crow's-feet etched like whiskers around his crystal-blue eyes; the long, sharp features; the bump on the top of his nose where he'd broken it playing basketball in high school. Dash had never told Laurel that he'd been a basketball star in high school; it was his parents who'd told her that their son had gotten multiple scholarship offers to Division I schools but turned them down to do his undergrad at Harvard. Dash had always been shockingly modest, especially for a surgeon. Did he think he didn't deserve anyone's admiration? Did he think the good things he did were canceled out by the bad? Were they?

"What are you thinking about?" he asked her.

"Did you know that, in med school, before we knew your name, there was a group of us who called you the Nordic Superhero?"

Dash laughed, loosening just a bit. "I didn't," he said. His long arm reached over the back of the chair to light on her shoulder, and she let him touch her, pretending, like so many times before, that his touch was welcome and okay. What would those women from Laurel's med school class think now? Most of them were doctors: Laurel and another student named Elizabeth were the only ones to drop out. Laurel took comfort in remembering how they'd all thought Dash was superhero-like in his physical and academic strengths, and that not one of them pegged him as villainous. "And then when we learned your name," Laurel said, "we called you *Dashing* behind your back. I think we thought we were really clever. It's funny; I remember that like it was yesterday. I miss those friends." Laurel had been so close to the women she started med school with that first year, but then things intensified with Dash, and she mistakenly let her friendships fall away. A few college friends had tried to be in touch, too, and even Laurel's old high school boyfriend, Mark DeFosse, had called a couple of times, leaving thoughtful voice mails wondering how she was doing, and if she was okay, and asking if they could catch up. But Laurel never called any of them back. Dash had been so demanding of her time; plus there was all the course work, and then suddenly it was Dash and Laurel against the world, getting pregnant and married and starting down the dark path that was theirs alone.

"Would you change it?" Dash asked.

Laurel took a sharp breath. Dash didn't often ask questions like this, dangerous questions with potential for ugly answers, and she couldn't risk an argument. "You mean dropping out of med school?" she asked, and Dash took a sip of his wine. They were quiet for a minute, trying to recover from the turn their conversation had almost taken. Outside of the therapy sessions they'd tried, they had never explicitly discussed what Dash did in bed. It was like it happened, and then they tried to erase it from their memories. "I'm glad I was home to raise Mira and Anna," Laurel said plainly, just as she'd told him so many times before.

"If you wanted to go back to finish med school, you could," he said. He had no idea how often she thought about it. "I would help you," he went on. "I would help you study, and it would be like old times."

Old times. What Laurel needed was new times—and that meant she needed to stick to her plan.

"I should go, Dash," she said, checking her watch. "You'll call me if Mira gets in touch?"

"Where are you going?" Dash asked.

"I need to pick up a few things for the fundraiser tomorrow," Laurel lied.

"I thought you had everything?"

"Except protein bars," she said. "For anyone who forgets to eat breakfast. We don't need anyone passing out, do we, Dr. Madsen?"

Dash forced a quick smile, and Laurel returned it.

"I'll just run to Target," she said, and the lie came so easily and naturally that she was sure she'd get away with it.

VOICE MAIL RETRIEVED BY THE RAVENDALE POLICE DEPARTMENT FROM MIRA MADSEN'S PHONE, LEFT BY ANDREA WHITE AT 7:32 P.M.

Mira, it's me. Are we still on for tonight? I can't get through to you. I know you're going through some messed-up stuff right now, but just text me so I know you're coming. Don't flake on me, okay?

LAUREL

7:57 p.m.

Laurel's nerves raced as she pulled up to the small shop in White Plains. It was so ironic, really. Wasn't this how men and women met now, on the internet? If she ever dated again after Dash, isn't this how she'd do it? She imagined a stream of dates with older men—they'd be older, right?—maybe fiftysomethings who still appreciated Laurel's looks and thought of her as a younger woman, because isn't that what divorced men wanted in the second half of their lives?

That was obviously a broad overgeneralization, and Laurel really hated generalizations, just like she hated being part of the sexual assault statistics. She told herself she was still an *individual*, and she tried to hang on to that, even though she knew no one would see her story as special. *Happens every day, all over the world.* The statistics often floated through her mind, actually, just like the facts had in med school. She'd be sipping her coffee, and she'd see the numbers parade like a warning: the 43.9 percent of women and 23.4 percent of men who'd experienced sexual violence during their lifetimes; the 10 to 14 percent of women raped during the course of their marriage; the 14 to 25 percent of sexual assaults experienced by an intimate partner; and the one that scared Laurel the most: the 18 percent of women who claimed their children witnessed the sexual assault. The most recent stat she'd read on Huffington Post reported that the number of American women murdered between 2001 and 2012 by intimate partners (11,766) was nearly twice the amount of troops killed in Afghanistan and Iraq during that time. It was an epidemic, obviously, and it made her feel less alone, no matter how sick that was.

Intimate partner violence . . .

Laurel knew all the correct terms. She studied them on internet searches in the middle of the night when she couldn't sleep. Because wasn't sexual assault what it was? Or was she a fool for even thinking that? If she took part in the sex, did that make it just run-of-the-mill S&M? Was she consenting by going along with it?

Laurel shuddered. Her car idled, the lights illuminating a *Do Not Enter* sign on a chain-link fence. She turned off the engine and everything went dark.

Just go inside, Laurel, go inside and get what you need.

She opened the car door and stepped onto the gravel. A light rain fell on her bare arms. It was dark, and she was so desperate not to trip and fall that she crept inch by inch over the ground. There was only a dim light on inside a shop, and Laurel checked the number beside the door: 1071, the correct address. The man had sounded so gruff on the phone, so impersonal.

Laurel opened a rickety screen door and knocked on the wooden one behind it. No one answered.

Come on, please be here.

She knocked again. Two full minutes later the door opened to reveal a man in his fifties. Short-cropped gray hair covered his head, and his eyes were a piercing blue. He was short, maybe five six or so, and his thin lips curved into a smile at the sight of her. "A pretty lady," he said. "I figured by your voice on our call."

Laurel's skin prickled with goose bumps. Coming here alone wasn't smart, but what was the alternative?

"Thank you for seeing me," Laurel said, trying to make her voice sound professional, and trying to hide how scared she felt.

"Come in," the man said. He stepped aside so she could enter, but he didn't leave enough room. Laurel felt ill as she brushed against his protruding stomach.

The shop was long and narrow. A waist-high counter like you'd see in a jewelry store lined every wall, along with floor-to-ceiling shelves. Except instead of jewelry, the shop was filled with guns.

Statistics.

What were the statistics on gun violence?

Laurel had always been so vehemently in favor of stronger gun laws, especially to protect children. But what about in her particular situation? It wasn't like all those parents of young children who were so crazy to keep a gun in their homes that could accidentally fire off and kill someone. Wasn't what Laurel was doing okay? Or was it wildly irresponsible to have a gun hidden in the house with Dash and two older children?

No, not at all.

Dash had never, ever been violent unless it was sexual. So unless she tried to leave during sex, he wouldn't hurt her, right? She had absolutely nothing to be afraid of.

This was just extra protection for the very slim chance she was wrong.

PART II

THE DAY OF THE ASSAULTS

CORA

8:23 a.m.

The next morning, Cora gripped her car's steering wheel in the parking lot of The Sweat Box. She was safely inside a parking spot, staring at the shining grill of a Range Rover. The gym was housed behind Buzzed, and rumor had it that a juice bar was moving into the vacant retail space next door, which thrilled all the mothers.

The radio blared one final, bleating note of a Christina Aguilera song before Cora turned off the ignition.

Quiet. Too quiet.

Cora turned the car back on and let Christina wail, cranking up the sound until her eardrums rattled. How in the world was she supposed to face Laurel today?

So glad I'm co-chairing this fundraiser with you, Laurel! You'll never believe this, but your daughter's diary turned up in my bed last night . . .

Cora squeezed the steering wheel until her fingers went white. Was there any chance it was Laurel who had left the diary for Cora to find? The whole thing felt like an insurmountable nightmare. Sam hadn't come home, as she'd instructed, and the bed felt huge and cavernous without him snoring next to her. Cora had finally fallen asleep around three, and woke when the twins did at seven. She changed them and fed them breakfast like a robot (but she didn't give them the iPad!). Today was Monday, so had Sam gone to work? Or called in? *Sorry, I won't be in the office today because I've gone and touched our babysitter right on the hip and then kissed her more passionately than I've kissed my wife in years!*

Cora tried to release her grip from the steering wheel. She'd been able to fake it just fine with the babysitter this morning, passing off the twins and listing instructions like an unfeeling drill sergeant. She would just do the same thing today, with all of Laurel's friends, and with Sarah and Jade, too. For now.

Cora let out a long, slow breath. It was 8:25.

Please, God, don't let Mira be inside. I won't be able to take it.

Cora turned off the ignition and then glanced into her rearview mirror. The Lululemon jacket she'd loved in the store looked like a radioactive raspberry in the daylight. She'd forgotten to wash her face this morning, and she looked like shit, but that seemed appropriate for a workout class, right? She smoothed her light hair into a low ponytail and then opened the door and stepped carefully onto the pavement. Her feet didn't feel like her own as she walked across the lot.

The Sweat Box logo announced itself in purple block letters. Cora tried to practice smiling, and when she thought she had it right, she swung open the door. Chilled air greeted her, carrying the sickening scent of sweat and Purell.

"Hellooo!" a voice called, and it sounded so young and high-pitched that Cora's brain didn't recognize it at first, not until she turned to see Laurel standing off to the side of a reception desk at a folding table. Anna stood next to Laurel, staring at Cora with her round brown eyes. Unlike Mira's perfect nose and chin, Anna's features were angular enough to give her face character.

A receptionist sat at the oval desk behind Laurel and Anna, but she didn't greet Cora or even look up from her *Cosmopolitan* magazine. Cora said hello to her anyway.

Laurel's blond hair was tied into a tight ponytail. Her late-forties skin looked impossibly young, and except for a spot of mascara smudged beneath her right eye, her makeup was flawless. Her eyes were slightly red, as though she'd cried that morning or the night before. Or maybe she was hungover? It always shocked Cora how many mothers drank copious amounts of wine at night. Raising children was hard enough without a hangover, as far as Cora was concerned. She was so busy studying Laurel's face—it was like something was slightly off—that she forgot to be freaked out. But couldn't she surmise from Laurel's greeting that she had no idea what had happened between Mira and Sam?

"Good morning," Cora said to Anna and Laurel, meeting Laurel's eyes.

Do you know what my husband did to your daughter? Am I supposed to tell you? Wouldn't I want someone to tell me?

Weren't they becoming friends?

Cora hadn't considered the possibility yet, but instead of trying to hide Sam's guilt, should she tell Laurel what had happened?

No. She was a mother—she had her own children to think about. "How can I help?" she asked instead.

LAUREL

8:27 a.m.

"Why don't you sit here and get ready to check everyone in," Laurel said to Cora, who looked even worse this morning than Laurel felt. Laurel considered Cora's sweet features, remembering the exhaustion of young motherhood like it was yesterday. She wanted to say to Cora, *They do start sleeping at some point,* but she was sure it would come off rudely, like she was accusing Cora of looking as crappy as she probably already knew she did.

What Laurel needed was a real friend. Could it be Cora? She watched as Cora lowered herself into the folding chair and started scanning the registered participants. Laurel scanned them, too, tallying the three mothers she always felt obligated to invite to everything even though she wished she never had to see them again. All three women grew up in Ravendale, and they were at the football game in 1986 when Laurel's dad hit her mom, and they all knew about the social shaming Laurel had endured even if they hadn't played active roles in it. Which meant today Laurel would grin and bear it like she always did when she was forced to interact with them—and she'd focus on her new friendship with Cora.

The nice thing about getting closer to Cora was that Cora didn't ask too many questions. Her head was buried in raising her babies, and that meant she wasn't paying too much attention to Laurel. Laurel knew there were friends she could pick who would challenge her to be more honest and vulnerable, or, God forbid: the ones who encouraged her to *share*. Asher Finch's mom had been like that—always inviting Laurel over and trying to become close until she finally gave up. But now wasn't the time to be pushed in a better direction—now was the time to survive.

"I can't believe we filled the class so easily," Cora said, counting the forty names in front of her.

Laurel smiled. Maybe more than anything else, Cora seemed gentle, and Laurel could use a bit of gentleness in her life. "Incredible turnout, right?" Laurel asked. "I'm just waiting for the manager to confirm we can eat these bars anywhere in the gym." She pointed to a few boxes of protein bars. "I just thought, in case people didn't eat breakfast yet."

"Smart," Cora said.

Laurel checked her phone. Any minute Mira would show—she was sure of it. Mira wouldn't miss the fundraiser; if Mira was supportive of anything Laurel did, it was the things that had the least to do with motherhood: the fundraisers like this one, a short-lived watercolor painting club, or even the French cooking class Laurel took a few years ago. It was Mira who suggested Laurel go back to medical school, and Laurel had thought about it many times, much more seriously now that the girls would both be in college. She wouldn't go back to become a surgeon—she'd be sixty before she finished her training—but she could do four years of med school and then go into family practice. She and Dash didn't have a prenup, so even after a divorce, Laurel could still afford to pay her way through school. Maybe later today she'd look into MCAT courses. It was over twenty years ago that she'd taken them the first time; everything had felt so new back then, and she'd been so full of hope (especially when she got her MCAT scores back and saw she'd nailed the thing).

Anna cleared her throat. She was standing listlessly beside the registration table, staring at Cora. Last week Anna had told Laurel she thought Cora was a really good mom, and then, to Laurel, she'd said, *And you know I think you're a great mom, too, right?* Three summers ago, Mira had given Laurel holy hell during the months before she left for college, but not Anna.

Goddamn it, where is Mira?

"Anna alphabetized the names for me this morning," Laurel said to Cora.

"Very sweet of you," Cora said, still scanning the names.

It wasn't unlike Mira to stay out, but not to call? Laurel had been unable to sleep last night, and she'd ended up teaching herself how to use Instagram at two in the morning. She'd created an account so she could see if Mira had posted something that would give away her whereabouts, but as far as Laurel could tell, her daughter hadn't posted after the O'Connell twins' birthday party, when she'd snapped and posted a picture of herself with Anna and Asher by George and Lucy's new play set, the one Cora had called allergen free. (Was that really a thing for a play set? It seemed like Cora had misunderstood something.)

"The party yesterday was great," Laurel said to Cora, using a box cutter to open a cardboard box filled with water bottles.

Cora finally looked up. "I'm so glad you came," she said. Her right eye twitched. It was unsightly, and Laurel looked away. "Did you have fun, Anna?" she heard Cora ask. It sounded almost robotic. Was she all right?

"We did," Anna said, tossing her gum into a wastebasket. "But you know that one mom, Antoinette—Mrs. Campbell, I mean—she got so pissed at Asher. She accused him of throwing the ball at her kid's head." Anna let out an embarrassed laugh, like she was unsure of whether it was okay she'd said that about one of Cora's friends.

"Oh well, she'll get over it," Laurel said, but then she noticed how concerned Cora looked. "Look how great these bottles came out,"

Laurel said, pulling one from the box to show Cora. The slim plastic bottles had light-pink tops, and *Women Against Sexual Harassment and Assault* was emblazoned in tiny letters at the bottom of the bottle.

Cora held out her hand to take the bottle. She considered it, and smiled. "They look even better than they did online."

Laurel nodded her agreement. To Anna, she said, "Honey, can you check your phone to see if your sister texted?"

Cora's head made a strange, jerking motion. "Is Mira coming?" she asked, glancing from Laurel to Anna.

"I hope so," Laurel said, checking her phone. "She actually didn't call home last night, which is really unlike her, but I'm pretty sure she's at her friend Andrea's. I told her the fundraiser started a half hour earlier than it actually does because she's always running late, and nothing wrong with a little white lie to get your daughter to show on time, right?" Laurel asked, forcing a laugh that sounded unnatural. She was trying so hard not to worry Anna.

Cora's face was pale. She looked at Laurel, and then Anna, and then returned her eyes to the paper.

"Should we just stack these here?" Laurel asked about the water bottles. It probably made sense to put them directly on the registration table so the participants would know they were meant as gifts.

"Sounds good to me," Cora said, and then she, Laurel, and Anna silently arranged four dozen water bottles on the table. Cora had let Laurel take the lead on most of the planning, and she was really easy to work with, actually, which was a nice surprise. It wasn't always that way when Laurel asked someone to co-chair an event.

When they finished lining up the water bottles, Laurel said to Anna, "Let's set up the mats." To Cora, Laurel said, "If anyone comes early, just check them in and let them know they can change in the locker room if they haven't yet. And if Mira comes, send her straight into the Pilates studio to see me."

Cora's face went from white to slightly green as she nodded at Laurel. Maybe she was expecting another baby? She really didn't look well.

Anna and Laurel passed the receptionist, a girl in her twenties who chewed on a pen tip and ignored their existence. They headed into a spacious, airy room designated as the Pilates and yoga studio.

"You sure we need the mats?" Anna asked. She was wearing leggings and an oversize T-shirt that hung off one slim shoulder, showing off a hot-pink sports bra and making her look like a 1980s aerobic enthusiast. She'd been dressing quirkier lately, maybe in preparation for NYU. Yesterday for Cora's party it was a sack dress with a chunky beaded necklace featuring a four-inch claw-shaped shell.

"It's what the instructor told me," Laurel said. "I think it's so she can teach us how to throw an attacker onto the floor."

"Yikes," Anna said.

"Yikes indeed," Laurel said, praying her daughters would never need to know how to do any of this.

"You okay, Mom?"

Laurel bent to tug a fold-up gymnastics mat off a stack of five others. "You know that a lot of violence happens when you're already in a relationship, right? Not just with strangers?"

Anna met her gaze. Her wide brown eyes always looked surprised, but they looked steady now, too. "Of course I know that," Anna said. "You've told me."

"I hope it never happens to you," she said. "But if it does, I hope you'll leave right away. You can always come back to me, whenever you need me, for anything, you know that, too, right?"

Anna nodded, and then she bent to help Laurel with the next mat. They worked in silence, unfolding the blue-and-red-striped mats to shape a large rectangle that covered nearly the entire floor of the studio.

Just when they were about to finish, Anna turned to Laurel and asked, "Has it ever happened to you?"

Laurel turned to take in her daughter's slim frame bent to arrange the final mat into place like a puzzle piece. She weighed her options. She could shake her head no and the issue would be swiftly and neatly put to bed, or she could come clean and shatter Anna's world. She squatted to fix her shoelaces with a double knot. "Sweetie," she started, still looking down at the deep-purple laces, "there are things that have happened in my life that I'm not proud of, and I promise you I'll explain them when you're a little older." *After I leave your dad, when some time has passed.* "Would that be okay?"

Anna stared at her mom as though she were seeing her for the first time. She didn't answer.

Would Laurel ever tell the girls the truth about their father? Wasn't their sexual life far too private to share? Wouldn't it be inappropriate? Maybe she'd be more vague. But sooner than later she'd tell them about her own father hurting her mother so that they would know they could confide in her if something like that happened to them, too.

"I still meant what I said, Anna, if it were to ever happen to you—"

"I'd leave," Anna said. She steeled her skinny legs and stood up taller. "I promise you."

It's not always that easy, Laurel wanted to say. But of course she didn't.

JADE

8:32 a.m.

Jade was in her closet, getting ready for Cora's fundraiser and thinking about the things that had led her to this very moment, to living in her childhood home as Jeremy's wife. At Vanderbilt, if anyone had shown Jade this glimpse of her future, she never would have believed it could be true. Back then she was sure she knew what her life would look like: living in the city with Maggie, auditioning, frequenting coffee shops and book readings, and hopefully making enough money to travel overseas like she'd always done with her parents. She saw an artistic, bohemian life for herself, and never once did she imagine returning to Ravendale and mingling with families and suburbanites. (Not that anyone in Ravendale would consider themselves *suburban*.) But Jeremy had been so adamant that they start their real lives, as though the Tribeca apartment they'd lived in since they got married was fake. And maybe in some ways he was right. The years since Maggie died felt like a blur, and sometimes Jade couldn't shake the feeling that in some other reality, she and Maggie were still twenty-two and planning to take over the world together.

Now, Jade worried that her inability to let go of the past was detrimental to her marriage; maybe Jeremy could sense she was never really entirely present with him, and maybe the chasm between them was her fault. So she had agreed to move out of the city, thinking that maybe a new location could be a fresh start. But that wasn't how Ravendale was turning out for them, and that made her feel more desperate than ever.

Jade slithered into a too-tight pair of spandex. She hated working out. She did the occasional Pilates video on YouTube and spent the whole time wishing it were over. But today was about supporting Cora, of course, and plus: it was a worthy cause.

Really, when Jade was honest with herself, she'd never intended to marry Jeremy. She was in shock during the days and months following Maggie's funeral, and Jeremy had sought her out, and then one thing led to another and she was sleeping with him. Sex with Jeremy was a drug, a temporary cure, and it was the only way she could seem to escape her grief. But then things had escalated so quickly, and Jeremy was down on one knee, and Jade was so incredibly confused and unable to imagine a life without him when he was the person helping her hang on. And he loved her, and wasn't that what she was supposed to be looking for? Maggie had always been the romantic one—she believed in love above all else—and Jade had been the scared one, the slightly cynical one. But in that moment, when Jeremy was down on one knee, everything Maggie had ever said about love floated through Jade's mind, and so she'd said yes to Jeremy, to the chance of it.

Jade considered herself in the mirror. Her hair was falling free from her braid, and she tried to pin it back with a bobby pin. Even if she'd grown to deeply love Jeremy, what was she supposed to do if he never came around to adoption? Wouldn't that mean she'd have to choose between her husband and the chance of becoming a mother to the children meant to be hers?

CORA

8:39 a.m.

Cora sat at the reception table and stared at the pink top of one of the water bottles, letting her gaze relax in the absence of anyone to see her zone out. Laurel had said Mira never came home last night, and all Cora could think about was whether Mira had been with Sam. Was she overreacting to think that way? Or was it the obvious thing to assume?

Cora tried to breathe—to focus on the task at hand. She'd already checked three participants in, one of them a mother of two sets of twins. The woman was tall and lithe, and Cora didn't understand how she looked so incredibly good after having two pregnancies with multiples. Cora found herself trying to make a joke that her own stomach looked like an elephant's vagina, and the woman had laughed, but Cora sensed she'd said something a little too strange.

Ugh.

"It's so hot in here," Laurel said, and Cora jumped. Laurel was suddenly at the desk, taking off her jacket and laying it over the back of a folding chair. "The manager says we can pass out the protein bars when we register everyone, and they can eat them anywhere," she said.

Without the collar of her jacket, Laurel's bare neck was exposed, and Cora made out a quarter-size bruise on her neck. "Oh," she said. "Are you all right?"

Laurel froze.

"The bruise, on your neck?" Cora said.

Laurel's perfect skin blushed. "It's from a boxing class," she said, her eyes flashing, "here at the gym, actually."

"Really?" Cora asked. Could that be? They were hitting each other's necks during boxing classes?

Laurel grabbed her jacket from the chair. "Cooler out here," she said and then slipped back into it. Cora was about to ask if she was really okay, but then the glass door swung open and Antoinette Campbell waltzed in.

"Good morning," Antoinette said, smiling sweetly when she saw Laurel and Cora. Maybe she wasn't that upset about Asher hitting her son's head with the baseball?

"I meant to text you last night," Cora said as Antoinette strode toward her, "to make sure Henry was okay, but it got late so fast, and . . ." *I had just found out my husband has a thing for our babysitter, Laurel's daughter, actually!* "I hope he's all right? It was a foam baseball, of course, you know how careful I am! I wouldn't have a real baseball right by the play set!"

"Of course I know you wouldn't," Antoinette said, smiling at Laurel instead of Cora. She hiked her gym bag higher on her shoulder, and she waved a hand like the whole thing hadn't worried her for even a second. "Henry's fine! He's absolutely *fine*." Laurel took off without greeting Antoinette, who looked slightly deflated. She turned her attention back to Cora. "But how are *you*? Was the party a stress? I felt awful that you got so sick. Is it a bug, do you think?"

Cora gritted her teeth. Obviously she wouldn't have come today if she were contagious with a stomach bug. "No, not at all," Cora said. Should she implicate her cooking—should she say it was the food? *No.*

That would absolutely start everyone talking about widespread food poisoning from the party. "I think I might be pregnant," Cora whispered conspiratorially, because it certainly was a possibility, because she and Sam had had sex once this month, and though they'd used a condom, it was theoretically possible it could have broken.

Antoinette's eyes widened. She clapped her hands together and said, "Oh! How wonderful!"

"Please don't tell anyone," Cora said, her voice hushed and urgent. It was unsettling what a good actress she was for someone who supposedly didn't like lying.

"I *won't*," Antoinette said with a sly smile, but Cora didn't know her well enough to know if that was true.

"Now, let me check you in!" Cora said. She scanned the paper and found Antoinette's name. It was nice of her to come, actually; she was the only one of Cora's friends with children who'd made the effort to get a sitter. "Here you are," Cora said excitedly when she found Antoinette's name, like something really special had happened. She crossed off *Antoinette Campbell* and then handed the woman a water bottle. "You can go straight to the Pilates studio and get a spot on the mat," Cora said. *A spot on the mat?* Laurel hadn't said that. Hopefully the ad-libbing made sense for a class like this.

"Thanks so much," Antoinette said. "I'm so glad you invited me. I've wanted to get to know Laurel better and talk to her about how to get more involved in the school district. I hear you have to be personally *asked* to be class mom for kindergarten, did you hear that, too?"

Cora shook her head.

"It's not a *volunteer* thing," Antoinette went on, "so I just want to start showing my face around Ravendale Elementary before Henry enrolls in a few years."

"Right," Cora said, exhausted.

Antoinette lowered her voice, and said, "If you don't feel well in the class, just give me a sign, and I'll help you get to the bathroom."

Cora forced a smile, and Antoinette took off toward the Pilates studio. A glossy redheaded woman entered next and introduced herself as one of Laurel's friends from high school. "Where's Laurel?" she asked as Cora handed her a water bottle. "I brought her a coffee," the woman said, nodding toward a tray with two large to-go coffee cups that smelled like hazelnut.

Cora pointed Laurel's friend toward the Pilates studio, and then a muscular woman zoomed toward Cora. "I'm Alex Wainwright," she said formally, and Cora said, "Oh! Hi, I'm Cora O'Connell." Cora recognized most of Laurel's friends from around town, but not this woman. She ducked her head to look over the paper and felt a pit in her stomach when she didn't see the woman's name. "We don't have your name here, for some reason," Cora said, "but I'm sure we can fit you in?" She wasn't sure she could fit the woman in at all, but maybe . . .

"I'm the instructor," the woman said. She smiled with a line of very straight, fake teeth, the kind that look like Chiclets, aggressive in their perfection.

"Oh! Well, that makes more sense. It's nice to meet you."

The woman, Alex, reached out her hand and Cora shook it. Her grip was surprisingly limp for a woman who'd be teaching them self-defense in a few minutes. "You can just go right in," Cora started, but the woman said, "I know where I'm going! Not my first rodeo!" and took off down the hall.

Cora signed in another dozen or so women before Jade and Sarah entered the gym. Sarah looked immaculate in head-to-toe black spandex and pearl earrings. Jade's dark hair was adorably braided, her green eyes were bright, and she was somehow toned even though she never worked out. Rope bracelets were stacked on her arms, making her look younger than her twenty-eight years. Maggie used to wear them, too.

Sarah glanced around the gym and beamed at Cora, as though Cora were doing something truly impressive today. "I'm really glad you came," Cora said, warmed by the sight of them. She stood and hugged her mother first, biting back tears.

"We wouldn't miss it," Jade said, and Cora knew that was true. Sarah and Jade showed up to everything Cora invited them to: baptisms, birthday parties, and even a silly *Bring your family day!* at Musical Mother Goose. "How's your stomach feeling, sweetie?" Sarah asked, and Cora said, "Better."

"I'm so proud of you for doing this," Sarah went on, and Cora felt herself blush. She looked down at her paper and crossed out their names.

"Thanks, Mom," she said. "Save me a spot next to you?"

Jade nodded, and Sarah said, "Of course."

VOICE MAIL RETRIEVED BY THE RAVENDALE POLICE DEPARTMENT FROM JADE MOORE'S PHONE, LEFT BY JEREMY MOORE AT 9:05 A.M.

Jade, hey, it's me. I just wanted to talk to you about yesterday. I'm sorry for being such a dick. I just, I don't know, can we talk? Please call me.

JADE

10:58 a.m.

Later that morning, Jade sat in the waiting room of Mount Pleasant Hypnotherapy and Wellness and stretched her arms. They were a little sore from the self-defense class, actually, but Jade was glad to have been there and happy to see what a good job Cora had done organizing the thing with her neighbor. Cora obviously still wasn't feeling well, though; midway through the class, when the instructor was demonstrating how to fend off unwanted sexual advances, Cora had hurried to the bathroom, and Jade overheard one of the mothers whisper to another that she was pregnant. It was Laurel who went after Cora to make sure she was all right. It was nice to see Cora making a new friend, especially Laurel, who seemed as kind as Cora.

Jade stared at a clichéd Zen waterfall. The waiting room was tiny, with only four chairs and a magazine rack filled with wellness magazines sporting headlines like: *How High Is Your Spiritual IQ? Take Our Quiz and Find Out!* Two monstrous quartz crystals, the biggest Jade had ever seen, sat on the floor near her feet. She bent to touch the jagged edges, like glass at her fingertips. Maggie would have loved this place.

The door opened, and a small, curvy woman emerged. "Jade Moore?" she asked, smiling warmly. The woman's headband was made of real dandelions, like something straight out of Coachella, but it felt right somehow. Plus, she smelled like lemongrass, and Jade loved lemongrass. "Come this way, love," the woman said. She had a grandmotherly vibe, though she looked to be only fifty or so. She reminded Jade a little of her mother, with her pale skin and feline eyes. Jade missed her parents, but she knew they were happier in Florida. They were older than Clark and Sarah and most of Jade's friends' parents—they'd been nearly forty when they had her—and they needed the warm weather for their bones, they said when they moved two years ago.

In the woman's cluttered office, a noise machine next to the door sounded the rolling pattern of ocean waves. The air was warm and felt almost moist. Jade looked for a humidifier and spotted one in the corner. She felt a little woozy as she sat in a big comfy chair.

The woman sat across from her, and Jade was thankful that there was no table between them, no space for tarot cards or a crystal ball. There was just the woman, sitting in an identical comfy chair, facing Jade and smiling. "Hi, Jade," the woman said, and Jade murmured hello. "I'm Carina, and I'm very glad you've come today."

Oh God. That sounded so rehearsed. Did she say that every time, to each new client?

"On the phone you told me you were having some trouble with conceiving," Carina said. So it had been her, not a receptionist.

Jade's eyes scanned the framed photos of saints and other spiritual types that dotted the walls. A winged figurine perched on the windowsill, and the sun that glinted off its porcelain feathers struck Jade as wild and beautiful. She turned back to Carina. "Actually, that's not why I'm here," she said.

Carina raised an eyebrow. "No?" she asked.

"I'm here because something is wrong in my marriage, and I don't know how to fix it, but I think a part of it is that I can't let go of my past. There's this memory that runs through my head all the time—and I thought maybe hypnotherapy could help me move past it . . ." She cleared her throat. "I guess I'm not sure what's wrong with me, and maybe that's why I'm here."

The woman nodded. The lemongrass smell seemed to be growing even stronger.

"This is confidential, right?" Jade asked. "Like traditional therapy."

"Yes, completely," Carina said. She gestured toward a framed degree, and Jade's eyes scanned the words. It was a licensed social worker degree. Even better. Maybe this wasn't so out there.

Jade met Carina's gaze. "Six years ago, I was in love with a girl named Maggie Ramsey," she blurted, "and she was in love with me, too." There it was: the *truth*. It felt so good to say it out loud, and if Carina knew Maggie and her family, her expression didn't betray it. "We were getting ready to tell our families about us, and we were excited, and we weren't even that nervous, because both sets of parents are really open-minded. Um, and I think mine may have already known that I wasn't exactly straight. I'd had boyfriends, but my mom is pretty perceptive." Jade was artistic and her mother was *quirky*, but both qualities seemed to come from the same place, and they'd always gotten along, even if Jade felt the weight of the world, while her mom took everything far less seriously. When Jade was falling in love with girls, she always used to wonder if her parents knew, and now she wondered why she never told them. Why did everything seem so secretive back then? After Maggie died, there were so many times she wanted to tell her mom, Cora, and Sarah about their relationship, but it almost felt unnecessary, because they all seemed to completely grasp what the loss of Maggie meant for Jade. Whether or not they knew she and Maggie were in love, they seemed to understand the singular love Jade had for Maggie, and how devastating it was for them to be separated by her death. And did the difference between romantic love and deep, true love even matter? After you were together for a while, didn't *in love* blend to *deep love*, anyway? Wasn't that the better kind? Parents had it for their children; children had it for their parents. Friends could have it. Good marriages had it. Jade was almost positive Jeremy didn't have it for her, but did she have it for him?

"For Maggie, it was a little different," she went on, "because she'd had a lot of boyfriends and never any girlfriends before, so her family would have been surprised, for sure. But we were pretty convinced that, after the shock of it, they would be happy for us." Jade cleared her throat. "Maggie's sister, Cora, had just gotten engaged, and there was a party for her. Maggie was drinking way more than usual. She never drank like she did that night; I think she was just so nervous to tell her parents and her sister about us. It was a big deal for her, for us, obviously. So the party was winding down, and everyone was drunk, really, not just Maggie. We were all back in Ravendale together, which is where we all grew up; it was practically like a reunion because so many of us hadn't seen each other for a while, and it kind of became about that. We got really trashed. Even the adults were a mess, and all the mothers were sort of treating us like adults, which I guess maybe they shouldn't have been. Everything was going fine, but then Maggie started saying it wasn't actually the right night to tell everyone about us. And I totally agreed because we were way too drunk, but Maggie was so much drunker than me, and I started feeling really insecure and wondering why she was saying that we shouldn't tell them. She was too drunk to be logical about it, and I started worrying it was some secret desire she had to not tell them at all, ever. We got into a fight, and I lost her for a few minutes because she stalked off and I didn't go after her, but then I went to find her, and I found her next to the side of the house in the lap of a man who is now my husband." Jade was sweating. It sounded so incredibly fucked up. "Jeremy. That's my husband's name." How was she going to explain to Carina how and why she married Jeremy, after seeing him there with Maggie like that? "After Maggie died, I started sleeping with him, and at first it wasn't meaningful, it was just a trick to try to forget about her and make everything hurt less, but then it all got so incredibly convoluted. I grew to have feelings for him, real feelings, but it was just such a dark time, and I got so mixed up."

And now they were married, and something was missing, and how could it *not* be related to Maggie? "I've tried to move on, to get married, to have a life, but I keep comparing my husband to her. I love Jeremy. But I don't know how I could ever love anyone as much as I loved Maggie. And I don't know if it's because she was my first true love, and so nothing could ever measure up to that, or if something's very wrong in my marriage that I need to try and fix. And if I could just forget about that night, maybe I'd have a better chance at fixing myself," Jade said. She tried to clear her throat and get back on track. Carina was watching her without an ounce of judgment, and it made it easier.

"Tell me more about the night of your sister's party," Carina said, her voice gentle.

Jade took a breath. "Maggie and Jeremy were on the side of the house where no one could see them. Jeremy was sitting on a lawn chair, and Maggie was straddling him, and she was, well, she wasn't kissing him or anything, but the way her head was bent toward his it was like anything could have started at any second, if it hadn't already."

Jade flushed. This part was so painful, just remembering Maggie like that, all over Jeremy like her body fit perfectly with his.

"And what did you do?" Carina asked.

"I was so upset I just took off. I ran back to the party. I don't even think Maggie ever saw me. I went inside the house, where everyone was talking about who was going to pick up pizza and more alcohol so we could all keep partying, which was, of course, the last thing I wanted. In the living room I saw Maggie's mom, Sarah, and I wanted to tell her, to make her help me get Maggie inside and into bed. But Sarah was talking to her ex-husband, Clark, which was really strange, actually; they were in conversation, leaning into each other like I'd never seen them. I didn't want to interrupt them, and I'd calmed down a little by then and realized I just needed to go get Maggie myself. But when I returned to the side of the lawn, she was gone, just completely *gone*. I ran toward the front lawn right in time to see my car's taillights disappearing down the street. It was my dad's car, actually, his convertible; we'd decided to drive it that night because it was a special night." Jade started sobbing. Her head dropped into her hands. "When they found the car a mile down the road, Maggie's face was sideways, pressed against the wheel. I saw her and I knew right away she was dead."

Jade shook her head, still disbelieving after all this time.

"Cora's fiancé, Sam, was thrown out of the car," Jade said. "He and Maggie weren't wearing seat belts, but Jeremy was. He was in the back seat, and he was the one who called for help." Jade tried to swallow back her tears. "If I had done anything different that night at the party, if I'd just walked up to Maggie and Jeremy and told her I needed to talk to her, or if I tried to get her away from Jeremy and put her safely into bed for the night, if I'd done anything other than run away from her, she'd still be alive."

SARAH

11:06 a.m.

Sarah was in her garden pruning pink roses. She stopped to blow an ant off her finger, marveling at the way the little thing clung to her skin. She had her reading glasses on—her *gardening glasses*, as she sometimes called them—so she could see every detail of his little ant body as it crawled over her index finger. She really should be wearing her gardening gloves. She had her appointment soon with Dr. Madsen, and she'd already showered after Cora's self-defense fundraiser (she was so proud of Cora for organizing such a thing!), and she didn't want to have to shower again after gardening. Though she also didn't want Dr. Madsen examining her hand and spying dirt beneath her fingernails. Is that the kind of thing he'd note in her chart?

It was July, and another hot morning, just like the one before. Sarah and Clark had gotten married in July; Maggie had died in July. Both anniversaries were coming up, filling Sarah with dread. On the first anniversary of Maggie's death, Clark had mistakenly, insanely, suggested they spend it together. The sheer stupidity, the nerve of Clark to suggest that! He was dense, but could he really not see that if he hadn't cornered Sarah that night at the party, or if he hadn't left their marriage in the first place, that none of this would have happened?

Not that he should carry all the blame, Sarah knew. It was mostly her fault, and she was perfectly willing to admit that. She'd been so desperate to talk to Clark, to pretend she was still his wife at that beautiful party for their daughter, that she'd ignored how drunk Maggie had gotten and let her out of sight for five minutes—just five minutes!—and look what had happened.

If she and Clark had still been married, she would have been secure in herself as the only woman who held his attention, and then she would have had her eye on Maggie like a hawk. Maggie never drank like that! But maybe that was it? Maybe she didn't know her limit? *It could happen to anyone.* That's what all of Sarah's closest friends said. *When you're drunk like that, you don't know, you make mistakes.*

What had gotten into Maggie that night? Most likely, her and Jade's decision to tell Sarah and Clark that they were a couple. If only Sarah and Clark had sat Maggie down when she was a teenager and said, *And by the way, if you're gay, that's totally great! Don't even think twice about telling us! We'll be happy, actually! And I'll nanny your child if you and your wife both want to work!*

But instead they'd focused on things like making sure the girls' vegetables and fruit were organic. How blissfully unaware they'd been.

Still, Maggie had to have known that Sarah would accept her no matter what. And Maggie did, partly, or at least that's how Sarah interpreted it when she read her daughter's diary. She'd read the diary so many times, focusing on the lines where Maggie said she wasn't sure what her mother would think but that she mostly thought she'd be okay with it.

Of course I'd be okay with it, sweetie! Just come back and tell me. Pull me aside at the party, let me know right away, then you won't have to drink like that, you won't be so drunk that you get behind the wheel and accidentally kill yourself.

Sarah sat back on her haunches. Tears blurred her vision until the roses were a singular pinkish-white sheet streaked with green.

Clark had had plenty to drink at the engagement party, too, and that's why it was so pathetic that Sarah let him pull her aside right at the exact moment Maggie needed her.

We did a good job with the girls, Clark had said to Sarah that night. They were tucked in the living room behind the massive lemon tree Sarah had imported for the party. Bright balls of yellow lemons flowered everywhere among dark-green leaves. *We did,* Sarah had said in reply, and Clark stepped so close she could smell his woodsy cologne mix with the lemons. Was he going to kiss her?

And we were good, too, us, for so many years, Clark whispered.

Her heart exploded. *Yes, exactly!* she thought to herself. And then she said aloud, *I know that, Clark, I—*

But just then Clark's phone rang from the pocket of his jacket. He took it out, and they saw Jeremy's name flash across the screen.

Pick it up, Sarah teased. She was flirting. Jeremy was calling to say her daughter was dead, and Sarah was flirting with her ex-husband. Clark put the phone to his ear. *Hello?* he said, and he was still smiling a secret smile just for Sarah, and she was melting, but then his face changed. His jaw slackened. *Where are you?* he demanded of Jeremy. Then his eyes met Sarah's and he said, *There's been an accident.*

And then they ran.

CORA

11:26 a.m.

Cora was sitting at a table inside Buzzed and clutching a latte when Isabella arrived.

"I'm so sorry I'm late," Isabella said, slithering into the seat opposite Cora. The small round table between them was inlaid with chess squares, and a tiny vase with flowers sat next to a Mason jar filled with brown sugar.

"It's no problem," Cora said. "I got you a skim latte, I hope that's still what you drink?"

Isabella took off her sunglasses and put them inside her iridescent blue Balenciaga motorcycle bag. "It's perfect, thank you," she said, curling her delicate fingers around the porcelain mug. A whopping pear-shaped diamond caught the light and glistened on her left hand. "I don't remember this shop being so *busy*," she said, glancing around to take in the other diners and the long line that snaked from the register toward shelves stacked with fresh-pressed juices, cold soups, and gluten-free cupcakes. Directly next to them sat a woman with a child on her lap who unwrapped a banana muffin. A teenage girl in jean shorts the size of underwear sorted through packages of silver and gold cocktail napkins. (Did teenagers throw fancy parties in Ravendale just like the adults? What would Lucy be like when she was that girl's age?)

Cora shuddered. Mira barely looked older than the tiny-jean-shorts teenager. Cora turned away and tried to meet Isabella's dark eyes. *Just get this over with. Fake it like you did at the fundraiser.*

"I wish I could stay longer today," Cora said, checking her phone, "but I've been away from the kids doing a fundraiser this morning, and I need to relieve the sitter soon." She was losing count of the lies she'd told today. In fact, she'd already called the sitter to see if she could extend her hours, and the woman had said yes. Cora couldn't go back home yet, but she also couldn't stay with Isabella and make small talk when her life was imploding.

"I'll get to the point," Isabella said. "I know you're busy."

There was a chill in her voice. Wasn't this precisely what Isabella probably disliked about Cora now—her inherent busyness since becoming a mom? If only Cora had been better about returning Isabella's calls after the twins were born. She'd just been so buried, and it had felt daunting to call her friends and act like she was having the easiest and best time with motherhood, and that it was as wonderful as everyone promised. (It *was* wonderful. But it was also impossible!)

"I'm sorry," Cora said. She lifted her latte to her mouth and tasted chalk. Why had she ordered almond milk on a day like today?

"I'm sorry, too," Isabella said. She cupped her large mug. "I'm sorry that we haven't kept in better touch."

"It's hard—" Cora started, but Isabella interrupted.

"I know," Isabella said, taking a sip of her latte. "It's hard being a mom and balancing it all. That's what everyone says." It wasn't what Cora was going to say, actually. "I'm about to have my own in December," Isabella said, gently resting a hand on her navy-striped blouse.

"Oh! That's wonderful! Congratulations!" Cora said. She wanted to stand and embrace Isabella, but every inch of her body felt so drained from the past twelve hours, she didn't think she could. Isabella beamed for the briefest second, but then her lips pursed, as though she'd slipped by letting herself be so happy in front of Cora. It was in that moment Cora realized Isabella didn't ask her to coffee to talk about something pleasant.

"Cora, I . . ." Isabella started.

Glass shattered. Cora turned to see a boy in a bandana behind the counter staring down at the spot where he must have dropped a cup. A fortysomething woman Cora recognized as the manager emerged from the kitchen. "Get the broom," she barked to the boy. "And how can I help you?" she asked the next customer in line.

Isabella leaned closer. "Cora, what I want to discuss with you isn't an easy thing to say. I know that . . . well, I know that you and Sam are very close with Jeremy, but . . ." Isabella's voice trailed off. She glanced around her again.

"But what?" Cora asked, finding herself suddenly irritated. Isabella had asked her here to talk about Jeremy? Terrence probably had some kind of difficulty with Jeremy at work—it was exactly the reason Sam had been so hesitant to get Terrence a job with Jeremy in the first place. *He can be ruthless with his employees,* isn't that how Sam had put it? But Terrence had been laid off and out of work for nearly a year, and he'd needed the connection. So Sam gave it.

"You may know that Jeremy and Terrence were working on a deal together with Sam," Isabella said.

Cora didn't say anything. She didn't know that, actually.

"The deal went south, and now Jeremy is trying to ruin Terrence with false accusations. If the slander continues, he'll never be able to work again," Isabella said, her words like a freight train.

Cora blinked. "Why would Jeremy ever do that?"

"Because Terrence found out that Jeremy was leaking information to his father, which is very illegal, and Terrence threatened he would come forward if Jeremy didn't, and they got into a pretty heated argument one night, the same night, actually, that Terrence fell down a flight of stairs. He was out of his mind with stress."

Cora thought about the drugs Jeremy had said Terrence was using. She almost mentioned it, but the last thing she wanted was to upset a pregnant Isabella.

"Terrence didn't even want me to talk to you today," Isabella said, taking a quick breath. "We don't have any proof of Jeremy's misdoing, and there's no way we can proceed in any legal type of way. Sam is the one who has concrete evidence, but he's protecting Jeremy."

"Then I don't even understand why you're telling me this, if it's just a theory, and if you know how close we are to Jeremy."

"It's more than a theory, Cora," Isabella said, her voice hard.

"Is it?" Cora asked, bluffing. She didn't understand Sam's world. She had no idea how much of what Isabella was saying was true, or if it fell under some kind of gray area.

"I need your help getting Jeremy to back off of Terrence, to stop spreading rumors about him using drugs. We used to be good friends, Cora."

Cora didn't say anything, and Isabella tried again. "I still care about you and Sam very much, even if it's been years since we were all close." Her face betrayed nothing. She toyed with a diamond earring, also big and pear-shaped, and leveled her eyes on Cora. "Do what you wish with what I've told you," she said coolly. "If you won't help me, I'll find another way." She shifted in her seat, her stomach swelling beneath her top, her hands trembling just slightly as she gathered her things.

LAUREL

11:27 a.m.

Laurel was pacing outside Buzzed. Mira was supposed to show up for work within the next few minutes, and Laurel walked back and forth along the Main Street sidewalk past the library, the deli, the community center, and the cookware shop, praying she wouldn't run into anyone she knew who might want to make small talk. Her triceps already ached from the amount of punches the self-defense instructor had them practice, but the whole thing had gone off without a hitch. (Except for Cora seeing the bruise Dash had made, and Mira being a no-show.)

Goddamn it, Mira.

Mira was notorious for letting her phone battery die. When she wanted to check Instagram, she'd charge it again. Laurel could just imagine what Mira was going to say when she showed up to work: *I told you I was sleeping over at Andrea's! I'm in college, Mom! A little respect would be nice.*

Laurel checked her phone. 11:27. She could see activity inside the coffee shop: a young man with a bandana arranging muffins on a shelf above the counter. And was that Cora? Yes: Cora, with Isabella Gonzalez. If only Laurel had asked Isabella yesterday at the party how

Mira was doing at work, maybe she could have learned something meaningful.

11:28. Where was Mira? Was there any chance Isabella had heard from her? Mira wasn't due to work at her internship until tomorrow, but maybe . . .

11:29. One of the things Laurel hated most about being a mother was the way your nerves could go from zero to one hundred in a single breath. Everything could be just fine; *You have it all under control, that's right!* And then something—a fall, a missed call from school—and your heart was racing at the possibility of something happening to the person you loved most in the world.

11:30. Laurel could explicitly remember Mira as a baby with her big cheeks, huge dark eyes like her own, and the barely there peach fuzz that covered her head. She remembered the bout of fevers Mira got around four months of age, and how Laurel couldn't sleep unless she was on Mira's floor, just next to her crib, soothed by the sound of her tiny breaths.

11:31. No Mira.

Laurel started typing an e-mail on her phone about the hiring of a new principal for the high school—she was on the parent committee that approved prospective candidates—so that she'd look casual when Mira showed up.

It was 11:32 when she finished the e-mail. Her fingers were sweating on the phone as she pressed send, and then she headed into the coffee shop just as Isabella was pushing through the door. "Hi," Laurel started to say, but Isabella's head was down, and Laurel was suddenly overcome with embarrassment at the thought of having to ask such an accomplished woman if she'd heard from her daughter. Isabella would probably never lose her own daughter. Laurel watched Isabella walk to a green Jaguar and then pushed open the door to Buzzed and stepped inside.

"Cora?" Laurel said.

"Oh! Hi, Laurel," Cora said. They stared at each other. There wasn't much more to say about the fundraiser—they'd already talked about what a success it had been—and Laurel fumbled to make small talk when what she really needed to do was talk to the staff.

"You're leaving?" Laurel asked as she watched Cora corral sugar into a napkin. "I just saw Isabella."

"Yes, Isabella," Cora said, sliding her gym bag over her shoulder. It looked brand new. Laurel had never seen Cora at the gym, come to think of it. "We're old friends, from when Sam was in school."

Laurel knew Sam had graduated from Columbia Business School and that Cora had a master's from Columbia, too. It was nice of Cora to refer to it only as *school*; so many women would drop an Ivy League name into the conversation. Modesty was a lovely quality.

"I'll see you back in the neighborhood," Cora said, and Laurel leaned in to kiss her cheek.

"Good job today," Laurel said, because she knew it would mean something to Cora.

Cora smiled and headed toward the door, sounding a little *ding!* as she opened it.

Laurel approached the counter. "How can I help you?" asked the boy wearing a bandana.

"Hi there," Laurel said casually. "I'm Mira Madsen's mom."

The boy gave her a blank look, and then the manager emerged from the back room. "He's new. Hasn't met Mira," she said.

"Hi, Denise," Laurel said. Denise—what was her last name?—had run Buzzed for years, and Laurel came in every day for a triple almond-milk latte. Laurel was the one who asked Denise if Mira could work here this summer. "I'm looking for Mira," Laurel said.

"Me, too," said Denise.

"Oh, ha," Laurel said. Was she seriously pretending to laugh right now? "She hasn't shown up?"

"She's late. *Again.* Mrs. Madsen," Denise started. Laurel hated when Denise called her Mrs. Madsen; they were the same age! "Mira has been late quite a few times this summer, and the past week she's started skipping. I told her today was the last chance. I would've told you myself, but it seemed unprofessional to report her lateness to you."

"Of course, I understand," Laurel said. "Will you excuse me?" She turned on her heel and started toward the door.

"Do you want your latte?" Denise called after her.

Laurel shook her head and shoved open the door. She dialed Dash. His cell service at work was terrible, even worse inside the hospital, so she called his office and hoped he wasn't in surgery. His secretary picked up. "Westchester Orthopedics," she said.

"Dash Madsen, please," Laurel said. "It's his wife."

Dash answered on the first ring. "Laurel," he said, sounding surprised, as though she'd snuck up on him. She almost never called him at work.

"I'm at Buzzed," Laurel said. "And Mira's not here, and Denise said Mira hasn't been showing up to work."

"Who's Denise?"

"Her boss," Laurel said. Dash never bothered learning the names of people who served him things or cleaned his house and clothes.

"Hmm. Strange. We'll talk to her tonight. She'll need to be punished, obviously."

"But what if something's wrong?" Laurel asked. Could it be drugs? Was that why she'd been missing work?

"Call the police if you think something's wrong," Dash said. "I need to take a patient."

Laurel hung up on him. Did she think something was really wrong with Mira? No, not really. Most likely, her eldest daughter had been missing work because she was dealing with an unwanted pregnancy.

Laurel got into her car and drove home. She needed to talk to Asher Finch.

SARAH

11:38 a.m.

Sarah Ramsey? Follow me, please," said a heavyset nurse in white. She led Sarah into Dr. Madsen's examining room. Sarah moved toward the table covered in a white paper sheet and put her purse on it.

"You can put your things there, actually," the nurse said, pointing toward a lone chair. Sarah obeyed. Above the chair was a framed poster of a human body with all its fleshy muscles and sinewy tendons. "Sit here," the nurse said gently, like she was talking to a child.

Sarah sat on the exam table. She wondered about the heavyset nurse: Did Dr. Madsen ask her to lose weight out of fear for her joints? The nurse wrapped a blood pressure cuff around Sarah's barely there biceps. She puffed it up, and then let it slowly deflate.

"Nervous?" she asked Sarah.

"Yes, I often get white-coat hypertension," Sarah said. She was quite proud of herself for knowing the terminology. "But I've taken my blood pressure at home with one of those Omron devices, and it's in the normal range." Sarah spent a lot of time on WebMD.

The nurse smiled. She handed Sarah a clipboard with a few sheets of paper attached. "Just fill this out, and Dr. Madsen will be right in."

The nurse left, and Sarah looked around the room. Her eyes settled on a skeleton hanging from a wooden stand. Now that was something you didn't see every day. Sarah could practically hear the joints creaking. She'd have to tell Cora about it. Cora loved science things. There were so many awards she'd won growing up for science fair projects and math tournaments. She was extremely smart, and now she was just a mother, and not that there was anything wrong with that, but didn't she want to finish her dissertation? Would she ever want to? Did Maggie's dying suck the math right out of her bones?

Bones. The paperwork.

Sarah looked down at her clipboard to see the outline of a body sketched out on the paper. She used a pen labeled *Westchester Orthopedics* to circle the areas where she felt pain, as instructed, rating the pain on a scale of one to ten, and then she moved on to the section for family history and started scanning the boxes.

Well, you see, my family history is really so complicated, and you don't quite have the right boxes for me to check.

Sarah felt like one of the absolute worst parts of sharing what had happened to her family was seeing how people's faces changed when she told them not only that her daughter had died in a drunk driving accident, but that her daughter *had been the driver*. Of course she usually just said *car accident*, but when she got closer to someone, or if they asked for details, she'd tell them what had really happened. And it always seemed like somehow, in some way, the fact that the accident had been Maggie's fault took away from her death for almost everyone whom Sarah told, and that felt so ragingly unfair. If Maggie had just walked in front of a car and gotten hit by a drunk driver, or if she'd fallen off a cliff—those were things people could wrap their heads around, a tragic accident that wasn't her fault. And Christ, technically, Maggie *was* at fault! But it had still been all wrong—it still was a *mistake*!—and Maggie was supposed to be alive, not dead because of the first big mistake she'd ever truly made.

Sarah finished her paperwork and unlocked her phone. She found the video she'd texted herself that morning and pressed play to see a thirteen-year-old Maggie at a piano recital. The plinking, opening notes of "Für Elise" filled the exam room. Sarah loved watching Maggie's tiny, determined shoulders as she made her way through the song, and she remembered how hot it was that June afternoon, and how after the recital, Clark and Sarah had taken the girls for ice cream to celebrate. When Maggie stood to take a polite curtsey, Sarah found herself grinning at her phone, warmed by the look on Maggie's face.

The door clicked open, and Sarah started.

"Mrs. Ramsey," Dash Madsen said.

Sarah pressed stop on the video and put down her phone, filling with nerves as though she'd been caught doing something illicit. Dash shut the door behind him and smiled. God, he was handsome. Sarah found she liked thinking of him as *Dash* instead of *Dr. Madsen*—it felt like a secret.

"How are you?" he asked. He wore a long white coat over khaki trousers and crisp brown shoes. One of his silver-blond eyebrows arched.

"Oh, I'm fine," Sarah said, embarrassed to find herself in the middle of a girlish wave. *This isn't a cocktail party, Sarah!* And obviously she wasn't really that fine, or she wouldn't be here. "Well, it's just my hand," she said. "This one. It's been so painful from my wrist to my thumb. I think it's carpal tunnel. I read about that on WebMD."

Dash sat his tall frame on a stool and did that thing doctors do where they ride the stool toward you at a fast clip, stopping right before they crash into you. He reached out his hand, and Sarah folded hers into it. "Actually, I'd just like to see your paperwork," he said.

Sarah, embarrassed again, took her hand from his and passed him her clipboard. He perused it, and Sarah fought the urge to make nervous conversation. Really, what was her issue with doctors?

Dash stood from the stool, still looking down at the clipboard. His eyes—so icy blue—roved over her paperwork.

He had to be mid- to late forties. If Sarah weren't his patient, if she just sat across from him at a coffee shop, would he find her attractive?

Or at sixty, was she simply too old for him to look at her like that? Not that this was appropriate *at all* to be thinking . . .

Dash glanced at her. He came closer, this time standing right next to her. Had a man been this close to her since Clark on the night Maggie died? They both faced forward, toward the skeleton. "Can I see your hand?" Dash asked. He was so tall that Sarah had to lift her hand to put it into his. His fingers were warm. "Show me where it hurts," he said. His grip was so gentle.

"Well, mostly right here," Sarah said, pointing to a spot on the side of her hand, right between her wrist and her thumb joint. "And then, often, the pain travels into my thumb. And I get it in the exact same spot on my left hand, too, sometimes."

Dash nodded. He ran the pad of his own thumb over the path Sarah had described. *Oh God.* Sarah shivered. *Shit.* Could he see goose bumps? This was so incredibly inappropriate. What was wrong with her?

"Tell me how often you use your smartphone to text?" Dash asked.

"Not that often," Sarah said. "Maybe six or seven times a day." She almost didn't want to say it, but she did: "I scroll a lot on my phone and computer to watch videos and such, and I guess that makes my thumb work at an awkward angle."

Dash nodded. "Any kind of repetitive fine motor activity can lead to pain in the muscles and tendons," he said, "and we do quite often see tendonitis from smartphone and computer overuse." He touched the fleshy muscles on her palm beneath her thumb, and said, "Often there's pain here, in the thenar eminence."

Sarah thought about Laurel Madsen. What was it like to be married to Dash? Did he touch Laurel like this, so gently and with great concern for all the inner workings of her body? Did he run his expert hands all over her, knowing exactly what lay beneath her skin?

Sarah flushed with heat. *Get yourself under control, sister.*

"Are you all right?" Dash asked.

"Oh yes," Sarah said. "Just a hot flash."

A hot flash? Why had she said that? Now he was sure to think she was elderly, just like all the rest of his patients.

You are *just like all the rest of his patients.*

Sarah needed to start dating again.

It came to her just like that, sitting there with her hand being professionally caressed. Sarah needed someone to properly touch her again. Could she do it? But where? She couldn't date in Ravendale; she knew everyone, and there were no widowers or divorced men she wanted anything to do with. Would she have to join one of those terrible dating sites for old people?

Dash set down her hand and moved to his computer. Sarah let go of a breath as he typed. "I'd like to start with physical therapy for four weeks," he said. "If you don't improve, we'll do an MRI. But I'm nearly positive this is a repetitive strain injury."

"A repetitive strain injury?" Sarah asked. That sounded a little serious. Wait until she told Jade and Cora.

"We're all using our hands in different ways than we were meant to because of technology," Dash said, "which brings me to the next part of your treatment. I'd like you to stop using your phone and computer as much as possible. If you can completely take a break from them, even better. For a few weeks, say. Is that possible for you?"

Sarah swallowed. What about Maggie?

"It's possible, I suppose."

"I know," Dash said with a smile. "It's not easy."

You don't know, actually.

Sarah had been going backward again through the videos, and she was at the end of second grade, when Maggie made her First Communion.

"Are you doing work on your computer, or just using it for pleasure?"

"Just for pleasure," Sarah said, though she wasn't sure she could call it entirely pleasure. It was pain, too. "So it'll be easy to stop." A lie, of course. A small, insubstantial lie, one that wouldn't cause anyone any trouble at all.

Sarah met Dash's eyes. "Thanks for seeing me, Dr. Madsen," she said.

JADE

12:27 p.m.

Jade had rushed from her hypnotherapy appointment to make the open house in time, and now she was standing with tepid coffee in a Styrofoam cup. She peeled off the top of a French vanilla single-serve creamer and dumped it into her coffee, surveying the rectangular room with its light-gray walls and realizing she wasn't as nervous as she thought she'd be. It felt right to be here in this room, surrounded by the posters of babies and children. The posters were outdated—the haircuts and clothes on the children looked to be from the early nineties—but each child smiled. Not that Jade thought everything would run as smoothly as the posters and adoption brochures made it appear (*The challenges and rewards of being an adoptive parent!*), but there was a sense of warmth here inside the adoption agency, and of possibility.

Four couples milled about the room, considering brochures, eating donuts, and making timid conversation, and Jade tried not to be bothered by being the only single woman. *I have a husband,* she wanted to say. *He's just not on board yet!* She thought about the apologetic voice mail he'd left this morning; if today went well, she'd tell him all about this place, and if she could catch him in a mood where his guard was down, maybe she could convince him to make an appointment here, too, and they could go together.

All the couples in attendance were older than Jade—they looked to be in their late thirties to midforties—and they met Jade's glance with tired, careful smiles. Jade returned the glance of a woman wearing a paisley scarf, and the woman took a sip of coffee and left her husband's side to say hello. "Is this your first one of these?" she asked Jade. Her curly hair was wisped with gray.

Jade nodded. "I'm excited," she said. *And nervous, because I have to tell my husband I did this.* "A little nervous, too, but mostly excited."

"Me, too," the woman said. "I'm Cynthia."

"Jade." They shook, and then the man Jade assumed was Cynthia's husband approached.

"The coffee's cold, but this place comes highly recommended by friends of ours who adopted last year," the man told Jade. His square jaw and rimmed glasses reminded her of Clark Kent.

"How exciting for your friends," Jade said.

"A girl, they got a little girl named Sadie," Cynthia said. "The old-fashioned girls' names are so in vogue right now."

Jade thought about mentioning George's and Lucy's names, because she didn't really know what else to say. But just then the agency's smart-looking social worker, Claire, sidled up to them. "We're going to get started in a minute, so take your seats when you're ready," she said, and Jade spotted a small heart-shaped patch of chocolate from the glazed donuts at the corner of her lip. Jade didn't know her well enough to say anything, but she hated when someone didn't tell her, so she motioned to her own lip with a napkin, and the woman took the hint and blotted the chocolate. "Thanks! I'm always a mess," she said, laughing. She pushed her stylish, tortoiseshell glasses higher on her nose and then smiled warmly before leaving to approach a couple standing by the watercooler.

Jade, Cynthia, and her husband headed toward the dozen or so folding chairs. The other couples followed, and Claire made her way to the front of the room and said "Welcome to White Plains Adoption

Agency" in a voice both cheerful and authoritative. "I'm so glad you attended our open house today. I know that all of you have your own stories and that you've been through various life events that brought you here. We hope today is the beginning of your journey. There's so much I could say about the joy of adoption—I have two adopted children of my own—but today I want to make good use of your time by getting you thinking about what you really, truly want. Adoption is the search for a baby, and the nature of adoption means there are questions you need to ask yourself. You don't have to answer them today, but I want to get you talking to each other and to yourselves. I'd use the word *soul-searching* if I were a more touchy-feely social worker, but I'm not, so I'll just say that here are the initial hard and true questions you need to consider as you begin."

A few of the parents shifted their weight, the folding chairs creaking loudly, but Jade sat still, her body rigid and perched at the edge of her seat.

"First," Claire started, tucking a wayward curl behind her ear, "are you looking to adopt a baby, an infant, or a child? Are you open to a child of a different race than your own? Must your child be a healthy child? What *kind of parent* do you want to be: Can you see yourself parenting a special-needs child? If you're open to an issue, what kind of issue? A mental health issue? A physical issue? What about a physically disabled child who is otherwise physically healthy, for example, a blind or paralyzed child? What about a child who isn't healthy? Would you be open to an HIV-positive child?"

The room had gone extremely still. One of the men Jade hadn't met coughed and then excused himself. His wife flushed with color as he left the room.

"What are you thinking right now?" Claire asked them all.

Jade felt transfixed and on fire, and in her mind, the words *I'm open* came to her like a shot.

When Claire spoke again, her voice was gentle. "Or are you looking for the perfect white baby?" she asked. "If you are, and I'm not judging you for it, you should know that this adoption agency isn't the right one for you. If you're looking for the perfect white baby, you should be hiring an adoption attorney and going straight to private adoption, because we don't have those babies here."

The perfect white baby. Was there even such a thing?

The woman had called adoption the search for a baby, and Jade planned to keep her search wide open to chance, possibility, and fate. Tears ran over her face as Claire began to tell them more. What if this place—this very agency—was where she would find her first little one?

Jade's phone buzzed with a text from Jeremy, and she was startled to realize she hadn't even thought about him once as Claire spoke.

We need to talk, he'd texted. ASAP.

Jade turned off her phone.

LAUREL

12:36 p.m.

Laurel lifted a closed fist to knock on the Finches' door and froze. This could get really, *really* awkward. What if the Finch parents were home? How was she supposed to talk to Asher in front of them? Could she ask to talk to him privately?

No, she wouldn't do that. If one of the Finch parents answered the door, Laurel would simply say that she couldn't get hold of Mira and was starting to really worry (which was an understatement) and ask if Asher had possibly heard from her? And she'd avoid using terms like *unwanted pregnancy* or *fetus* or *abortion* or *your son is the father*.

Was there even an abortion clinic around here? White Plains, maybe? Or would Mira go all the way to New York for one? Dash and Laurel knew the girls' OB-GYN from med school, so there was absolutely no way Mira would go to her for advice.

Knock, knock, knock.

The Finches' door knocker was one of those old metal ones with a carved lion's head midroar. It was a little ridiculous, actually, Laurel thought as she waited.

Thirty seconds passed. Laurel was starting to feel itchy, like she was covered in mosquito bites. She slapped at her bare arm. Was that a gnat?

The sun bore down on her shoulders. She was about to go check the backyard when the door opened.

Asher greeted her with the same half smile he'd worn since he was seven. "Hi, Mrs. Madsen," he said. He wore mesh shorts and a T-shirt that said: *Ravendale Lacrosse: In the Grass Is Where It's At!*

It seemed like a vaguely sexual reference, but Laurel couldn't think straight enough to figure it out.

"Asher," Laurel said. A wooden table in the Finches' foyer was filled with pictures of the Finch family (mostly Asher and his older brother) on vacations and in various poses. Laurel made out a close shot taken underwater of the boys wearing scuba masks.

She turned back to Asher and suddenly felt near tears. He was good-looking in a classic Ralph Lauren kind of way, with his sandy-blond hair and blue eyes, but he was still such a *boy*. He was maybe five foot nine or so, with the same skinny legs and knobby knees he'd always had, and all Laurel could see were the years of Asher playing in her yard, wielding sticks as swords and climbing their swing set, running back and forth with her girls across the stream that separated their properties. Once, after Anna tripped and cut her knee trying to keep up, Dash built a makeshift bridge that Anna used for a few summers to cross the creek. The remnants were still there, cracked and overgrown with brush.

Asher looked at the floor between them, and Laurel could see a smattering of freckles across his nose. She looked down, too, as though she wanted to see what Asher was staring at. Why couldn't he look at her?

Asher wore athletic socks pulled up almost to his knees. Was he trying to be ironic? Or was this just how he'd started dressing? And when and why did Mira start to feel something different for him? It had surprised Laurel, mostly because Asher seemed so much younger than Mira, especially with her being mature for her age and him being slightly less so for his age. Plus, Mira had always treated him like a little brother. There were years Laurel was sure it was Anna who had a crush on Asher. Two months ago, around mid-May, when Mira came home from Colgate and started to go to the movies with Asher, Anna had slunk up to her room, and she didn't want to talk about it with Laurel, no matter how she prodded. Anna had seemed pissed and depressed about being left out, until all at once, maybe around mid-June, she'd snapped out of it.

"I'm here because I can't find Mira," Laurel said. "Have you heard from her?"

Asher shook his head. Laurel waited, but he didn't say anything more.

"Nothing at all?" Laurel asked, hearing the desperation creep into her voice. "A text or anything? Or maybe a post on one of those sites you all check?"

"I haven't talked to Mira since the party yesterday," Asher said.

Laurel nodded slowly. That seemed so unlikely. Mira and her friends were all so overly in touch with each other. Was he lying? Laurel didn't know how much more she could press him without giving away what she knew about the pregnancy. What if Mira hadn't told him? "So, um." Laurel stalled. "I know things haven't been easy lately between you and Mira."

Asher went bright red. So maybe he did know.

"Right now, Asher, I'm just really starting to worry," Laurel said. "I know college kids forget to call home all the time, and blah blah blah." *Blah blah blah?* Was she trying to sound like a teenager? "So if you hear from Mira at all, I just want you to call me." Laurel whipped out a crumpled pink Post-it note from her bag and scribbled down her number. "Can you do that for me, Asher?" she asked, her voice rising steadily in pitch. "Because I really need to know my daughter's okay."

JADE

1:57 p.m.

Jade was back at her house and googling *uses for hypnotherapy*. She'd replied to Jeremy's text with: Let's talk tonight, but she hadn't heard back. She was reeling from both the adoption agency and the hypnotherapy, and she sipped a massive mug of chamomile tea, trying to calm her nerves.

The hypnotherapy appointment had gone better than she'd expected. Carina had explained in detail what she thought she and Jade should do together. She said Jade would remember everything that happened to her during hypnosis and that it would feel like a state of extreme relaxation. Carina didn't want to hypnotize Jade right then and there; she wanted her to go home and think—and journal, she'd suggested—and at their next appointment, if Jade was ready, they'd begin with the night of the party. Sights, smells, sounds: Carina said they'd use sensory information to prompt Jade's memory, and then they'd use hypnosis techniques to take down Jade's panic and anxiety over what had happened that night. The goal, Carina said, was to soften the memory and teach the brain that the trauma was in the past and ultimately to help Jade let go of the stranglehold that night had on her. Jade had tried talking about that night with Jeremy, to process it, but every time she asked him the how and why of Sam, Maggie, and him getting in the car together, he said,

What more is there to say, Jade? She had your keys. We were all wasted. It was the biggest mistake of my life to let her drive.

Still, the memories haunted her. Jeremy and Sam were both conscious when Sarah, Clark, Cora, and Jade had arrived on the scene of the accident. Sam was writhing on the ground twenty feet in front of the smashed-up fender, but Jeremy was nearly untouched other than the bruises where his seat belt caught him, keeping him safe. Even now, six years later, the image of Maggie against the wheel sent chills throughout Jade's entire body. Like always when the memory took over, she felt paralyzed, stuck in a flashback. She closed her eyes, the mug of tea warm in her hands, taking deep breaths until she heard the front door click.

Her eyes opened. "Hello?" she called out.

Jeremy was at work in the city, and no one else had the key. Or did Sarah still have it from when she'd watered their plants during vacation? No—she'd returned it, Jade was sure of it.

Nelson was sleeping at her feet. He was the world's friendliest dog, but not exactly a champion watchdog; plus his hearing was going.

Jade's bare feet were freezing as she padded over the cold tiles that led from the mudroom to the foyer, where Jeremy was hunched over and taking off his shoes. He straightened. He was as striking as ever in a slim-cut gray suit, holding a bouquet of creamy tulips.

"For you," he said, extending them to her. Jade stepped closer, and he passed the flowers into her arms. They were beautiful. "I'm sorry about the way I acted yesterday," he said, "when you brought up everything at the tailor's, the adoption thing. I wasn't ready to hear that, and maybe I'm still not, though maybe I should be. I don't know, Jade. I want a baby. I want *our* baby."

"I do, too!" Jade said, cradling the tulips. "And if the typical way of getting there doesn't work, I really think we would feel that way whether I carried the baby or not—"

"I got a few tests run," Jeremy interrupted.

Jade blinked, taking in what he was telling her.

"On my end, all looks fine down there," he said. "I mean my sperm motility and all that stuff." He looked so embarrassed that Jade momentarily felt mortified for him, even though nothing about what he said was embarrassing.

Jade tried to smile. "That's good," she said. So did he think she was the problem, then? Her nerves spiked. The last thing she wanted was to start down the path of fertility testing.

Jeremy's hazel eyes burned into hers. It was hard to see him want something so badly for so long. Other than work, which always held his interest, Jeremy lost momentum in most of the other things he initially found interesting. He might get excited about playing fantasy football in a league one year, and it would be all he talked about, and then the next season he'd shrug when she asked him why he didn't sign up again. *He likes the highs and lows; he likes the newness of things, and the ability to conquer.* That's what Jade had told her therapist. It was one of the things that scared her so much about the idea of having his baby. Cora had told Jade how hard the day-to-day work of having children was. Cora obviously loved it more than anything, but Cora also had that dogged, pounding-the-pavement type of work ethic. What if Jeremy finally achieved what he set out to—getting Jade pregnant—and then lost interest in the whole thing? He was hot and cold with everything: with other people and with Jade. So what if he was like that with a child?

Jade shuddered as Jeremy pulled her close. She could smell the tulips crushed between them. "You're ovulating now, right?" he said into her hair, and the question brought tears to her eyes.

"Yes," she managed. *And that's why you came home.* "Do you want to?" she asked, because she swore she couldn't bear to hear him say the words.

"I do," he said, and then he scooped her into his arms. Jade let out a surprised laugh.

"What's gotten into you?" she asked as he carried her back to the bedroom. He tossed her gently onto the bed and pushed aside the blue silk throw pillows. He climbed over her, and Jade opened her legs so he could be closer.

"I guess just the thought of doing this with you," he said as he slid the fabric of her skirt up over her thighs.

"Doing what?" she teased, relief washing over her. In moments like these she could almost fool herself that things were as they once were years ago, when Jeremy desired her, when he still listened intently to her feelings about adoption, and when he still pretended he would go along with her plan. And what about *her*? There was so much she never told him when they first got together. *Lies of omission.* Why had there been so much pretending when they first courted each other? Did all couples do that?

Jade turned toward the gilded mirror hanging on their bedroom wall and took in the scene of the tall, handsome man running his hand over her breasts, finding his way inside her. She closed her eyes and said a silent prayer, asking whoever was up there for forgiveness.

CORA

2:04 p.m.

Hey, Mom, I stopped by your house, Cora texted Sarah. Any chance you'll be home soon?

Cora sat on her mother's porch and waited. The sun was boiling.

After the horribly awkward interaction with Isabella, Cora had tooled around Mount Pleasant, trying to run errands and occupy her mind with bulk diaper and baby-wipe purchases at Target, stalling until she figured out that what she really needed to do was talk to her mother.

(She also wanted to call Sam and tell him what Isabella had said about him and Jeremy, because Sam was the person she confided in when she was riled. But she couldn't, obviously.)

Birds chirped around a stone birdbath. Sarah loved birds. There were at least three birdbaths and six feeders around the property. And was that some kind of labyrinth cut from hedges at the corner of the property? Was her mother getting increasingly spiritual? Cora hadn't been here in a while. Usually, Sarah was the one coming to her house to visit the twins. *Visit the twins.* It was how Cora thought of her mom's visits, because it didn't usually feel like her mom was there to see her. Nothing bad had ever really happened between Cora and her mom, not even the typical teenage screaming matches. They just weren't a whole lot alike, and Cora felt that difference even more since Maggie died, because she'd been the glue that held them together.

Cora tapped the leather seat near her thigh. Was it *her*? Cora knew she sometimes came off as aloof. Maybe she needed therapy. She checked her phone for a reply from her mom, but there wasn't one. At the fundraiser, Sarah had said something about an appointment this morning with Dr. Madsen for her hand, so maybe she was still there. Cora could wait. It was nice, actually, sitting alone and staring out at the brightly colored bougainvillea. She was so rarely without her twins, which meant she always felt *on*. Of course sometimes she could stare off into space, but not without feeling guilty, and not without one of the twins snapping her back to attention with whatever they needed in the very next moment. Once Cora had counted, and between the two of them, George and Lucy had needed forty-seven things over the course of a single hour.

When the twins were quiet and occupied with their toys, Sam jokingly called it *homeostasis*. Cora once overheard him explaining the term to Jeremy: *When they're like that, playing quietly, you don't ask them a question, you don't offer them water, you don't do anything at all. You just enjoy it.*

Sam often spouted parenting wisdom, and Jeremy didn't seem to entirely like it. Cora questioned Sam's motivations, too: Wasn't he showing off a bit? He knew Jeremy wanted children of his own and that it hadn't happened yet.

Cora had been surprised, actually, when Sam told her that Jeremy and Jade were having a hard time getting pregnant. Jade had always said she wanted to adopt, even when they were in college. Why wouldn't she tell Cora they'd been trying for their own baby? Not that Cora thought there was anything wrong with her keeping it private, she just genuinely wanted to know what it was about her that kept people from telling their secrets. Maggie had been the one who inspired people to share and confess, to *spill*, as she called it. Cora didn't have that particular knack.

You see things so black and white, but there's gray everywhere, Cora, Maggie had once said. Did she mean that was why other girls didn't tell Cora their deepest, darkest secrets?

Was there gray now? With her and Sam? With what he'd done?

Cora glanced down the street to see her mom's car. When Sarah pulled into the driveway, sunlight reflected on the windshield, but Cora still caught the look of surprise on her mother's face. Had Cora ever dropped by Sarah's house unannounced? Wasn't that something mothers and daughters typically did? Had Cora's mother ever seen her without the twins since they'd been born? They certainly hadn't gone out for any mother-daughter trips to the spa or even to lunch.

Sarah parked and got out of her car. "Sweetie, hi! What a surprise."

Cora studied her mother's face and then remembered to smile back. "Hi, Mom," she said.

"Beautiful day, isn't it?" her mother said as she walked toward the front porch, where Cora sat. "And you did such a great job at the fundraiser. It was really a very nice morning."

Cora nodded. "Can we chat, Mom? Can we go inside?"

"Of course," her mom said. She unlocked the door, and Cora stepped inside the house and took off her sandals. She walked barefoot along the floorboards she'd run across with Maggie so many years ago as little girls, thinking about the game they called *animal*, which entailed their dad transforming into some kind of jungle beast and chasing them all over the downstairs. Would George and Lucy remember these early years? Would they remember how much Cora loved them?

Cora followed Sarah wordlessly into the kitchen and set her keys on the granite countertop. Sarah stared at her, waiting. "Do you want lemonade?" she finally asked. "Water, coffee?"

Cora shook her head. Her mom didn't make herself anything, either. She sat down at a stool at the counter and gestured for Cora to take the one next to her.

Cora sat. Maybe she did need some water. "This thing happened," she said, holding her mom's blue eyes. Cora had gotten her mom's light eyes; Maggie had gotten Clark's dark ones. "Sam, he . . ." Cora started. "Well, you know my friend Laurel, she has two daughters; Anna was there this morning at the gym, and the older one, Mira, she's twenty-one. She babysits for us." Cora suddenly felt embarrassed and worried she was going to hurt her mom by admitting they used babysitters instead of calling her each time they wanted to go out. Of course she asked her mom to babysit some nights, but she'd always felt it was important that she and Sam had their own babysitters so that her mom didn't feel pressured. Bad call, apparently. "She was babysitting one night last month," Cora said quickly. "And when we came home, I went upstairs with the twins, and then Sam, well, he, I guess he made a move on her."

Sarah's eyes widened just the tiniest bit. God, this was so mortifying! *Fuck you, Sam!*

"Mom, please say something to me, because I just, I don't know what to do," Cora said, and then she burst into tears.

Sarah stood from her stool and wrapped her arms around Cora's shoulders. She tightened her embrace and didn't let go until a few minutes later, when Cora's sobs turned to whimpers.

"Was he the one who told you about it?" Sarah asked, holding out a tissue like a peace offering.

Cora blew her nose. "No, that's the worst part. Well, not the worst part, I guess. I found it in a notebook. In Mira's notebook. Someone left it for me on my bed during the twins' birthday party."

Sarah narrowed her light eyebrows. "How strange," she said, sitting back down on the stool. "Did he fuck her?" she asked.

"Mom!" Cora yelped. She'd never heard her mother say the f-word, and she had the outrageous urge to laugh.

"Sorry, darling," her mother said. She reached forward and squeezed Cora's hand. It felt so good to be in her mom's kitchen.

"He says he didn't do anything other than what Mira wrote in her journal," Cora said, "which is that he kissed her. While I was upstairs!"

"That's all?" her mother asked. "I mean, that's awful, obviously, I'm just clarifying."

"That's all, or so he says," Cora said. "When I confronted him, he admitted it. He said he was drunk, and that it was so completely stupid."

The window was open in the kitchen. Through the screen, Cora saw a blue jay land on Sarah's bird feeder. Weren't blue jays supposed to be the cruelest birds?

"Do you believe him?" Sarah asked.

Cora turned slowly back to her mom. "I don't know, and I don't want to be stupid."

"You're not stupid, Cora; you've never been stupid."

"You know what I mean," Cora said. She shifted her butt. It was starting to fall asleep on the stool.

"It seems so unlike Sam," Sarah said, shaking her head.

It wasn't at all what Cora expected her mom to say, and it felt like such a relief to hear those words. "I know!" she said. "That's what I keep thinking."

"But he did it," Sarah said carefully, and Cora deflated. "And when a man does it once . . ."

"This is nothing like Dad," Cora said, sharpness in her voice.

"I didn't say it was."

"Dad lied to you over and over," Cora said. "He had a whole secret life with Abby. He made sure she loved him back before he told you he was leaving."

"I know what Dad did."

"Sorry," Cora said, feeling a lump rise in her throat. "I didn't mean it to come out like that." Tears sprung to her eyes again. "I'm sorry, Mom." She looked up at her mother, the tears making Sarah's face blurry.

"This isn't about Dad and me," Sarah said. "It's about you and Sam, and every marriage is different, and maybe you two can figure this out."

Figure this out? Cora barely had the energy to read more than five pages of a book at night after she put the twins to bed. How was she going to figure this out?

"If you want to," Sarah finished.

Cora thought of her husband in the kitchen with their babysitter. She thought of him closing the distance between them and reaching out a hand to touch her.

If you want to.

Did she want to?

JADE

2:35 p.m.

Jeremy was having sex with Jade and giving it everything he had. Really, it was an A for effort. *Well done!* Jade thought to herself. *Now please finish.*

Normally she wanted this, but today it was making her sad, truly sad: the kind of sad that makes you feel like you've fallen into a deep, dark hole. It was something about the way he'd been holding those flowers, and the way he told her about the sperm testing, and now how hard he was trying to make the sex good. And she couldn't even relax enough to enjoy it because she was feeling so incredibly guilty about the simple fact that he desperately wanted something she couldn't give him.

Jade held on tight to Jeremy's muscled back as he kept pounding away. *Enough, really, it's not happening . . .*

Her gaze roved over the books on their towering, heavy wooden antique bookshelf: classics like *Anna Karenina*, memoirs like *Coming Clean*—Jade had always figured out her way through other lives and stories. It was one of the reasons she'd loved the years she'd spent acting, when she unearthed all the things she was capable of feeling by inhabiting another person's life. Jade had once told Maggie (high on coffee in a West Village espresso bar): *If you haven't played Hedda Gabler night after night, you won't likely have a chance to know what it feels like to be driven to death because of a man's position of control over you.*

Jade had been only twenty-one when she said that. It was such a young thing to say. And now, lying beneath her husband, she felt decades older than the girl who had sat across from her lover in a coffee shop and uttered those words, words made precious because Maggie understood them.

Jeremy groaned into her hair. "Jade," he said softly. She moved her hips a little faster to keep up with his, and then it was all over.

She put her hands in his hair, feeling his warm skin beneath her fingers. Her eyes went to the wall, where Jeremy had hung a seventies-style print with big red bubble words printed on pink paper: *Love For Ever*, it said, one word stacked on top of the other. It looked like the kind of artsy thing you'd see in an LA bungalow featured in *Elle Decor*. He had startlingly good taste.

Jeremy rolled off of her. "Want to grab a shower together?" he asked. She shook her head. He kissed her and said, "Come with me to Copenhagen next week. It'll be good for us."

Jade smiled. "Maybe I will," she said.

Jeremy turned, and Jade admired his perfect male form stride into the bathroom. She waited until she heard the shower running before moving to her vanity. She retrieved a tiny key and took it to a locked jewelry box hidden inside her closet. She opened it up and took a birth control pill.

LAUREL

3:04 p.m.

Laurel flung open the door to her home to see Anna sitting on the sofa watching television. A soap opera? Yes. Laurel could tell by the soft music playing beneath a woman's low voice. How many times had Laurel told her not to watch soap operas? *But they teach the art of story, Mom!* Anna always said.

Laurel dropped her keys on the slim wooden console. A framed picture of Mira, age seven, stared up at her. In the photo, Mira wore a white dress and held a basket full of Easter eggs. The town held an annual egg hunt at a nature preserve, and the girls had always returned home excited and flushed with heat and exhaustion. Dash made sure to have a bag of candy ready because he didn't want the girls eating the candy placed in the eggs by a random town worker. *You can't be too careful,* he'd told Laurel once.

Maybe you should be more careful, Dash, Laurel thought, rubbing the bruise on her neck. She could barely hide it without a scarf, and it was July, so maybe next time Dash could be a little more precise with his dark side. God, she hated him when she thought of Cora asking about the bruise today. Had Cora bought the lie?

Focus, Laurel. You need to find your daughter.

"Anna, we need to talk," Laurel said. "Will you turn off the TV?" Anna let out an overdramatic groan, and it set Laurel's already-frayed nerves on edge. "Turn off the TV and sit up," she ordered.

Anna did as she was told, and Laurel came to sit beside her, closer than she normally would.

"I'm starting to get very worried about Mira, honey," she said. She tried to keep her voice as calm as possible. Anna already looked pale. "So I need you to really think, and remember if she said anything to you before she ran off, anything at all."

"Mom, she didn't," Anna said, and her voice came out a little barking, like a cough, and then she started to cry.

"Sweetie," Laurel said, giving Anna's hand a squeeze. "You're not in trouble or anything like that. I just want to make sure Mira's off doing something Mira-ish and not calling us like usual, right? That's your sister!" Laurel could hear her voice starting to edge toward hysteria as she tried to comfort Anna.

Anna's dark eyes were filled with tears and slightly bloodshot. Anna and Mira both had Laurel's big brown eyes. They were so beautiful with their dark eyes and blond hair.

"We got in a fight at the community center," Anna said, her tiny shoulders starting to shake, "and Mira ran off, and that's all I know, she just wasn't in town anymore. And the whole time, she was checking her phone, and it was buzzing with texts, maybe her and Andrea trying to coordinate Andrea picking her up, or maybe she was meeting someone?"

Laurel put a hand on her daughter's knee. She rubbed a tiny circle. "What did you get in a fight about?" she asked carefully.

Anna suddenly looked ill, like she could be sick at any moment. She started crying harder, and then said, "I don't know, stupid sister stuff!"

The girls fought all the time; they had since they were small. When Anna was born, Laurel had felt resigned to the fact that she was meant to be a mother to girls, to spend her entire life trying to keep them safe from harm. But she hoped that having two girls meant a sisterly bond for them, one Laurel never got to have. Unfortunately it hadn't turned out that way between Anna and Mira, and Laurel managed to blame herself, even if she couldn't figure out what she'd done to make it so. They fought so often that by the time Anna was three, Laurel moved them into separate bedrooms. Now Anna refused to even share a bathroom with Mira; she used Laurel's instead.

Laurel pulled Anna to her chest. *Stupid sister stuff* was how the girls fought nearly every day. So it wasn't likely that a typical fight with Anna would cause Mira to run away or do something dangerous.

Anna nestled her face into Laurel's neck. Laurel almost cried out when Anna's forehead pressed into the tender spot, and she thought about Cora again. Was Cora suspicious about the bruise she saw? Would she tell anyone?

"It's going to be okay, sweetie," Laurel murmured, unsure if she was telling the truth.

Was it drugs? All the experts the high school brought in to present to parents and teachers said young adults could hide drug use more expertly than ever before.

Laurel held on to Anna and said a quiet prayer. *Please, God, I'll do anything to keep these girls safe. I've loved them since the day you gave them to me. Please help us.*

"Mom?" Anna asked.

Laurel answered by kissing Anna's silky hair.

"Mira said she had to go back to our house to get a book," Anna said, "remember I told you that? She took the car keys and her phone, but she didn't take her schoolbag. When she came back like twenty minutes later, I don't know, she was really upset, I mean the kind of upset she gets where she starts shaking, and she didn't have a book with her. So she went somewhere, but it wasn't home to get a book. She just had her phone and the keys, and she kept checking her phone, and then we got into our fight."

Laurel held Anna tighter. When Anna eventually pulled away, Laurel stood on trembling legs. She started toward the door, and Anna called after her, "Where you are going?"

Laurel lifted her keys from their spot next to the silver-framed photo of Mira with her Easter basket. "I'm going to the police," she said.

VOICE MAIL RETRIEVED BY THE RAVENDALE POLICE DEPARTMENT FROM MIRA MADSEN'S PHONE, LEFT BY ANNA MADSEN AT 3:13 P.M.

> Mira, what the hell? Mom's all over me, and I swear to God if you don't call her, I'll tell her every single thing you've been doing and I don't care if you tell her what I've been doing. You need to stop being so selfish and call Mom.

SARAH

3:18 p.m.

Sarah found herself really regretting making her first physical therapy appointment for four thirty that afternoon. Why was she always such a go-getter? What if Cora wanted to stay here in the kitchen all afternoon? Sarah would love that, even under the circumstances (*That damn Sam!*), but if Cora sensed there was any small reason not to stay—like if Sarah asked her how long she could stay because she just needed to cancel this small, unimportant appointment—Sarah was sure Cora would bolt, and she really didn't want that.

"Let me make tea," Sarah said, rising from the stool in her kitchen. She could smell the lilies she'd arranged that morning in a blue ceramic bowl on her granite countertop, right next to the stack of Ina Garten cookbooks.

Sam. God! And with a twenty-one-year-old? Mira was very beautiful, but she was a *girl.* He had to know better than to do that! What if he'd really messed with the girl's mind? He likely had! Twenty-one-year-olds weren't meant to be on the receiving end of sexual advances by thirtysomething adult men. It was criminal! Though, by definition, it actually wasn't. Still!

Sarah poured cold water into the teakettle. She glanced over her shoulder to see Cora's petite frame slumped in her chair, staring down at her pale-pink nail polish. Her poor daughter! Sarah just hadn't seen this one coming: Sam didn't seem like the type.

Although, Sarah hadn't sensed Clark cheating, either . . .

"Do you love him, honey?" Sarah asked as she set the teakettle onto the stove. She hadn't felt this free with her daughter in a long time. It was like Cora's permanent look of skepticism was on vacation, leaving behind an open, beautifully vulnerable face. Ever since Cora had been small, she'd looked at her mother with such doubt, and Sarah couldn't shake it. It was as if Cora questioned everything Sarah did, and from such a young age. It made Sarah incredibly insecure. But then Maggie came along, and everything Sarah did, in Maggie's eyes, was perfectly wonderful.

Cora nodded her head just slightly. "I do love him," she said. "I mean, you know, I'm tired with the kids. And there are so many times I'd rather sleep than snuggle up with him . . ."

"Or have sex with him," Sarah said. "I remember those days."

This time Cora didn't seem surprised. She just nodded.

Cora *did* look exhausted. Maybe Sarah should have been more vocal about wanting to help with the twins. She babysat only once a month or so; maybe she should have suggested a standing day—every Friday night, say—so Cora and Sam could go on date nights. *Yes.* If Cora and Sam got past this, that's what Sarah was going to do. *Date night every Friday,* she'd say to them. *I insist!*

"But there are good times we have, too," Cora said, "like with the kids. I guess, maybe too much of *us* is really *the kids*, you know? It's all about the kids, and that's probably my doing. But Sam's, too, I think."

Sarah lowered herself back onto the stool. "When Maggie was a teenager and you were off at college," she started, "maybe ten or so years ago, there was a whole movement to parent like the French, to be less hands-on, for adults to be very separate from children, to be less enmeshed, I guess, and to do more adult and sophisticated things." Sarah toyed with her pearl earring and then tucked a lock of hair behind her ear. "The thing is, I always disagreed, because, really, Cora, the moment the doctor put you and then Maggie into my arms, we were one. You were a part of my skin, it felt, and certainly my heart. So I don't think you'll ever look back and think that you and Sam were too involved, or that you spent too much time with George and Lucy. I don't look back and think that now, for Christ's sake, and Clark left me. And I'm not saying you shouldn't prioritize Sam, too, of course, and maybe during these years, that just means more coffee so you have the extra energy to snuggle up at night, or talk to him about his day, or to do whatever you need to make him feel noticed and beloved. That's all we want, right?" Sarah shrugged. "I thought I was doing that for Clark, I really did. I don't know how much you remember, or if you paid attention to your father and me, but I loved him so much. I mean, really, I even found him sexy right up until Maggie died."

Oh, why had she said that? Sarah looked away, embarrassed.

"What do you mean?" Cora asked carefully.

Sarah considered her hands. They were so wrinkled, honestly. "It was deluded, but I thought he'd come back to me," she said, looking up at her daughter. "And up until the night Maggie died, I wanted him to."

There was such empathy on Cora's face, which was a bit unlike her. Often Cora looked away when things became emotional or pushed the boundaries of what she was comfortable talking about. Sarah and Cora had hit walls in nearly every conversation about Maggie's death, until they stopped talking about it all, or at least the painful parts. But they never, ever stopped talking about Maggie herself. Their conversations were always peppered with what Maggie would have done or said. It made it easier to be with each other; it was like pretending Maggie was still there.

"After Maggie died, I couldn't even imagine a world where Clark and I belonged together," Sarah said. She'd never really said it like that even to herself. But it was true.

"That makes sense to me, actually," Cora said, sitting up straighter, "because I felt like when Maggie died, it was an entirely new world. Like how could anyone think that the universe we were living in hadn't completely changed? I even started reading these crazy quantum physics books that proposed alternate universes on the space-time continuum, and of course I didn't believe it could really be true, but it still made me feel better to think of a whole different world where Maggie was still alive, where I was blissfully unaware of how bad it would be to lose her." The look on Cora's face was as though she was still mystified by how all this had happened to them. "It was just like one day, we were here, and then Maggie died and that whole life was gone, and we were somewhere entirely new and uncharted, and not somewhere I wanted to be at all."

Sarah burst into tears. Cora had described exactly how she felt, too.

A breath later the teakettle shrieked, and Sarah jumped up and took it off the burner. She wiped her eyes with the back of her hand. She opened a cabinet and searched until she found chamomile, and her hands shook as she poured the hot water. Sarah brought the mugs back to the kitchen island, and she and her only living daughter drank them together in silence.

LAUREL

3:35 p.m.

I'm here to see Detective Mark DeFosse," Laurel told the cop sitting at the front desk of the Ravendale Police Department. Her name tag said *Officer Lisa Hoxie*, and she considered Laurel like she couldn't possibly be in the right place.

"He's expecting me," Laurel added.

Officer Lisa Hoxie raised an eyebrow at Laurel. She set down her lunch—kung pao chicken from Tao Palace; Laurel recognized the logo—and left her post at the desk, presumably to find Mark. She opened a door marked *Staff* and disappeared.

Laurel stood still, feeling her heels tingle against the linoleum. She hadn't seen Mark since last year, and it was from afar, when he was at ShopRite with his wife and looking terribly bored as he perused the frozen food section. If he hadn't been with his wife, Laurel would have said hello, but instead she'd cruised past the aisle toward the organic produce section. When she was finished grocery shopping, Laurel had driven home thinking about high school sex with Mark. It had been good sex, actually, and so incredibly sweet. Laughably different than sex with Dash.

Laurel glanced around nervously. The police station was entirely beige: beige floors, beige counters, and beige walls. The reception area held just one ergonomic chair and a computer for the officer working the front desk, which looked onto a small waiting room with wooden chairs. The rest of the officers and detectives must be in the back, out of sight. It was just so different from what police stations looked like on *Law & Order*. Was there even a jail cell?

Officer Hoxie returned and gestured for Laurel to follow. They walked through a long corridor past a few closed doors, stopping in front of the one marked *Detective Mark DeFosse*. It was slightly ajar.

"Go ahead, he's waiting," the officer said. Laurel thanked her and pushed open the door. Mark was seated behind a metal desk with a laptop on it. Next to the laptop was a clay paperweight adorned with rhinestones, similar to the ones Anna and Mira made during preschool. Mark stood right away. He'd always been the kind of man who stood the moment a woman entered the room, even when he was a teenager. He was tall, not quite as tall as Dash, maybe six foot or so. His almost-black hair had thinned only a little since high school.

"Thanks so much for seeing me," Laurel said. Her voice betrayed how on edge she felt.

"Of course, Laurel," he said, but then he corrected himself. "Mrs. Madsen."

"Please call me Laurel," she said.

"Laurel," he said, "please sit."

She sat in the chair across from him. He sat, too, and considered her. "Tell me what I can do," he said. His voice was deeper than she remembered.

Laurel tried to take a slow breath, but it was useless. She felt like she hadn't breathed properly since last night, when she sat on Mira's empty bed, staring around the room at the magazine tear-outs Mira posted on her walls. The tear-outs were always changing, just images that Mira said she found beautiful.

Laurel opened her mouth. *My daughter Mira is missing.* It's what she wanted to say, what she should say. But somehow she couldn't get herself to say it.

"My daughter Mira never came home last night," she said instead. The words seemed to bounce off the walls of Mark's office. Laurel leaned closer to the desk and stared into Mark's dark-blue eyes. Looking at him steadied her just like it had in high school. There had always been something about him, a feeling of *safety* and a certainty about what was right and what was wrong. Why hadn't she married *him*? She'd been in love with him, that was for sure. How different her life could have been if only she'd married someone else! And what would Mark think if he knew how far Laurel had strayed from who she was in high school, and from the life she thought she'd have? Mark knew how much Laurel had wanted to be a doctor back then because she talked about it all the time, she signed up for journals and clipped articles, and she made minimum wages in doctors' offices as a receptionist just so she could be around the world of medicine. Maybe Mark looked at her now and thought her plan to become a doctor was all she'd lost? He couldn't know about the part of her that had died the second Dash squeezed her throat that first time during sex. *You're the one who stays, Laurel,* she reminded herself. Though she knew that wouldn't matter to Mark; she had a feeling Mark would show Dash exactly what he thought of sexual violence.

"Yesterday we spent the afternoon as a family at a birthday party at our neighbors' house," Laurel said slowly, "and after that, a little after five, Mira went into town with her sister. She was texting a lot, buried in her phone, or at least that's what my younger daughter, Anna, told me. Anna also told me that Mira said she needed to return to our house for a book and left, but Dash and I were home, and Mira never made it to us. She must have gone somewhere else, somewhere she didn't want Anna to know about. Maybe to meet someone, I have no idea. She returned to town, to the community center where Anna was, and they had an argument. Mira left, and we haven't seen her since. It isn't unlike Mira to run off and not tell us where she's going. Ever since her first summer home from college, she's been very vocal about how she's an adult and needs the same freedom she has at college."

Laurel paused. Hearing the words out loud, she realized how spoiled they made Mira sound. Should Laurel have been stricter, maybe told Mira that as long as she lived under Laurel and Dash's roof, she lived by their rules?

"The second time Mira left," Mark started, "the last time your daughter Anna saw her, did she drive off in a car? Or was she on foot?"

"On foot," Laurel said, feeling odd about the turn of phrase. "Or, certainly someone could have picked her up. There's a girl Mira knows named Andrea White who lives in the apartments near the train station . . ." *Right by where you and I used to live, when we used to date.* Laurel straightened in her seat. "I thought maybe Mira could be with Andrea, so I got her number from the coffee shop where both girls work."

The trip to the coffee shop for Andrea's address and number had also provided the chance for Laurel to again ask Denise, the manager, if she'd heard from Mira, but Denise was certain Mira hadn't called in to the shop to announce her absence. *Does she usually call you when she's going to miss work?* Laurel asked, and Denise threw up her hands and said *Nope, she doesn't!* in a way that inferred Mira was the most self-absorbed brat on the face of the earth. Maybe Mira *was* the most self-absorbed brat on the face of the earth, but she was Laurel's brat, and Laurel wanted her home. She'd forced a smile at Denise and told her it was imperative to call immediately if Mira called in to work or stopped by. Denise had looked at Laurel like she felt terribly sorry for her, and also like she knew every single thing that was wrong in Laurel's life and therefore pitied her, which completely infuriated Laurel. She even found herself wanting to say mean things, and she purposely tried never to do that. It was unbecoming for a grown woman to behave like a cruel Queen Bee.

"I called Andrea and left a voice mail," Laurel told Mark, "but she never called me back, so I drove over there and rang the buzzer, but no one answered."

Mark raised an eyebrow.

"Mira didn't show up at work this morning, and this is just really unlike her," Laurel said, her voice starting to tremble a bit.

"How unlike her?" Mark asked.

"Of course she's unreachable sometimes, but never for too long. This is absolutely the first time something like this has happened."

Mark sank back farther into his seat. Laurel could feel herself losing him; he was probably thinking that all of this sounded like typical young adult stuff, that Mira would waltz in later tonight with a bad hangover that matched her bad attitude.

"Mark, look, the reason I'm so scared is that Mira is *pregnant.* Newly pregnant, going by the fact that I know she had her period last month because I had to buy her tampons." Was she seriously saying these things out loud? *Your daughter is gone, Laurel, you need to say these things.* "My husband, Dash, doesn't know yet, but that's why I'm so concerned, because what if she's had an abortion and something went wrong, and no one knows to contact us, or what if she's been kidnapped, or, I don't know, and I know it hasn't been forty-eight hours; it hasn't even been twenty-four hours, so I know she isn't officially missing yet, but I have a terrible feeling, and if you could just . . ."

Oh God, she was crying.

"Laurel," Mark said gently. "How about I come by your house after work this evening around six thirty and talk to Dash and your daughter Anna?"

Laurel nodded. "Yes, thank you! Please come. Thank you so much, Mark. Really, thank you."

"Before I arrive tonight, it would be helpful if you could think about the possible fathers of the baby."

Possible fathers? "Oh!" Laurel said quickly. "Mira has a boyfriend. A neighborhood boy named Asher Finch." Had Mira used the word *boyfriend* to describe Asher? Or had Laurel just assumed?

"Good," Mark said. "I'll pay him a visit tonight, too."

JADE

4:42 p.m.

Everything felt so messed up.

That's what Jade was thinking as she stared at Maggie's gravestone. It was speckled gray granite, and remarkably pristine-looking considering it had marked Maggie's grave for nearly six years. The grave site was positioned at the top of a hill beneath a willow tree, and during Jade's daytime visits, sunlight danced between the leaves.

A gust of warm air worked through Jade's hair like fingers, and she bent to place the bouquet of wildflowers on Maggie's grave. To the right of the gravestone was a curved pattern of stones, shaped like an M. She'd never seen them before.

Jade gazed at Maggie's grave, her thoughts quieting and wandering as they always did when she was at this spot. She knew the baby thing would come to a head soon, and she thought about what she'd say when Jeremy inevitably asked her to get tested with a fertility doctor. She wondered how a fertility doctor would broach the issue of the extra estrogen coursing through her system.

Jade had always been so honest with Maggie, but now look at all the lies she told. She knew how wrong it all was, so why couldn't she stop?

She needed to talk to her mother. Jade had called her on the drive to the graveyard about planning an upcoming trip to Florida, and right away her mother had said, *We'd love to see you!* just like she always did. When Jade was down there, she would tell her mom everything. Her mom always had a way of dealing with anything as though it were just something Jade had to walk through gracefully, something she could absolutely do if she set her mind to doing it. Maybe Jade would book Mira for dog sitting for that week she was in Florida, too, so she could stay a little longer than usual and figure it all out with her mom, and then Jeremy wouldn't have to worry about coming home from work earlier to walk Nelson. She knew Mira would say yes, partly because she wanted the money and partly because she had such an obvious crush on Jeremy. Jade sometimes wondered what it would be like to be Jeremy, to be always and forever on the receiving end of someone's unrequited desire. She could tell even Cora was attracted to Jeremy (in Cora's own safe and faithful wifely way), and it didn't bother Jade in the slightest. Jade thought Jeremy was too deep inside himself to want sex with another woman. He barely wanted sex with her, unless it was the middle of her cycle. So she didn't worry about Jeremy sleeping with their twenty-one-year-old dog sitter, or anyone else, really.

Could she be sure of that? She thought so. Though certainly she kept her secrets from him—so how well could married people really know each other?

She shook off the thought. No, not Jeremy. She knew him well enough to know he'd never.

CORA

5:05 p.m.

Hey. I'm home. Sitter is here so I told her to just go. Please come home, Cora. I need to talk to you.

Cora had shown her mom the text from Sam, and Sarah had canceled her physical therapy appointment and convinced Cora to go home to talk with him, promising she'd take the twins out and keep them occupied. Now both Cora and Sarah were in the car, pulling into Cora's driveway past neatly trimmed hedges.

Cora steered around George's tricycle and parked. She stared at her house, letting go of a breath she hadn't realized she'd been holding. It was such a beautiful house, painted all white, including the shutters. A gray stone chimney climbed into a bright-blue sky, and Sam had just painted the solid, gleaming navy front door with a special kind of shiny paint Sarah had recommended. A grand house like this one wasn't ever what Cora had pictured herself living in—she thought she'd be working in academia, living on a salary too small to afford anything like it—but she loved this house because it was where she raised her babies.

"I'll just take them to the park," Sarah said carefully. "Just an hour or two, all right, dear? Too hot for anything longer, anyway. Just time enough for you and Sam to talk."

Cora turned off the ignition. What were the other options? She couldn't avoid him much longer; that was for sure. It wasn't like she could force him to go to a motel for the week. She didn't even know which days the recycling needed to go out.

"There's not as much to say as you might think," Cora said. They were still buckled in their seat belts, and the car already felt hot without the AC.

"There's a whole marriage worth of things to say," Sarah said. She tapped a finger on her thigh, and Cora noticed how bony her mom's wrinkled knees looked poking out of ikat-printed shorts. She needed to eat more.

"I'll try," Cora said, and then she unbuckled her seat belt and got out of the car. She and Sarah walked slowly along the stone path, and at the front door Cora had the ridiculous urge to ring her own bell. She shook off the feeling and unlocked the door.

"George! Lucy!" she called out.

George came toddling from the kitchen, his face covered with something red. Blood? "George, sweetie," she said. She got closer and saw it was some kind of sauce. Cora ducked down for a hug, knowing her new T-shirt was going to be forever stained. "Hi, sweetheart," she said into his blond curls.

"Mama!" Lucy cried out. She appeared in the hall, trailed by a pale-looking Sam holding a washcloth.

"Hi," Sam said as the kids raced to hug Sarah. His brown hair was a mess, and he looked mortified to see Sarah standing there.

"My mom wanted to take the kids to the park. It's so nice out," Cora said, looking pointedly at Sam. "George, Lucy, what do you think?" Cora asked her twins. She scooped Lucy into her arms and nuzzled her nose.

"Park! Nana!" George said. Did that count as a two-word sentence? The pediatrician had asked at their recent visit if George was making two-word sentences yet, and Cora had said, *Not really,* and she'd been inwardly freaking out ever since she saw the concerned look on the pediatrician's face.

"Go to park, Nana!" Lucy said. Four words.

"Yes, let's!" Sarah said. "Should I bring a bag?" she asked Cora.

Cora nodded. She moved into the twins' playroom and grabbed the army-green canvas diaper bag her mother had bought for her. *It's stylish enough that you won't look like you've given up,* Sarah had said. Cora always tried to laugh and play along when other mothers lamented all the ways having kids had changed them for the worse, but she didn't exactly feel that way. Up until the twins' birth, Cora had never felt sure of anything, or grounded by something real and true. Before George and Lucy, there was so much she doubted, and certainly doubting had served her in a way; it was partly what had made her so good at math—the way she questioned everything, the way she doubted anything she couldn't prove. But when George and Lucy came, Cora felt sure of something for maybe the first time in her entire life.

"Mama, juice?" Lucy asked from the hallway as Cora packed a change of clothes for both kids.

"Do we still have the juice?" Cora called out to Sam. *The juice you weren't supposed to buy because they never stop asking for it?*

"I'll get it!" Sam called back. Matt Damon had a lot of children, didn't he? Four, maybe? Had Cora read that? Did Matt Damon listen to his wife when she asked him never to buy juice?

Sam appeared in the playroom just as Cora was slinging the diaper bag over her shoulder. He was holding two juice boxes, but they were opened, the straws poking right out of them.

"Are you kidding me, Sam?" Cora said, her voice hushed.

His eyebrows shot up.

"The juices are open," Cora said. "Should I pack *open* juices in our diaper bag?"

Oh God, she was getting hysterical. She might cry. Oh yes! She was crying. She slumped down on the floor of the playroom, pinching her right butt cheek on the corner of a Lego. She shoved the diaper bag toward him. "I don't want the twins to see me upset," she said, frantic. "Get two unopened juice boxes and give them to my mom with the bag."

"I'm sorry, I . . ." Sam started, but Cora glared at him and he left the room.

Cora dropped her head into her hands. She listened to the sound of Sam's footsteps in the hall, and when he finally got the correct juice boxes and she heard the front door open, she called out, "Bye, George and Lucy! I love you!"

"Love you, Mama!" came Lucy's voice.

"Mama, bye!" George called. Two words! That had to count as a two-word sentence, didn't it?

Cora carefully got to her feet and peered out the window of the playroom to see her mom walking the twins down the stone path. Sarah opened a car door and managed to lift George into his car seat while getting Lucy to stand still and not run down the driveway. Cora watched as Sarah buckled all of their seat belts and then backed onto the road. She always found it so hard to watch her twins drive away, even with Sam. It was like putting them into someone else's hands and praying for the best. She didn't feel quite right until they were back home and in her arms. Maybe she really did need a therapist? Or maybe this was just what being a mother felt like.

"Cora," said Sam.

Cora turned slowly. The afternoon was turning into early evening, and the sun came into the twins' playroom through the slits in the blinds. Sam was striped with yellow light.

"Can we sit?" Cora asked.

"Of course," Sam said. "In the living room?"

Cora shook her head. "Here," she said, and she lowered herself onto the twins' rubber play mat. Sam followed, sitting on top of the letters *E* and *F*. Near his feet, a happy gray elephant smiled maniacally at them.

"I just," Cora started, shaking her head. "Why did you do it?" What else was she supposed to ask? Wasn't that the crux of things?

Sam's face dimmed.

"And please don't tell me because you were drunk," Cora said.

During his midtwenties, Sam had smoked pot on the weekends. It didn't fit with the rest of his personality—he was such an achiever, a hard worker—but pot was how he chilled out on Friday nights after a week at work. The night of Maggie's death, when Cora arrived to see the convertible crushed against a line of trees, when she saw the paramedics lifting Sam from the ground and placing him onto a stretcher, she ran to her soon-to-be husband, praying he was alive. She threw her arms around him despite the warnings of the EMTs, and smelled pot all over him. He must have just smoked, maybe with Jeremy. (Maggie didn't smoke anything. She barely drank, which Cora thought was just one of the many cruel ironies of her death.)

The cops had to smell it on them. But the first cop on the scene in charge of the investigation was an old friend of Clark's—he had a daughter Maggie's age, and he and Clark coached the girls' softball team together for years—and Cora had always wondered if the police had spared her family by focusing only on making sure Jeremy and Sam were okay, not dragging them through the press with reports about how high they were as Maggie's passengers. Maggie's blood tests had come back with no drugs in her system, only alcohol at a level high enough that the social worker told Cora and her parents that Maggie wouldn't have been able to use any reason to make a decision about whether it was safe to drive a car.

Sam didn't touch drugs or alcohol for four years after Maggie died. He had to have blamed himself for letting her drive—who wouldn't? He never said it out loud, but he could still hardly bear to be in the room when anyone talked about Maggie. He was close to her, and plus, he hadn't had much experience with death. He was an only child, and both his parents were from small families, and no one had ever died who really mattered to him. At the center of his pain, Cora knew, had to be his overwhelming guilt for being drunk and high and letting Maggie drive that night.

Four years after Maggie's death, when the twins were born, Sam's boss came by the hospital and brought a bottle of champagne. Sam drank a glass with his boss to be polite, and one glass turned into two, and that got him drinking again. But he never had more than three or four drinks in a sitting, so Cora never made a big thing about it. And he never smoked pot.

The night everything happened with Mira, he'd had at least three drinks at the sushi place, and he would have been buzzed when they returned home. So had Sam always looked at Mira like that? Had he wanted to cheat (with Mira? with anyone?) for months (or years)? Maybe the alcohol only fueled a desire that was already there?

Had he cheated before?

Sam sat cross-legged on the play mat so awkwardly it was almost painful. Is this how he always sat when he played with the twins and Cora just never noticed? His back was curved, and his elbows rested on his knees. Blond-brown hairs paraded over his exposed skin.

"I'm sorry, Cora," he said and then cleared his throat. "You have no idea how sorry I am." He blew out a breath. "I get it if you want to leave me. What I did was very wrong, and I swear to you I regret it with every bone in my body."

Leave him? Was that seriously what she was going to do?

"I need you to tell me why," Cora said. "I mean, why you wanted to do that, why you wanted to kiss Mira." The words felt so creepy coming out of her mouth; it felt like throwing up.

Sam looked as ill as she felt. He shook his head as if he could free the words from the air between them, but they hung there, true and painful.

"I don't know," he said. "I mean, obviously I recognized Mira was beautiful, but before that night, I only thought of her as our babysitter."

He looked so young all of a sudden, like a boy caught with his hand in a cookie jar. He wore an old blue T-shirt, and he was unshaven with a coating of light stubble over his face. Had he gone into the office at all today?

"What I mean is, I wasn't having some fantasy about sleeping with her," Sam said.

"Do you have fantasies about sleeping with other people?" Cora asked him, rolling back on her butt, feeling the rubber play mat against her sit bones.

"Well, I guess sometimes. Don't you?" Sam asked. "Ever?"

Cora considered this. There had been a very elaborate Leonardo DiCaprio fantasy she frequently entertained, where she and Leo were at a garden party. (She wasn't even sure what a garden party was, but she was pretty sure it entailed an outdoor party with cocktails, and ivy trailing up the side of a house, or at least that was how her fantasy garden party always looked . . .) Leo always found her in the crowd, and he furtively grabbed her hand just as the sun was about to set. Then he pulled her against the side of the white-brick house and pushed her dress over her hips. They had standing-up sex, and it was always incredibly amazing. Did that count?

"With celebrities, but not with people we actually know," Cora answered. But wait, what about Jeremy? She'd always found him so hot, and sometimes—okay, maybe once every few months?—she thought about what it would be like to have sex with him. "Sometimes I think about having sex with Jeremy," she blurted.

Sam's eyes widened. "Are you serious?"

"But I *don't*!" Cora said. "I purposely do not have sex with anyone other than you! And I also don't go around town kissing people."

It was so incredibly urgent, like he had to kiss me because if he didn't he would die.

A toy spatula fell from the twins' kitchen and clanged against the floor. Cora flinched.

"It was a mistake," Sam said.

"The biggest you've ever made?" Cora asked. It didn't come out like a question: it came out like an accusation.

Sam didn't answer. He glanced toward the window. Through the slats, Cora could see Mr. Feinstein's landscapers cruising across the lawn on ride-on mowers.

"Have you ever cheated on me before?" Cora asked.

Sam whipped his head back around to look at her. *"No,"* he said. "Never."

"Was it something I did?" Cora asked. "Or didn't do?"

Sam looked like he didn't understand the question.

"Was it not sleeping with you enough?" she asked.

"Cora, *no*. Are you kidding me? It wasn't you—it was me. I looked at Mira that night in our kitchen, and something about her felt so young, so incredibly *young*, like we all used to be not that long ago, before everything got ruined the night Maggie died. Seeing her standing there made me feel like I used to feel: young, no responsibilities, and no fucking overwhelming guilt that feels like a constant knife in my stomach."

Cora took in a sharp breath.

"The seconds Mira and I were standing there, I forgot everything, all of it," Sam said. "I was free." His shoulders shook and he started crying, the first time he'd cried since the night of Maggie's death. He hadn't even cried when the twins were born, he'd just stared at them, unbelieving.

"I want *you*, Cora," Sam said, his voice low and determined. "I want our life together. I don't want anyone else but you. Please, believe me. Help me fix this."

LAUREL

6:57 p.m.

Laurel flitted around her kitchen making coffee and setting out the sandwiches and cookies she'd picked up from Buzzed on the way home from the police station. She saw no reason not to stop by and ask the manager again if she'd heard from Mira, and Laurel had found it extremely rude the way Denise had said, *I told you I'd call you.* Denise acted as though Laurel was some annoying customer, when Laurel had always thought she was one of Denise's favorites!

Dash was sulking at the computer in the kitchen. This morning, he'd seemed to think Laurel was overreacting about Mira. But somewhere around noon, something changed in him, and he finally became worried. By two, he'd started calling Laurel every half hour or so between patients. When Laurel told him that a detective was coming later to question them, Dash left the office and came straight home.

Now he was working on the computer, which is what he always did when he was stressed and one of his daughters was home so he couldn't turn Laurel into a sexual punching bag. No matter how quiet Laurel had tried to be when the girls were younger, she couldn't help crying out when Dash hurt her, and the thought of Anna and Mira hearing her like that still haunted her. She tried to assuage her guilt by reminding herself that other women cried out because sex felt *good*, and that maybe the girls, tucked away for the night, never heard anything at all. And then it was so confusing, because sometimes Laurel did cry out because it felt good. Never to be hurt, but the sex part. When Dash was in a phase where he hurt her less than usual, she was able to relax a little during sex, which meant sometimes she had an orgasm. It was such a release in the moment, but it was followed by a sinking sense that she herself must be as depraved as her husband, because how could her body still respond to him sexually after he'd hurt her so badly? After they'd started using Rachel, Laurel never again had an orgasm during sex. How could she with another woman watching?

A crash sounded upstairs. "Anna?" Laurel called.

"I'm fine!" Anna yelled back.

Dash pounded at the keyboard as Laurel arranged tomato-and-mozzarella sandwiches on a platter. Would Mark even like a sandwich like that? She grabbed a few turkey and ham options, too, and arranged them in a circle around each other. Would Mark come alone, or would he bring another detective?

Nerves overtook Laurel. She put a hand to her forehead and said, "Dash, I just, I swear to God if something happened to her . . ."

Dash stood and came to where Laurel leaned against the kitchen island. He put a strong hand on her back and pulled her close. He rarely hugged her, and she'd forgotten how good it felt. She started to cry against his crisp white button-down. "We know that Mira can be incredibly thoughtless," he said, his voice breaking for the first time in years. "And God knows I will regret those words if something is really wrong."

Laurel looked up at her husband. His light eyes were so clear, so crystalline.

"If it's drugs, like you mentioned today," Dash said, "there are places we can send her. We'll start arranging logistics as soon as she gets home."

Now both of Dash's arms were around Laurel's waist, pulling her against him. She wiped at her eyes. She had an insane urge to kiss him.

"How did we even get here?" she asked softly.

Dash didn't answer, but Laurel was sure he knew she wasn't talking only about Mira.

"I don't know," he finally said, and Laurel waited for him to say more—was there any chance, in this vulnerable moment, that she should ask him to go for help again? Wouldn't he try? Shouldn't he? Laurel would feel so much better about leaving him if he were already undergoing intense therapy with someone he trusted. He'd hurt her so badly yesterday—the bruise on her neck was the biggest mark he'd left since they'd started using Rachel. He had to know that.

"Dash," Laurel said, her voice a whisper. *I'm leaving you at the end of the summer* . . . "If the worst has happened," she started.

"It hasn't," Dash said. "It hasn't even been twenty-four hours, Laurel."

Technically, it had. But Laurel didn't say so.

The bell rang. Laurel broke from Dash and hurried toward the front door, swinging it open to see Mark DeFosse holding his keys and phone. Seeing him just standing there like that reminded Laurel of when he was just a teenager picking her up to go into Mount Pleasant to see a movie. (Mark always called Laurel fancy when she referred to movies as *films*.) But that wasn't the Mark that Laurel wanted to see right now. She wanted to see him looking like an imposing detective, ready and able to find her daughter.

Laurel lifted her hand in a greeting. "Please come in," she said, and Mark stepped inside. "Let's sit in the living room. I made coffee. I just need to get Anna."

They walked into the living room, where Dash was standing in the middle of the carpet, unanchored. "I'm Dash Madsen," he said to Mark, extending his big hand. "Thank you so much for coming."

They shook as Laurel called up the stairs for Anna. Laurel retreated to the kitchen and grabbed the sandwich tray with shaking hands. She brought the tray back into the living room and set it down on the shagreen coffee table like she'd done so many times for PTA meetings, playdates, and the Mother's Night Out gatherings she often threw as the perpetual class mom. She couldn't help but volunteer for class mom each year: the e-mail went out looking for willing mothers, and Laurel responded in the affirmative. Why were some of the other mothers so easily able to ignore those e-mails? And where had it gotten her, being class mom? In her beautifully appointed living room, serving overpriced sandwiches to a detective to discuss her missing daughter?

Anna's footsteps sounded on the stairs. Her face was pale, and at the sight of the detective, she looked like she could be sick. "Come and sit, honey," Laurel said gently. Anna stalked into the living room and sat on the sofa with Dash. Laurel sat on the other side of Dash, and for a brief moment, she felt united with her family.

Mark looked them over. He sat forward on the sofa, his back arched, and his hands folded. He didn't even look at the sandwiches.

"Anna," he said, "I'm Detective Mark DeFosse, and I'd love to hear your story first, since you were the last one to see your sister. Please know that you're not in trouble, and that nothing you tell me, even if it's something you know about drugs and alcohol, or anything like that, is going to get you in trouble. I just want to help your parents find Mira."

Laurel's eyes flooded with tears. He was speaking so kindly. What was it about unexpected kindness that always made Laurel cry? She reached for a tissue, trying not to be obvious about crying so she wouldn't upset Anna.

"Mira and I were at the community center studying," Anna started, and Laurel wasn't sure if it was because she'd heard Anna's story already, but it almost sounded rehearsed. "She said she needed to go back and get a book from our house. She took the car, and I know that because it wasn't where we first parked. I found it across the street. But she didn't come back with a book. She came back from wherever she went extremely upset, and she was checking her phone and it was buzzing with texts. Then we got into a fight and she left. And that's the last time

I saw her, and she didn't tell me where she was going or anything like that, because *obviously* I would have told my mom and dad."

"That's a good start," Mark said. "Any chance you want to tell me what your fight was about? And Dr. and Mrs. Madsen," he said, turning to them, "now would be a good time to tell me about any arguments you've had lately with your daughter." He settled his eyes back on Anna. "Anna, do you want to start?"

"I don't even remember," Anna said, but her face flushed at the cheeks.

"It was yesterday, Anna," Laurel snapped. "I'm sure you can think back and try to remember."

Anna's hands folded the bottom of her baggy T-shirt with a silk-screen of a girl's face, captioned: *Poor Little Me!*

Laurel's phone rang and she jumped. "Oh, just a second!" she said. "Maybe it's . . ." Her voice trailed off when she saw the 914 number. "Hello?" Laurel said into her phone.

"Mrs. Madsen?" came a young, nasally voice on the other end. "This is Andrea, Mira's friend."

Laurel felt a pit in her stomach like a punch. She whispered, "Mira's friend Andrea," to Mark and then put the phone on speaker.

"Um, so Mira didn't come to my house last night," Andrea said to all of them.

"Okay," Laurel said, heart pounding. "She told me she was planning to, so was she in touch with you to cancel?"

"Nope. I waited at my apartment until nine, and then I went out, so I guess maybe she could have come after that, but I don't think so."

"And you never saw or spoke to Mira?" Dash barked.

Mark flinched. Laurel shot Dash a look. They didn't need to scare Andrea.

"Did you hear from her at all, last night or today?" Dash asked, more carefully this time.

"No," Andrea said. "She was supposed to work my shift at Buzzed, and I know she didn't show up because Denise called to yell at me for both of us."

"I'm sorry about that," Laurel said, feeling inane for apologizing for her daughter. "Andrea, we're really worried about Mira. Could you call us if you hear anything?"

"Sure, okay," Andrea said, and then she hung up.

Laurel started sobbing, and Dash put an arm around her. "She's pregnant, Dash," she said. "Mira's pregnant."

Laurel caught Anna's face first, and the way her dark eyes widened made Laurel almost sure it was the first time she was hearing about it.

"What did you just say?" Dash asked, his voice so low she could barely make it out.

Laurel managed a nod to confirm what she'd said.

"Is it Asher?" Dash turned to Mark. "Mira is dating a boy named Asher Finch," he said. His voice was cold and clinical like he was talking about a patient. Only the rage simmering beneath his words gave him away.

Our daughter is pregnant, and now she's gone.

Laurel couldn't keep her thoughts straight. She felt like she was missing something, but she wasn't sure what it was.

"Let's go," Dash said to Mark, standing. "I'm coming with you to Asher's."

"No, Daddy!" Anna shouted.

They all turned. She hadn't called him that in years.

"There's something going on with Mr. O'Connell," Anna blurted. She sat forward on the sofa, so close to the edge she looked like she was about to topple. "Mr. O'Connell, he . . ." Anna's voice trailed off.

"Are you talking about Sam O'Connell, *our neighbor*?" Dash asked, his skin deathly pale.

Anna nodded. All three adults stared at her. Laurel couldn't breathe.

"Um, he, well, he kissed her once. I have no idea if anything else happened, but Mira definitely wanted something to happen, so I'm pretty sure if Mr. O'Connell wanted that, too, which it sounds like he did, then it probably did, right?"

Laurel's throat had closed. She could take in only the smallest bit of air. She turned to Dash, unable to speak. Sweat had broken out along his hairline, and a single bead slipped over his temple.

"How did you learn this, Anna?" Mark asked slowly, carefully, *professionally*. "Did Mira tell you herself?"

Anna shook her head. "Mira had a notebook on her desk, I guess she was starting a journal, and I snooped in it."

Mark looked at Dash and Laurel. "We'll read the journal and go from there. Anna, can you go and get it for us now?" he asked gently.

Laurel's neck hurt as she turned to look at her daughter.

"Mrs. O'Connell has it," Anna said, her voice cracking.

"What?" Dash asked. He was no longer pale; his face had flushed with color and he looked like a monster, a roaring beast about to pounce. It was the first time in her marriage that she was ever relieved to see him that way. *Our daughter, our blood.* Laurel clutched her stomach, feeling pain like a knife.

"I gave it to her!" Anna said, starting to cry. "I like Mrs. O'Connell! I think she's really nice, and I thought she should know what Mira and Mr. O'Connell were doing!"

"I'm going over there," Dash said, starting toward the door.

"No, you're not," Mark said. He got to his feet and grabbed Dash's arm. "I am."

It was precisely that moment, with Dash and Mark staring at each other over the pristine coffee table, that Laurel realized just how very possible it was that her daughter was dead.

JADE

7:16 p.m.

Jade pulled into her driveway next to an unfamiliar car. She glanced to the front porch to see Terrence Washington in docksiders, green shorts, and a light-blue button-down shirt. He looked uncomfortably vulnerable standing there with his posture not quite right, stooping forward slightly and clutching an oversize cream envelope. The house was built so long ago there wasn't a garage (much to Jeremy's chagrin), and Jeremy's car wasn't in the driveway. So was Terrence just waiting for them to return?

Jade's hands trembled as she turned off the ignition. She hated confrontation. Terrence had always seemed like a good man, but something nefarious had obviously gone down.

Jade opened her car door and stepped into the hot sun. "Hi, Terrence," she said as she walked up the driveway.

Terrence reached out his hand when she got to the porch. That had to be a good sign, at least. Jade took his warm hand and shook it. "I'm sorry to barge in on you like this," he said.

Jade could see the outline of a back brace beneath his shirt. "It's no problem," she said. Was she supposed to invite him inside? Did he want to talk out here? There was something so easy about this man's presence, even now when she had no idea what he wanted. He'd always seemed so peaceful and kind the few times Jade had met him at Jeremy's office. Were some men just like this? Had she simply picked the wrong one?

"What can I do for you?" Jade asked, immediately regretting her choice of words. She sounded way too formal, like a line had been drawn and they weren't friends anymore.

Terrence considered her with his deep-brown eyes. "This hasn't been an easy time, as you can imagine," he said.

Jade nodded. She felt the sudden urge to cry. *For us, either,* she wanted to say.

Sweat marked Terrence's hairline. He was clearly nervous, and he had to be melting in that long-sleeved button-down. "Do you want to go inside, and I can make you something to drink? Lemonade? Iced tea?" Jade asked.

"I'm okay out here," Terrence said.

Jade considered him. Nothing about him seemed okay right now. She inched back against the porch railing.

"Your husband asked me to sign these papers," Terrence said, giving the envelope a small shake. "But I can't. I wanted to talk to him today, but maybe it's best I don't. Would you give them to him for me?" he asked. He passed the envelope to Jade. It felt so warm in her hands.

"Do you want to tell me what's going on?" Jade asked. "At the party yesterday Isabella kept looking at me like I'd done something."

Terrence ran a hand over his short black hair. "You didn't do anything. But your husband, well, first of all, he's spreading rumors that I was on drugs at the office. I can't work for him anymore, but the drug rumors are making it nearly impossible for me to find work. I wasn't on those kinds of drugs. I was on antianxiety medication. I was on it during my early twenties, too, when the banking hours and the pressure were insane, but then I got good therapy, and I didn't think I needed them anymore. But when I started working for Jeremy, things got bad again. So I went back on them. I was planning to leave the company sooner than later, and then . . ." A pained look crossed Terrence's face.

Jade sensed he wanted to tell her more, but he didn't. "I just need you to give those papers to your husband. Tell him I can't sign them. Tell him I just want to put all of this past us and move on. I'm not out to hurt him. I want a job with a different fund; I want my life back. That's all I want, okay?"

Jade nodded. "I'll tell him," she said. *I'll try my best to help you.*

The air between them felt charged. "Thank you, Jade," Terrence said, and then he turned and stepped carefully off the porch. Jade watched his guarded steps over the lawn and the way he scoured the ground for possible spots that might cause him to stumble. One foot in front of the other, gingerly, he made his way to his car.

Jade clutched the envelope. When Terrence's car disappeared from sight, Jade headed inside. "Nelson?" she called out, and found the dog thumping his tail on his bed. "I'll walk you in just a second, buddy."

Jade made her way into the kitchen and grabbed a butter knife. She slipped the knife beneath the taped lip of the envelope.

"What are you up to, Jeremy?" she whispered as she sliced through the tape.

CORA

7:17 p.m.

Cora and Sam were watching *Breakfast at Tiffany's*.

It seemed crazy to watch a movie, but it had just happened. What would Sarah say when she returned? *I told you to talk, not watch a movie!*

But they were exhausted from talking and crying, and when was the last time the twins were gone long enough for them to watch a movie?

It was Cora's favorite movie—she knew how sorry Sam was when he suggested it—and everything seemed magically okay in Cora's world as she watched Audrey Hepburn flitting across the screen. She knew that wasn't true, but wasn't it okay to forget for a couple of hours?

Sam and Cora had started off watching the movie on opposite ends of the couch. Then they migrated to the middle, and now they were sitting close with Sam's arm resting on the back of the couch. Cora felt like a teenager, wondering if he was going to put his arm around her, wondering what she would do if he did. They'd gotten together at Vanderbilt, when there was such newness to everything; Cora had even lost her virginity to Sam! She'd thought they'd lost it to each other, actually, but that hadn't been true. Sam hadn't exactly lied about it, but he hadn't been forthcoming, either. Early on when they were dating, Sam told Cora he'd never had a serious girlfriend and that she was the first person he'd ever fallen in love with—*my first everything,* he'd said—which Cora took to mean she was the first person he'd had sex with, too. Then, at Sam's five-year high school reunion, a drunk, blond twenty-three-year-old practically leaped into Sam's arms when she saw him. It was the kind of thing you could just spot: first love. The girl's voice was fluttery and high-pitched when she said, "Sam O'Connell! How ever have you *been*?"

How ever have you been?

Cora didn't even think that was correct grammar, but it sounded so romantic coming out of the girl's glossy mouth. After hours of socializing with Sam's old high school classmates—Sam was the big man on campus with his finance job; he was already making six figures at twenty-three while most of his friends were still figuring out their lives—Sam and Cora drove back to New York, and she spent the car ride grilling him, and he admitted he'd lost his virginity to the girl. Cora couldn't bring herself to ask him if he'd loved her. She didn't want to know.

Ding-dong!

The doorbell pulled Cora from the unpleasantness of her memory. Audrey Hepburn was looking into the camera with her doe-eyed stare.

Hadn't they given Sarah the keys?

Sam paused the movie and Cora stood. Without the dialogue and music swelling around them, the room suddenly seemed cramped and too bright. Was it really already seven? The twins were usually getting to bed by now. Cora might need to skip the bath to get them down on time.

Cora swung open the front door, but it wasn't Sarah and the twins. It was a fortysomething man wearing a button-down shirt and trousers. "Can I help you?" Cora asked.

The man pulled a badge from his pocket and held it up for Cora to see. "I'm Detective Mark DeFosse, and I'm investigating a missing person. May I come in to ask you a few questions?"

Cora's pulse picked up speed. "Of course," she said, opening the door wider. "Is in here okay?" she asked as the detective stepped inside. She gestured to the living room, flinching when she saw her butt print still on the couch cushion. Maybe they should go into the kitchen?

Sam walked across the living room. He reached out his hand to meet the detective's. "Sam O'Connell," he said.

"Detective Mark DeFosse," the detective said again.

Cora followed Sam numbly to the sofa, and the detective sat opposite them in an armchair Cora had been meaning to reupholster. *It's not easy to find mid-century furniture,* Maggie had said when she convinced Cora to buy it at a yard sale. *It would be divine with the right fabric.*

The detective cleared his throat. "Mira Madsen has been reported missing," he said.

"Missing?" Cora heard herself say. Panic swelled in her chest. "But we saw her yesterday. She was *here*, actually."

Detective DeFosse pulled out a small notebook and checked it. "Yes," he said, "at your party, is that correct?"

"For our twins. It was their birthday party," Cora said, feeling oddly defensive about throwing a birthday party for George and Lucy. She turned to see Sam staring blank-faced at the detective.

"And do you remember what time Mira and her family left?" the detective asked.

Cora waited for Sam to say something. Wasn't he going to talk at all?

"Guests started to leave around five thirty, I'd say?" Cora said. She was so nervous she felt like she could hardly breathe, like she was about to have another panic attack.

"And did Mira say or do anything at the party that seemed at all out of the ordinary?" the detective asked.

Cora's heart pounded. What about what Mira had said to her in Lucy's room about being involved with an older man? Did that count? And had Mira meant *Sam*?

Oh God.

All at once Cora's breathing slowed. She wasn't having a panic attack: this was something else—this was the clear-eyed space she used to feel before the twins came. It was what she used to solve the problems before her on the paper: the equations; the beautiful proofs; the myriad things she could solve that so many others couldn't, the ones that would have earned her a PhD in mathematics from Columbia if she hadn't given birth and fallen apart.

"Do we need a lawyer?" Cora asked. She suddenly felt like someone entirely different. She felt like the *old* her, the one who'd existed before her children—the one who'd existed long before Maggie's death.

"Why would you need a lawyer?" the detective asked. His face betrayed nothing. He'd done this for so many years, but so had Cora, in her own way.

"Well, you're here, aren't you?" Cora asked. "You must be here for a reason, and if that reason is to implicate us in the disappearance of a twenty-one-year-old girl, I'd say we need a lawyer."

The detective stared at her. Her husband stared at her.

"There's a journal I was told about," the detective said. "A journal belonging to Mira that's in your possession, one that suggests your husband and Mira may have been romantically involved."

"No!" Sam blurted, as though he'd suddenly woken up. "No lawyer, no nothing, because I didn't do anything to Mira. If she's missing, then you're wasting your fucking time talking to us." Sam stood. "I'll get you the notebook."

He left them sitting there and stalked up the stairs. Cora stared at the detective, her nerves starting to fray. Where had that clear-minded place gone? Cora's thoughts suddenly felt transient and weighted by the reality of being a mother whose husband may or may not have had something to do with the disappearance of a young woman. It was her reality, wasn't it? Maybe that was the crux of her predicament as a mother—the *reality* of it all, which was that two babies had been placed screaming in her arms, and she now had to navigate a world where the two hearts she loved the most were beating outside her body.

A drawer slammed upstairs, and Cora met the detective's narrowed gaze. *I know as much as you do,* she thought, *and you should know better than to look at me like this! As if I'd ever hide anything about another woman's child!*

But hadn't she already done that?

Sam pounded down the stairs. He came into the living room and stood before the detective. "There's only one entry," he said, passing Mira's notebook into the man's hairy-knuckled hands. "And all of it's true."

The detective opened the notebook and started to read. Cora's pulse was skipping beats now in an irregular rhythm that was making her feel insane. She was about to say something like *See, we don't know anything!* because she couldn't take the silence anymore, but then the doorbell rang.

"Oh my God, George and Lucy," Cora said to Sam, rising from her seat.

"Ask your mother to put them to bed," Sam said, his voice firm. His features had folded into a mask Cora couldn't recognize.

The detective didn't even glance up from the notebook. Cora headed toward the front door and swung it open. "Mom!" she found herself saying. She bent to kiss George and Lucy, and their lavender baby smell made her eyes fill with tears.

"The playground was too packed with older kids roughhousing," Sarah said as Cora breathed in the scent of her babies. "So we ended up at the diner, if you can believe that, and guess who ate all of their vegetables! George and Lucy! And, honey, there's a police car in the Madsens' driveway. You should check on them tonight."

"Mom," Cora said, straightening. She forced her voice to stay calm. "There's a detective here to ask us some questions about Mira, actually. Do you think you could put the twins to bed?"

Sarah's face blanched.

"Mama! No!" Lucy screamed. "Mama do bed!"

The sound of Lucy's cry made Cora feel animalistic. She wanted to claw out the detective's eyes and scream that they had nothing to do with this. They didn't have anything to do with this, right? *There's no way he hurt her.*

"There are lollipops upstairs in the closet, remember, Lucy?" Cora cooed.

Lucy wouldn't remember, because Cora had hidden them, but she knew the promise of lollipops would stop Lucy's crying.

"Pops!" George cried out. A stripe of sunblock marked his nose.

"In the blue basket in Lucy's closet," Cora told her mother. "Emergency lollipops."

Sarah nodded, her face pale.

"They can't find *Mira*," Cora said. She was trying not to set off the twins by seeming upset, but saying the words in an upbeat voice made her feel sick.

Sarah's lips pursed into a tight circle, and wrinkles etched the skin around her peach lipstick. "I see," she said. She turned to George and Lucy. "Come on, now, let's go get lollipops!" She scooped them up like she was half her age and carried them up the stairs, her kitten heels clicking the hardwood like a metronome.

Cora returned to the living room, drenched in sweat after the exchange with her twins. Was the sweat coming through her shirt? Could the detective see it?

Sam was back in his seat. He looked like a small, guilty version of himself. *Sit up straight!* Cora wanted to say as she sat next to him.

Watching the detective read Mira's words felt like waiting for a verdict. Cora couldn't feel her legs, and her fingers had gone numb, too.

"And is this all?" the detective asked, still looking down at the paper. He flipped through the pages of the notebook twice, presumably checking to make sure there were no other entries.

Cora heard the start of bathwater upstairs. Was her mom seriously giving them a bath? *Just get them to bed, Mom!*

"That's all," Sam said, "because nothing else happened."

The detective looked up. "And did you know Mira was pregnant?"

A queasy feeling hit Cora's stomach.

"I did not," Sam said, but his voice hitched. Cora whirled around to face him. Was there any chance?

"Mira has a *boyfriend*," Cora said, her eyes back on the detective. "Asher Finch. He lives on the other side of the Madsens' house. If someone got Mira pregnant, I would imagine it was him."

"I'm about to go over there now, actually. I'll need to take this with me," the detective said about Mira's notebook, and Cora imagined Mira's diary entry splashed across the front page of the *Ravendale Daily*. Sam and Cora deserved it, didn't they? All of this happiness they'd had while Maggie lay buried deep underground; wasn't it a sure thing it would all come crashing to an end? Cora and Maggie were *sisters*. Weren't their fates somehow intertwined?

"When did this notebook come into your possession, Mrs. O'Connell?" the detective asked.

"Last night at the end of the party," Cora said, "probably around five, like I said. I came upstairs and found the notebook in an envelope."

"And do you know who gave it to you?" the detective asked.

"I don't," Cora said.

"And did you show your husband this journal last night?"

"I did," Cora said. "When the party was finished."

Sam was glancing back and forth from Cora to the detective like a Ping-Pong ball. Wasn't he acting strangely, even under the circumstances?

"What did your husband say when you confronted him?" the detective asked Cora, as though Sam wasn't even in the room.

"He said he was sorry," she answered, her voice lilting like a song. Everything felt wrong.

"And can you provide an alibi for your husband last night from six p.m. on?" He stared at Cora as though he could see right through her.

"I can't," she said, the words barely making it out.

The detective turned to Sam. He sniffed, considering him for a moment. "Can *anyone* provide an alibi for you last night, Mr. O'Connell?" he asked. He sounded like he thought Sam was the most pathetic man on the face of the planet.

"No," Sam said flatly, a yellow hue all over his olive skin. "Cora asked me to leave around seven, so I took a drive to Castle Point. I hiked there for an hour or so, maybe stayed at the summit for another hour, and then came back down. And then I stayed in a motel, but I didn't check in until eleven or so."

"I see," the detective said. He arched forward on the sofa. "I'm going to ask you both one more time if there's anything, *anything at all*, you'd like to tell me regarding the disappearance of Mira Madsen."

Cora shook her head, and Sam said, *"No."*

"Then I'll see myself out," he said. He stood and didn't look back at them as he walked with long strides toward the foyer.

At the sound of the front door shutting behind him, Cora turned to her husband.

"Now you're going to tell me exactly what the fuck really happened with that girl," she said.

LAUREL

7:40 p.m.

Anna was sobbing on the floor next to the piano. Dash had flipped the coffee table in a fit of anger, and it was the first violent thing Anna had ever seen him do in her entire precious life. Not Laurel. Laurel knew that Dash smashing the coffee table was the best thing that could have happened, because it dulled his rage just enough that he was able to hear her when she said he had to stay put and let the detective do his job.

"Why the fuck is he leaving the O'Connells'?" Dash asked now, his face pressed against the glass panes that framed their front door. He was dripping sweat. Laurel squeezed next to him to see Mark leaving Cora and Sam's, walking quickly toward Asher Finch's house. Laurel watched Mark, mesmerized, as he took out his cell and made a call. It couldn't be a good sign the way his eyebrows were knit together as he spoke to whoever was on the other end. He ran a hand over his brow, then disconnected his call and started jogging. Laurel felt the urge to vomit. She bit the top of her lip and turned to see Anna huddled against the piano, horrified. Dash moved to a window on the side of the house to watch Mark complete his trip to Asher's. Laurel joined him, arriving at the window just as Mark rang the doorbell. Asher answered immediately, but Laurel couldn't make out the look on his face. "Why did he leave the O'Connells', Laurel?" Dash asked again, as though Laurel were personally responsible for Mark's investigation.

"I have no idea!" Laurel said.

Mark disappeared inside Asher's house. Dash whirled around to face Laurel. "Where the fuck is our daughter?" he screamed.

"Dash, calm down," Laurel said.

"Calm down? *Calm down?* You knew she was pregnant and you never told me! Did you know it was *him*, Laurel, did you know it was Sam? Is that what's going on here? You and Mira keeping secrets from me?"

"Mira has no idea I know she's pregnant," Laurel said, and this time she couldn't hold back her sobs. "And I found out about Sam O'Connell at the exact same moment you did." She put a hand on Dash's arm, but he flung it off. He headed back into the living room, where Anna was still crying. "I'm going to the O'Connells'," Dash said. "I'm finding our daughter."

"You're not!" Laurel said. She moved quickly to Dash, trying to restrain him, but he was already sliding his feet into sneakers. "You heard Mark!" she said, realizing her mistake too late. She should have called him *Detective DeFosse*, because *Mark* made it sound like they knew each other. And how had Dash always reacted to her prior lovers, even from the very beginning of their courtship? He'd become jealous and enraged, of course. (*Clues, Laurel. See: there were* clues!)

"Dash, listen to me," Laurel said, and Dash turned, his eyes glazed. "Detective DeFosse said he would deal with Sam." Laurel tried to sound as calm as she possibly could. "You could mess everything up if you go over there, and we could lose Mira!"

Anna whimpered. Two sheets of piano music fell to the floor.

Dash's blue eyes were burning brighter than Laurel had ever seen them. For just a second, Laurel thought he'd heard her. But then he took two hands, placed them on Laurel's chest, and shoved her hard. "Mom!" Anna cried out as Laurel crashed against the liquor cabinet.

Dash ran toward the door.

Anna started screaming and raced to her mother's side. "Are you okay?" she asked, breathless as Laurel stood on shaking legs.

"Call nine-one-one and report your father," Laurel told her daughter. "Send the police to Cora's house."

Laurel lifted her purse from the console. Her feet were numb as she raced up the stairs. In her bedroom, a window was open and she heard crickets and creek water. She inserted her key into the lockbox and got her gun, and then she raced back down the stairs and out the door after her husband.

CORA

7:50 p.m.

You have to believe me, Cora, please," Sam was saying in their living room. Audrey Hepburn's face was still paused on the television. Sam and Cora stood there, staring at each other.

Upstairs, the bathwater had just been turned off. Cora heard the sound of her mother's voice singing to quiet George, who'd started fussing.

> Taffy was a Welshman
> Taffy was a thief
> Taffy came to my house and stole a leg of beef!

It was a song Clark used to sing. Cora hadn't heard it since she and Maggie were small. Cora started crying again, for what felt like the thousandth time that day.

"You can't think I've done something to Mira, can you?" Sam asked, his voice so low Cora could hardly hear him.

She looked up. Over Sam's shoulder was a window, and Cora caught movement on the lawn. The darkening sky made it hard to see, but she was sure she saw a man on the lawn, coming toward them. Was it the detective, returning from Asher's?

Cora returned her gaze to Sam. "How am I supposed to believe you haven't done something like this before with another woman?"

She'd never seen Sam look like this: a trapped, wounded animal. *"I haven't,"* he said, but it was like he could barely get the words out, and then his features fell.

"I can see it on your face, Sam, you're lying to me about something!"

He opened his mouth slowly and then closed it.

"Sam," Cora said, "*please.* You need to talk to me, or this is going to be over. *We* are going to be over, do you understand me? Tell me why I'm supposed to believe you!"

"Because I've never done a single fucking thing wrong in my entire life other than what I did with Mira and killing your sister!"

The room stilled.

"What did you just say?" she asked softly.

"I killed your sister," Sam said, and his face was incredulous, like he couldn't believe what he was saying. He tried to extend his arms to her, but his hands were shaking so violently he put them back at his sides. "I was driving that night, not Maggie," he said, his words wavering, "and I was drunk and high, and I drove that car into those trees, and your sister is dead because of me."

Cora took a step back. She had the distinct sensation of sinking, as though the house could no longer bear the weight of her, as though a dark hole had opened at her feet and she was falling *down, down, down*, losing her grip on everything she thought she knew.

VOICE MAIL RETRIEVED BY THE RAVENDALE POLICE DEPARTMENT FROM SAM O'CONNELL'S PHONE, LEFT BY JEREMY MOORE AT 7:51 P.M.

You need to call me back. Terrence won't sign the nondisclosure agreement. We're fucked if he comes forward with this, you realize that, right?

LAUREL

7:52 p.m.

Dash!" Laurel cried out as they sprinted across the grass toward the O'Connells' house. He was only twenty-five yards ahead of her, but he was gaining pace, and Laurel wasn't sure she could cross the stream with the agility Dash had. "Stop!" Laurel screamed, knowing how useless her voice was. Had Dash ever stopped because she cried out?

Laurel looked down at the grass, trying to maneuver through the lawn in sandals without breaking a bone. This was *Ravendale*, not Chappaqua or Scarsdale or the other Westchester suburbs with their pristine lawns. In Ravendale, it was the thing to have a mildly unkempt property with woods, streams, tall grass, and scattered rocks that announced just how different Ravendale was: it was laid-back and country-like; it was fucking *idyllic*.

Laurel didn't see the fallen log before her sandal caught on it. "Shit," she cried as she braced for a fall. Her hands hit the grass first, and then her knees. *You're okay, Laurel, get up!*

Dash was barely visible now as he neared Cora and Sam's house. There was a light on in their kitchen and in the upstairs bedrooms, too, which meant the twins were still awake.

Laurel pushed to a stand, feeling a bright streak of pain through her left ankle. She started running.

SARAH

7:53 p.m.

Sarah's mind spun as she tightened the diaper around George's chubby legs. Obviously Sam wouldn't do anything to hurt Mira; there was just no way. Couldn't you tell by the looks of a man if he was violent?

Couldn't you?

A flicker of doubt hit Sarah's chest. She was finding it a little hard to breathe, actually, and there was a distinct pressure in her lungs and throat. Maybe that high blood pressure reading from Dr. Madsen's office was more accurate than she'd thought. Were these *symptoms*? Sarah hadn't had any health symptoms, ever, not unless you counted the pain in her hand. She was aware of how very fortunate she'd been; she didn't take it for granted. But what if it all was about to come crashing down? Maybe she was having a heart attack?

No, she told herself as she carefully folded George into his footed pajamas. *It's just anxiety.* Sarah had had anxiety even before becoming a mother, and when she gave birth to her girls, the anxiety seemed almost useful, practical; Sarah prayed that the anxiety could magically protect her from all the bad things that could befall her beautiful family, as though by worrying about the bad things, she could cancel out the possibility of them ever happening. She'd been so very wrong.

"Nana, pee pee!" Lucy said from her pink chair.

"Okay! Let's do the potty!" Sarah said. She gave George a kiss and put him in his crib so he'd be contained while she walked Lucy down the hall. He barely whimpered, unlike Cora at his age, who wouldn't let Sarah put her down until she was three and Maggie was born. The best bond Cora and Sarah ever had was during those first few years together, and Sarah thought about how she'd never told Cora how close she had felt to her as a baby. As Lucy held out her tiny hand, she resolved that she would.

Sarah and Lucy walked slowly toward the bathroom, and Sarah noted how quiet it was downstairs. The detective had already left—Sarah saw him march purposefully across the lawn toward the Finches' house—so the quiet meant at least Sam and Cora weren't fighting.

Sarah unzipped Lucy's pajamas. "Here we go," she said, helping Lucy onto her little potty. Lucy's face brightened as she did what she was supposed to, and just as Sarah was lifting her back up, a pounding sounded from downstairs. It was coming from directly below Sarah and Lucy. Was someone at the back door? Sarah glanced out the bathroom window to see Dash Madsen below on the patio, slamming his fist against the French doors. His wife was crossing the lawn, and she was limping.

"Come on, darling," Sarah said to Lucy, her throat tightening again. "It's bedtime now."

CORA

7:54 p.m.

"What the fuck?" Sam said when he heard pounding at the back door.

Cora sobbed softly. She and Sam had stood rooted in place since his revelation, and Cora had been unable to do or say anything except push him away when he'd tried to embrace her. Images of a dead, helpless Maggie flooded her body. Her *husband* had done it? He was an adulterer, and now the person who killed her sister, and certainly, above all else: a *liar*.

Bang. Bang. Bang.

The pounding made Cora lift her head and glance toward the kitchen. It sounded visceral, and for a split second she had the bizarre sensation that she herself was making the noise, as though her fury had come alive and was emanating from her body.

"What the *fuck*?" Sam said again as the pounding grew louder. He straightened, and the teary, vulnerable man he'd been a moment ago was gone, and in his place was *Sam*: Cora's husband, her protector, a man who didn't take pounding on his home as anything other than a threat.

He flew past Cora. "Sam, wait," Cora said, suddenly finding her voice as she ran after him. She trailed him into the kitchen, and that's when she saw Dash Madsen's face fragmented through the rectangular panes of glass. His hair was silver in the moonlight, and his large hand was curled into a fist and pounding even as Sam neared the door.

"Do *not* open that door, Sam," Cora said. "Our kids are upstairs!"

"Fuck him," Sam said as he grabbed the handle. "I didn't hurt her!"

Sam swung open the door, and Dash was inside like a flash of light. He was running at Sam before Cora had the chance to scream.

"Where the fuck is my daughter?" Dash shouted.

Sam was strong, but Dash was bigger. Dash's hands landed on Sam's chest and tried to shove him against the wall of the kitchen. Sam struggled against him, shouting, "Get your hands off me!"

Cora fumbled for the telephone. Her head was filled with pounding, thrumming white noise. She heard footsteps on the stairs, and then her babies crying, and she screamed, "Stop it!" at Sam and Dash, and then Sarah was in the kitchen, too, throwing her hands over her cheeks, getting to the phone just before Cora.

Where were her babies?

"Where are the kids?" Cora screamed at her mother. Had Sarah just left them at the top of the stairs?

Dash wrapped his hands around Sam's neck. "How could you touch her?" he shouted into Sam's face. *"Where is Mira?"*

Sarah had the phone pressed to her ear. "Please send the police to Thirty-Six Crawford Farm Road," she said into the receiver. "My son-in-law is being attacked by his neighbor!"

Sam threw out a fist and hit Dash on the chin, but then Dash grabbed hold of Sam's shoulders and shoved him hard. Sam flew across the kitchen, and on the way to the ground, his head struck the pointed silver handle on the cabinet beneath the sink. Cora saw the blood immediately, and she lurched for her husband. "Sam," she said, her hands going to the top of his shoulders, trying to keep his slumped body from toppling. She heard the cries of her twins from upstairs, and she turned to scream that Sam needed help, but Dash was still coming for them. "Stop!" Cora screamed at Dash, and then she saw her mother.

Sarah's willowy frame stood very still except for her shaking hands on the glinting, trembling butcher's knife.

LAUREL

7:56 p.m.

Laurel's ankle was white-hot as she ran across the grass toward the bright lights in Cora's house. The house was right there; she could see it—the French doors open to a long wooden table. She couldn't see anyone, but she heard screaming. *Please, God, don't let Dash hurt them.*

And if Sam had done something? If he'd hurt her daughter? Then would she want him to be hurt, too?

Tears streaked Laurel's face. She finally hit the patio, her sandal broken and dangling from her injured foot. "Dash!" she screamed. She stepped through the open doors into the O'Connells' kitchen. Dash was on top of Cora and Sam, and Sarah was screaming bloody murder, inching toward them with a knife.

Laurel reached into her bag and took out the gun. "Stop it!" she screamed, but no one listened. Dash continued pounding on Sam's limp body as Cora tried to fight him off, and then Dash raised his hand to hurt Cora, and that's when Sarah raised the knife above her head.

"Stop it or I'll shoot!" Laurel screamed. The kitchen lights were suddenly too bright, and Laurel felt everything in the room quiet; she saw each person turn to her as if in slow motion, giving her time to take in the details of every face: flared nostrils, sweat beading on foreheads, muscles clenched. She heard every voice fall silent, and it was as though the silence itself had a sound. For a moment, she was sure something was very wrong with her, or that she was about to pass out, but she didn't. She held the gun steadily, aiming it directly at Dash. "Get away from them, Dash," she said, her voice somehow in control.

Dash backed up against the stove, but he was still right beside Cora and Sam. "Laurel," he said, panting like an animal.

Sarah dropped the knife. It clattered across the kitchen floor toward Dash.

"Put the gun down, Laurel," Dash said, his voice a growl.

"Get away from them," Laurel said again. Her palm was sweaty against the metal.

Sarah fell at Cora's feet. Both women tried to get Sam to wake up, but he was unconscious. He looked dead.

"Get up, Dash, we're going home," Laurel said. *Home.* What an insane word to call the torture chamber in which they lived. *"Get up, Dash,"* Laurel repeated. She still had the gun pointed at him. With her other hand, she rummaged in her bag for her phone. She tried to swipe the bar so she could call the police while still holding the gun, in case Anna hadn't already. But just then Anna slipped through the open door into the O'Connells' kitchen.

"Mom!" Anna screamed when she saw Laurel holding the gun, and then she saw the scene on the kitchen floor: Sarah sobbing, Cora trying to wake Sam, the blood on Dash's shirt and hands, and Sam just sitting there with his head tipped forward like an overstuffed toy. The sound of Cora's children crying came from upstairs, and then, blessedly, came the sound of sirens.

"Oh my God, *Dad*?" Anna cried out.

"Go home, Anna!" Laurel said. "Go back home!"

Anna's hand flew to cover her mouth. She whimpered, and then, into her fingers, she said, "It's me." She turned her gaze to Laurel, her eyes watery. The sirens grew louder, drowning out Anna's soft words, so that she had to shout the very next thing she said:

"I'm pregnant, Mom, *me*, not Mira."

CORA

7:58 p.m.

Cora looked up to see Anna standing next to the kitchen table, quivering.

"Please," Cora said to Laurel, needing her to refocus on Sam, no matter what Anna had just said. "Laurel, please, go meet the ambulance and send them back here!"

The sirens sounded so close; they had to be here any second.

Sarah cried softly next to Cora. "Sweetie," Sarah said softly, and Cora wasn't sure if she was talking to her or Sam. Did she think Sam was dead? *He isn't. He can't be—he's still so warm.*

Cora kept her palm pressed against the wound at the back of Sam's head. Blood gushed through her fingers. She looked over at Dash hunched against the stove, immobile for now and staring at Anna.

"What did you just say, Anna?" Laurel asked. She still had a gun aimed at her husband, but it was shaking now. Dash was staring at Anna, his breath coming hard.

Anna opened her mouth. She hesitated, and then spoke. "Me and Asher," she said. "He's been cheating on Mira with me, and we were going to tell her together, but then I felt so bad I told her last night. That's the fight we got into, Mom. I'm so sorry, I really am, I . . ." Anna tried to finish, but she was sobbing so hard it was hard to understand anything she said.

Laurel flipped the safety on the gun and put it back into her handbag. She embraced her daughter, both of them crying now.

"No, Laurel, you need to . . ." Cora started, but just then Dash started to get up. "Stay away from us!" Cora screamed at him. How could Laurel put the gun away with this maniac on the loose? Dash rose to his full height and towered over them. The knife was right beneath him. Blood flecked over his forehead, and his right eye was swelling, making him look like a deranged monster. Cora started screaming, sure he would come after them again. But he didn't. He hobbled across the kitchen to his family.

JADE

7:58 p.m.

Jade was on the way to Cora's house to pick up Sarah, who was at Cora's now without her car. She stopped at a red light and thought about Terrence. The document she'd found inside the envelope was filled with legalese and was definitely some kind of nondisclosure agreement. Jeremy was merciless with ex-clients and ex-employees (and some current employees, actually), but Terrence was a friend of Sam's. Couldn't Jeremy play nice for once? She would talk to him, though she doubted he'd listen. He certainly didn't think she could ever understand what his world was like and how nothing was as it seemed. He'd once told her he did what he needed to do to survive, and then, almost as an afterthought, he'd added: *For us.* But didn't that seem overly dramatic? Did other finance guys talk that way? Or was it that her husband had a dangerous and narcissistic viewpoint?

Jeremy against the world . . .

Jade glanced in her rearview mirror and saw the manager of Buzzed, Denise, whom Jade knew personally, because there was once talk of Jade selling her jewelry inside the coffee shop.

It would be so Ravendale to sell jewelry alongside baked goods from a local vendor! the owner had said, but it hadn't worked out.

Jade turned and squinted. Didn't Mira work at Buzzed? She needed to ask her about dog sitting while she and Jeremy were in Copenhagen.

A driver honked behind Jade, and she flinched and looked up to see the light had turned green.

Text Mira about dog sitting, Jade put on her mental to-do list, along with: *finish the jewelry order for Bendel's, try to find wholesale topaz, book flight to see Mom and Dad.*

Jade accelerated down Ward Hill past a horse farm and thought about Jeremy. The trip to Copenhagen would be good for them. At some point, Jade needed to tell him that she wouldn't—she couldn't—have his biological children. She needed to tell him about the birth control, and she knew that meant he might leave her.

What would she do if he left?

She'd mourn him. She knew how to mourn; that was for sure. And she wouldn't be with anyone else. The only relationship she would be interested in was one with a child. She'd call the social worker from the adoption agency and schedule another meeting to figure out exactly what she needed to do to successfully adopt as a single woman. It would be harder, of course, but single people adopted babies all the time.

Could she do it? Could she be a mother all by herself?

She was getting ahead of herself—there was still a chance Jeremy would come around—but why did she feel such excitement when she thought about doing it alone? Wasn't she supposed to be scared?

Her fingers tightened around the steering wheel and something swelled inside her. She could, she *would*, become a mother. She swore she could see the baby: little fingers; little toes; a smooth, round belly—and then she heard laughter, years ahead, as though she'd plucked a memory she hadn't even made yet.

Sirens sounded. Jade pulled to the side of Crawford Farm Road as a screaming line of cop cars and ambulances passed, trying to ignore the pit in her stomach. Only recently had she stopped thinking of Maggie every time she saw an ambulance, but with a parade of at least half a dozen cop cars, there was no way not to go back to that night. There had been an EMT there when they'd pulled Maggie from the convertible—a young girl, maybe a teen volunteer—and she'd gotten sick when they'd laid Maggie's limp body on the stretcher. Jade hadn't thought of that girl in a while, but she thought of her now as she pulled away from the curb and carefully followed the police brigade. *Don't slow down,* she tried to telegraph to the cops and ambulance driver. *Keep going, please, right past Cora's house, please keep going.*

They didn't. Jade rounded the bend, and Cora's gleaming white house came into view, nearly all the lights inside blazing. Sirens screamed, lights flashed, and police officers ran inside. Jade gripped the steering wheel. The twins? Sarah? Sam and Cora? So many people she loved were inside that house. She flung open the car door and started sprinting up the driveway. An EMT shot toward her. "The house isn't cleared for entry," he said, but Jade ignored him and kept running. "There's an assault going on, ma'am. You cannot go inside. Stay back!"

Jade fell to her knees on the grass. She stared at the house, tears streaming down her face.

LAUREL

8:01 p.m.

Laurel watched as the paramedics carried Sam O'Connell out of the kitchen on a stretcher followed by Cora and her mother. She held Anna tight against her.

"Dash Madsen, you'll come with me down to the station now," Mark said.

Dash looked so tall standing there beneath the lights of Cora's kitchen. "And why would I do that?" Dash asked, his breath coming hard.

Could he really think he hadn't done something wrong?

"Because if Sam O'Connell dies, you'll be charged with a homicide," Mark said. "So you can either come down to the station voluntarily, or I'll cuff you and put you in the back of the car."

Dash let out a noise that sounded like a disbelieving grunt. "I had every right to try to find my daughter," he said, but his voice had an uncharacteristic quaver to it.

"Your daughter Mira is home right now, actually, in your living room, unharmed."

Laurel let out a cry and buried her face into the top of Anna's head. Dash's crystal-blue eyes widened. Anna was the first one to speak. "She's okay? Mira's okay?"

"She's perfectly fine," Mark said. "She was hiding out at the Finches' home. Mr. and Mrs. Finch are out of town, as you may or may not have known."

"Asher lied to us?" Anna said.

"Can we go to her? Please?" Laurel asked.

"First I'll need you to confirm as an eyewitness what the phone calls to the police have already reported, which is that your husband assaulted Sam O'Connell in his home tonight."

Laurel caught Dash's stare. She saw his silent pleading, and she looked away, her gaze settling on the floor. All the times Dash had hurt her flooded through her, and she remembered the searing pain of each one as she looked up and met Mark's eyes. "Yes, that's right," she said. "When I arrived Sam was already immobile on the ground, but Dash was still attacking him."

"Laurel," Dash snarled.

"Go home and stay with your daughters," Mark said to Laurel. "Patrol officers will be over to take your statement."

Goose bumps swept across Laurel's skin. She looked up to see tears in her husband's eyes. Tears of rage? Of regret at hurting Sam? Of relief at finding Mira?

She didn't care. She grabbed Anna's hand, and they ran out of the O'Connells' house. Her ankle screamed as she raced across the lawn, but the trip felt faster this time. Anna carefully helped Laurel across the old, overgrown bridge, and then they were back on their property. There was a light on in the living room of their home. Was that Mira passing in front of the window?

Anna didn't let go of Laurel's arm as they crossed the lawn and stepped onto the front porch. Laurel flung open the front door. "Mom!" Mira cried as Laurel and Anna crossed the foyer and closed the distance between them. Laurel flung her arms around her daughter.

"Oh, sweetie," she said into Mira's flaxen hair. "What have you done?"

SARAH

8:42 p.m.

Sarah glanced around the ER's packed waiting room at Westchester General Hospital. Across the room, a woman about Sarah's age plunged her hand into a bag of potato chips, and two children at her hip did the same. An elderly man clutched his stomach, and a woman who looked like she might be homeless called out for help.

Jade, Cora, and Sarah sat on yellow and orange plastic chairs. Sam was likely in surgery or at least that was the incoherent relaying of information Sarah had gotten from Cora when she met her at the hospital.

"I just don't understand," Jade said. Cora had been in the ambulance with Sam, and Jade had driven Sarah and the twins to meet them at the hospital. "Dash thought Sam got Mira pregnant and hurt her?"

Cora's eyes seemed like they weren't focusing properly, like she couldn't even see Jade as she stared at her, not answering her question. She'd grown so wild and agitated that Sarah was having a hard time watching her without breaking down.

The twins were sleeping in their massive double stroller. *This thing is like an SUV!* Sarah had said when the twins were six weeks old and Cora bought it. *It's my only option, Mom,* Cora had said, appearing more exhausted than Sarah had ever seen another human being. Why hadn't she helped her daughter more? She should have been there, no matter how many times Cora assured her they were all doing fine.

After the ambulance left Cora's, Sarah couldn't just stay behind at the house, and she knew George and Lucy would be so spent from crying in their cribs that they'd fall asleep on the car ride and transfer easily into a stroller. Sarah spent the drive singing the twins to sleep while Jade tried to get information out of her.

"I could have sworn I saw Mira earlier today in town, actually," Jade said.

"Her sister is pregnant," Cora spat. "Not her. And Sam did *not* hurt Mira. He wouldn't do that!"

"Honey, goodness, of course we know Sam didn't hurt Mira," Sarah said, putting a hand against her daughter's back.

The homeless woman screamed something nonsensical, but no one came to help her.

"Really?" Cora asked, starting to cry. "How can you know that? You think he isn't capable of hurting another person? He is, Mom." She was hysterical now. "He hurt *Maggie*."

Sarah's pulse picked up. "What are you talking about, sweetheart?" she asked softly.

Jade straightened in the seat beside her.

"Sam killed Maggie," Cora said, sobbing, lifting her eyes to meet Sarah's. "He was driving the car that night, Mom, he just told me an hour ago!"

Sarah's heart stopped. When it started again, it plunged ahead rapidly as if it were trying to make up for lost time. "I don't understand," Sarah said. Her words sounded hollow, like they were coming from the end of a long hallway.

Jade's hands were over her mouth, and she was making a noise that sounded like she was choking. The plastic chair squeaked beneath Cora as she tried to adjust her weight. Her features slackened, and slowly, she said, "Tonight, when we were fighting, I asked Sam how I could ever trust that he hadn't done something with another woman, and he said because he'd only done one other bad thing in his entire life: driving the car that night and killing Maggie."

Jade burst into tears.

Sarah watched Cora carefully, trying to piece together what she was saying, but it felt impossible. Maggie had been a *passenger*, which meant that Sam had committed manslaughter and then made her sweet daughter guilty of what he'd done. It was unfathomable. Sarah tried to reimagine the scenario she'd been replaying for six years—instead of Maggie sliding into the front seat, she'd let someone else drive her. Sarah's brain almost couldn't reconstruct the thing she'd thought about every day for so long: she had to force the image of Maggie—her thin angles and wide dark eyes blinking beneath her smooth blond bob—to round the car, and instead of sliding into the driver's seat, to move into the passenger seat like a ghost.

"I can't believe it," Sarah said to Cora and Jade, tears running down their faces.

Jade was shaking, still not saying anything, and Sarah leaned into both of them and put her arms around their shoulders. All that worrying and wondering, all that doubting of how incongruous the night felt, all that *blame*. Was it still hers to carry? And did it matter, except in the retelling? Maggie was still dead.

"Our Maggie," Sarah whispered to Cora. She held her daughter tight against her and swore she'd never let her go.

LAUREL

8:44 p.m.

In the living room, Laurel sat on the sofa between her daughters. Mira clutched her knees to her chest, and Anna cried into her hands as Laurel stroked her hair. Later tonight, Laurel needed to find out how far along her daughter was. If Anna wanted to keep the baby, Laurel needed to make sure she was making OB appointments and taking vitamins and doing all the things she was supposed to.

All the things she was supposed to.

Years ago, Laurel would have said that she herself was doing all the things she was supposed to, but now she knew that wasn't true.

"Is this my fault?" Anna asked. Mascara had smudged beneath her lower lashes. "For not telling the police about Asher and me, and me being pregnant?"

Mira sat in stony silence as Anna cried. How baffling that Anna, her quiet, sensitive child, had stolen away Mira's boyfriend.

Laurel closed her eyes for a moment. "You should have been honest," she said weakly, feeling like a hypocrite, "but it's not your fault that Dad hurt Mr. O'Connell." This kind of stress wasn't good for a baby, and what was Laurel supposed to say? *Some of this mess is your fault, girls!*

Sam O'Connell needed to not die. Those beautiful babies of his! And Cora! And how would Laurel's girls ever live with themselves?

Laurel looked over at Mira. Her light hair covered half of her face, and she was staring down at her skinny fingers as they toyed with the hem of her T-shirt. Did she feel sorry at all for what she'd done? Was Laurel supposed to tell her she should? Was Mira a narcissist, or just young and selfish?

Mira cleared her throat like she'd heard Laurel's thoughts and wanted to respond, but she didn't say a word. Earlier, she'd told Laurel that she'd overheard the detective questioning Asher (in his own home, where Mira was hiding upstairs), and that she'd marched down the stairs screaming about how everyone had to *Stop being so dramatic*.

But then Mira heard the sirens and saw Sam carried out on a stretcher, and now she knew her father had been brought to the police station. *You've set something in motion you can't stop,* Laurel almost said, but she held her tongue. Whether or not Mira felt sorry was another matter entirely, and now Laurel was thinking she'd better have her daughter properly evaluated by a psychologist. This week, if she could get an appointment.

"I just don't understand why you didn't call Dad and me back," Laurel said carefully to Mira. "We tried you so many times. You must have known we'd be terrified."

Mira didn't cry or make any show of emotion at all. Her face was still as she tucked a lock of hair behind her ear. Why wasn't she saying anything?

"I need to talk to Mom by myself," Mira finally said to Anna.

Laurel swore she saw a tiny swell to Anna's belly, but maybe she was just imagining it. "Lie down and rest, sweetheart," Laurel said to Anna, and she was surprised when her daughter didn't argue. Anna bent to kiss Laurel's cheek and dutifully climbed the steps to her bedroom, hanging her head like she used to when she was in trouble as a preteen.

At the sound of Anna's door closing, Laurel turned to Mira. "Why didn't you tell me about what happened between you and Mr. O'Connell?"

A flush crept up Mira's neck. She twisted to face Laurel. "Do you tell me everything, Mom? Do you tell me about all the things you do that aren't okay? Or the things Dad does to you?" Laurel tried to open her mouth to ask Mira what she was talking about, but she couldn't get the words out. "Why do you think I hid from you and Dad at Asher's?" Mira hissed. "I came back here last night to get a book, and I went around back to the patio because I actually thought I left my book there, but I heard all this commotion, so I looked through the window in the kitchen, and I saw Dad throwing you against a wall, Mom! What the hell? And then I saw him put his hands around your neck! And I was about to come help you, but then I saw Dad having sex with you! Or raping you, or whatever that was!"

"Mira," Laurel said, her entire body shaking.

"And who the hell was that woman?" Mira asked. "You and Dad have threesomes? Violent threesomes? What the *fuck*, Mom?" Mira was screaming now, and Laurel's body felt like it was filled with a venomous force that could kill her.

"Mira," Laurel said, trying to reach for her daughter. *Explain, give her the truth.* "We don't have threesomes," Laurel said, her voice trembling. "That woman was a . . . well, she's a professional to help Dad and me . . . I don't even know how to explain it because it's so messed up," she said, and then Mira collapsed into her arms, sobbing, and Laurel held her as tightly as she could. "I'm so sorry, honey, I'm so, so terribly sorry." She pulled Mira's slight frame into her arms and cradled her just like she'd done when she was a baby.

"Do you know why I went to Asher's after what I saw Dad do to you?" Mira asked, not waiting for an answer. "It was because no matter how pissed I was at him and Anna, Asher was the one who told me earlier this summer that he saw Dad hurt you. He said he saw it through your bedroom window." Mira buried her head against Laurel's chest. "I didn't believe him when he told me. But then, after what I saw . . ."

Laurel's heart thudded. How could she have thought they could hide it? Why had she even tried to? "I'll fix this," she said. "I'll leave him, I will. Tonight, I promise." But even as she said the words, she knew it wasn't enough. Leaving Dash couldn't make Mira unsee what she had. How could she have done this to her daughter?

Mira pulled away and looked at Laurel. "You're going to leave Dad?" she asked.

"I was planning to wait until you and Anna left for school," Laurel said. *I'm never going to lie to you again.* The words came to Laurel, unbidden, and her life as she knew it felt over. Her new life started *now*, staring at her daughter, planning her next move, the one that would take them far away from this house and Dash's violence.

Mira nodded slowly, and Laurel was shocked she wasn't arguing, even after what she'd seen. She'd always been so loyal to her father. "But what's wrong with Dad?" Mira asked, her voice suddenly steady. It was the first moment that Laurel saw a glimpse of a girl who could be a doctor—the ability to view an inexplicably dire situation and try to make sense of it. "Tell me this isn't something you want, too?" Mira asked, with the same calm clarity to her words.

"No, God, no. I've tried to get him to stop, but he . . . sweetie, I don't know what's wrong with him."

"He needs *help*, Mom," Mira said, her voice accusing again.

Laurel squeezed Mira tighter. "I know that, Mira. We all do, we all need help. And we're going to get it."

JADE

8:46 p.m.

Jade's head was in her hands as the sounds of the ER whirred around her. Cora and Sarah were embracing, crying softly.

The truth.

Sam had killed Maggie, her love, and he'd gotten away with it. And Jeremy? What had he *done* that night? He was the one who was the least injured—so how did Maggie's body get behind the wheel?

Jade felt like she was going to black out. She put her head between her knees and tried to breathe, but all she could see was Maggie.

"Cora O'Connell," said a woman's voice.

Jade raised her head just enough to see a young woman wearing scrubs.

Cora tried to stand, but she couldn't quite do it, so she just raised her hand and sat back down. Sarah arched forward, but Jade just sat there, frozen.

"I'm Dr. Lee," the woman said. Her shiny black hair was braided, and she looked like she was still in her twenties. "Your husband is doing just fine," she said, and Cora let out a gasp. "He's sustained a concussion, and he's going to seem very out of it for at least another twenty-four to forty-eight hours. He has no memory of what happened or how he got here, and we can't predict when or if his memory of his accident will return, but we do expect him to make a full recovery."

Jade turned to Cora. Did Sam remember telling her about Maggie?

"Are these beautiful children yours?" the doctor asked Cora, who nodded. Jade turned to see George and Lucy sleeping side by side in their strollers, angelic in their innocence, and even in her distress, Jade had the urge to protect them from the chaos of this place: to drive them safely back to their house, to carefully place them in their cribs, and maybe even to sing to them like Sarah always did. Was that what maternal instinct felt like?

"We've stitched up the wound on the back of your husband's head," the doctor told Cora, "and we expect it to heal with no complications. I can take you to him."

You have no idea what he's done, Jade thought as she stared at the doctor, and then she thought about Jeremy, and the tiny flame that had been burning inside her built in size and fury. All the times she'd begged to go over what had happened that night, he'd lied. She imagined the way Jeremy's face would fold whenever she asked to go over the details, his features composing into a saddened expression. An actor in a play, and shouldn't Jade have been able to tell?

Cora looked at Sarah, who nodded almost imperceptibly, her eyes still so wild. Cora hugged her mother, and then Jade. "I miss Maggie," she whispered into Jade's ear. "Me, too," Jade replied, choking up again. They locked eyes, and Jade watched as Cora disappeared with the doctor through the swinging doors.

Jade stared into her hands. *Maggie.* Could she see all of this? Was she looking down at them now?

We know what really happened, or at least part of it, Jade tried to tell her, and she felt herself letting go, unraveling. Who knew what was real anymore?

VOICE MAIL RETRIEVED BY THE RAVENDALE POLICE DEPARTMENT FROM LAUREL MADSEN'S PHONE, LEFT BY DASH MADSEN AT 8:48 P.M.

Sam O'Connell is perfectly fine, Laurel, and I've been released on my own recognizance. Why aren't you picking up? Avoiding my calls, are we? We need to talk, Laurel. Our lawyer's dropping me off. Be there when I get back.

CORA

8:51 p.m.

"It can be very disorienting to sustain a head injury like your husband has," the doctor said to Cora as they walked down a long tiled corridor. The hospital smelled like lemon and Clorox. An orderly passed with folded blankets, sending a sympathetic smile Cora's way without actually making eye contact. The fluorescent lights shined so brightly that Cora kept seeing white spots in her vision every time she glanced away. Her sandals clacked against the floor, too loud to her ears. Everything felt out of sorts; everything felt wrong. "So right now, your presence will be very comforting," the doctor was saying. Cora tried to listen and keep up, but her legs felt weighted with sand. She was terrified to see Sam. He wasn't just her husband and George and Lucy's father anymore; he was the man who'd killed Maggie and tried to cover it up. How could she ever get back to him, or their marriage? "And I'd advise you to stay as long as possible with him. Was that your mother out there?" the doctor asked, and Cora nodded. "Would it be possible for her to stay with your children tonight so you can be with your husband?"

"Yes, I'm sure," Cora said. Her *mother*—the person she could be most sure of. How lucky she was to be a mother and to *have* a mother, to love like a mother and be loved by a mother. She'd always taken Sarah's physical proximity and availability for granted; she'd always lamented all the ways they could and should be closer. But their relationship was *good*. It wasn't perfect, but what important relationships were? And as of now they had the luxury of time to grow it into something better.

The doctor knocked softly and pushed open the door to a small room. A curtain was drawn to reveal Sam beneath white blankets. The back of his head was bandaged, and Cora's eyes welled with tears to see him lying there like that. Sam turned carefully at the sound of the door and stared at her. Stripes of deep blue marked the bags beneath his eyes.

"Sam," Cora said softly as she entered the room. It felt chilly, and her bare arms prickled with goose bumps. She moved slowly toward him, wondering what she would have done if he'd died. The sight of him on that stretcher—just like Maggie—had been enough to shake her awake. What was she going to *do* about all of this—about Sam and his dark secrets?

His eyes were bloodshot, and he was blinking. Did he recognize her? Tears fell over Cora's face as she put her arms around him. "Cora," he said into her hair. "Are the kids okay? The doctor said the kids are okay."

"The kids are fine," Cora said.

"Did something happen at the party?" Sam asked.

Cora pulled away. She shook her head. She wasn't going to spare him the truth, not even in his current condition. He didn't deserve gentleness, not after what he'd done, not even now.

"What happened to me?" Sam asked.

Cora was unable to keep the edge from her voice when she said, "I think you happened to us, actually."

LAUREL

9:01 p.m.

Laurel was upstairs in Mira's room throwing clothes into a bag, and Anna stood in the doorway, already packed. Mira was still downstairs on the sofa.

"I don't understand, Mom," Anna said, her voice whiny and high-pitched. "Why do we have to go to the Finches'? Do you have any idea how awkward it's gonna be with Asher, Mira, and me in the same house? By *ourselves*? Seriously, it'll be like an episode of *The Bachelor*. Is that what you want, Mom, drama like that?"

Laurel grabbed a long-sleeved waffle T-shirt from Mira's top shelf. She stuffed it into the duffel bag along with a pair of leggings. "I expect you and Mira to behave yourselves, and I expect the *drama* of late to stop completely. Things are going to change, honey. We're going to be different. We're going to stop keeping secrets, for one."

"But why can't we be here when Dad gets home?"

As of now, Mira hadn't told Anna that she'd seen their father hurt their mom. Laurel just needed to get the girls out of the house, because there was no telling what Dash would do when she announced she was leaving. She had to do it tonight—otherwise, what message was that sending to Mira? Laurel had messed up enough. It would be over tonight because it had to be.

You can do this, Laurel. One step at a time. First, protect your daughters.

Maybe it was cowardly to send the girls to Asher's, but Laurel knew that if she called one of her mom-friends to take the girls on a moment's notice, she'd have to explain *why*. There was no explanation necessary with the Finch parents away.

Laurel thought about the girls growing up next to Asher Finch and his older brother, and all the years of shared sandboxes, swims in the stream, and hours spent riding bikes in the Finches' long driveway. In some ways it didn't surprise Laurel that Asher could have feelings for both Mira and Anna. In his own way, he probably loved them both.

Or maybe Laurel was too soft; maybe Asher Finch was a hormonal prick.

"I know you don't understand right now," Laurel said. "But I need to talk to your father alone tonight. Just, please trust me, Anna."

Anna gave Laurel a look that said *I'm not happy, but I'll do it,* and then toted her bag down the hall. Anna had packed her things in an old diaper bag, one of those waterproof vinyl numbers that had always made Laurel feel like such a *mom* with her stack of diapers and snack containers filled with Cheerios and sliced grapes.

Laurel tucked a fleece for Mira into the duffel bag. Mira got so cold at night, always sleeping in layers. So would the girls be sleeping at Asher's? Maybe. Certainly yes if Dash didn't cool down in time. Laurel left Mira's room and started down the stairs. "Remember," she said to the girls, "I'll call or text when it's time to come home, okay? You'll stay at Asher's until then. Or there's a chance I'll actually pick you up at Asher's."

"Pick us up at Asher's?" Anna repeated. She was sitting on the piano bench, far away from Mira. "Like to take us somewhere?"

Yes, possibly to a hotel.

Laurel was shocked at the thrill she felt thinking it. It was electricity shooting through her—*I can do this! I can leave him!*

Mira got off the couch. She came toward Laurel slowly, and Laurel held out the duffel. But Mira didn't take it right away. Instead, she reached forward and hugged Laurel. "I love you," Mira said.

Anna started crying, and then she came over, too. She wrapped an arm around Mira and one around her mother. "Me, too, Mom," she said.

CORA

9:07 p.m.

Cora held her husband's hand as he slept soundly. At home, Sam typically fell asleep minutes after his head hit the pillow, and every night, Cora snuggled up to him, still wide awake. Sam's sleep was forever marked with fits and starts—he never seemed to actually enter a deep sleep. But now, as Cora watched the rise and fall of his chest beneath the hospital's crisp white blanket, Sam seemed to be sleeping soundly for the first time in years. Maybe it was the concussion, or maybe it was because he'd finally told her the truth.

When Cora, Jade, Sarah, and Clark had arrived at the scene of Maggie's accident, Sam had been thrown from the car, Maggie was dead, and the entire front of the car had been smashed to pieces. Jeremy, as the back-seat passenger, was the only one who'd escaped without injuries. He was pacing in front of the car with his hands in his hair, and a paramedic was trying to put a blanket over his shoulders and get him into an ambulance to be checked out, but he wouldn't cooperate. His face was crazed as he watched the paramedics pull Maggie from the car and load Sam onto the stretcher. He was screaming and crying, but so was everyone else.

Could Sam have moved Maggie into the front seat? He was lying so far away from the car; it seemed impossible, unless he had moved her and then tried to walk away and collapsed? Maggie was tiny; she didn't weigh much over one hundred pounds. But still, with his injuries, could he have done that? The other option seemed so much more likely: Jeremy, trying to protect Sam, had moved an already-dead Maggie into the driver's seat.

Cora thought about the enmeshed relationship Sam and Jeremy had had ever since the night of the engagement party. It was a friendship marked with rivalry and jealousy, but maybe Cora never sensed all the darkness that ran beneath it. What had they done in that car after it crashed?

Sam stirred. His eyes fluttered open, and Cora couldn't help herself. "How could you lie to me about Maggie?" she asked, her voice a whisper. Sam let out a groan. "How did she get in the driver's seat, Sam? You have to tell me."

Sam's eyes locked with hers. Did he remember telling her? Lying to her? It was still so hard to believe—if the Ravendale cops hadn't known their family so well, would they have investigated the accident for foul play?

Cora expected Sam to lie again, but instead, he blinked and asked, "Is Mira okay?"

"Mira's *fine*," Cora spat, rage descending on her. "Is it really Mira you're asking about?"

"She was missing," Sam said.

"You remember that part," Cora said, and Sam nodded. "Do you remember telling me that you killed my sister?"

Sam swallowed but said nothing.

"How could you keep the secret from me? I don't understand, Sam. I don't understand how you could look at me and lie for all of these years. How could you think it was better to keep how Maggie died a secret?"

"How could I *not* think that?" Sam asked, his voice croaking. He tried to prop himself up on an elbow but winced and fell back onto the pillow. He struck Cora as so incredibly vulnerable lying there like that, so weak and unlike himself. "I did the worst thing possible to you—I killed Maggie, who you loved more than anyone or anything, including me—and I knew you'd leave me, and that I'd go to jail most likely, and then you'd have lost both Maggie and me, and everything would be over."

Cora shook her head. "You do realize that no one gets the death penalty for vehicular manslaughter, right?" she asked. "If you went to jail, you would've gotten out. You could have given me the chance to forgive you for what you'd done, instead of this, which is so much fucking worse."

Sam started crying. Cora didn't care.

"Did you move her body?" she asked, but he didn't answer. *"Sam,"* Cora said, and then she started crying, too. "Don't you see that Maggie deserves for everyone to know what really happened? And my mother, you know what this has done to her! Her daughter died, and you could have made it just the tiniest bit better by telling the truth!"

"Are you sure about that?" Sam asked. "Would it be better for all of us if I was in jail and you lost your sister and your fiancé?" They stared at each other. "Cora," Sam said, "if we lost Lucy, would the details even matter?"

"It *matters*, Sam," Cora said, her throat tightening at the thought of anything happening to Lucy. How had her mother endured this?

"I wanted to tell you," Sam said. "There were so many times I wanted to tell you, until we had George and Lucy, and then I stopped wanting to tell you. It almost made it easier when we had the kids because I wasn't conflicted about telling the truth. What I'd done was so terrible I couldn't ever let them find out."

"What exactly did you do?" Cora asked, and then she sent up a silent prayer to the God she hoped existed. *Tell me only Jeremy moved Maggie, and tell me Sam tried to stop him, because I don't think I can take any more than that.*

But that wasn't what Sam said. He started crying so hard his breath came in gulps. "I moved her, Jeremy and me both," he started, his voice so low she could barely hear it. "It was Jeremy's idea, but I was drunk and high, and I did it, too. We moved her into the driver's seat together, and we let her take the fall for what I'd done."

Cora dropped her head into her hands, and the monitors beeped around her as she started to wail.

LAUREL

9:16 p.m.

Laurel paced the living room. She waited for headlights to illuminate the driveway and for the slam of a door and the inevitable crash of steps as Dash stormed into the house.

Anna and Mira were safely with Asher. Floor-to-ceiling windows in Laurel's living room looked out onto the Finches' house, and she could see a light on in the basement. Hopefully they were tucked away watching a movie rather than arguing over what had happened between the three of them; maybe they could even get back to what they'd had growing up—the girls would need that with everything Laurel was planning.

Laurel stared at her bare feet as she trod across the woven carpet. Her ankle still hurt, but it felt even worse when she stopped moving, so she just paced slowly back and forth until headlights streaked across the gravel. The outdoor lamps gave enough light for Laurel to see their lawyer's hands gripping the steering wheel, and the rage that played across Dash's face.

Embarrassment and shame.

It's what Dash would blame her for: *How could you embarrass me like that? How could you shame our family?*

"Don't you get it, Dash?" Laurel whispered as Dash got out of the car and watched it back down the driveway. "It's you."

Dash didn't slam the door; instead, he opened and closed it like a whisper. Was he trying to sneak up on her? Her heart raced as she heard him creep into the house. "Dash!" she called out, her toes gripping the carpet.

Was there any chance he'd apologize? He was a doctor. What if the sight of Sam's bloody body on the stretcher had been enough to finally make him realize he needed help?

Dash emerged from behind the staircase. "You fucking bitch," he said.

Laurel's mouth dropped. Of all the things he'd done, of all the ways he'd abused her, he'd never done so verbally.

"How dare you say that to me," Laurel said, her lower lip trembling. The words felt like cotton in her mouth.

Dash moved toward her, and Laurel braced for him, but she felt completely unprepared. He raised a hand like he was going to strike her, and Laurel cowered. "You're the one who did this, Dash," she said, her ankle throbbing and her legs quaking. "Did you expect me to lie to the police after you hurt Sam like that?"

"Sam touched our daughter. Do you not get that?"

"So, what is it, you were avenging Mira's honor? What about my honor, Dash? Do you think about that when you hurt me?"

Dash's lips curled into a snarl. "This is different," he said.

"You're a coward," Laurel said. "And I'm leaving you."

Blood drained from Dash's face. "What did you just say to me?" he asked.

"I said I'm leaving you," Laurel said. She could barely stand for another moment. Her legs felt like they were going to crumble beneath her.

Dash lunged and threw her onto the couch. She gasped, struggling for breath.

"Stop it, Dash!" she screamed, the weight of him nearly crushing her. Dash used a forearm to hold her against the couch, and her arm was splayed out toward her handbag on the carpet.

The gun.

It was so close, right inside her bag. She carefully closed her fingers around the straps, pulling it an inch closer, sliding her hand inside until she found the cool metal. She pulled the gun from the bag. "Get off me!" she screamed. Her other arm was still pinned down. The gun waved precariously in Dash's face—it was impossible to get her grip around the trigger properly. Laurel swore she heard a knock on the front door, but she couldn't be sure with all the commotion as Dash sprung off of her.

"Are you fucking kidding me, Laurel?" he said, and then the craziest thing happened, something Laurel never could have predicted: Dash started laughing. It was a cold, maniacal laugh, like everything was actually a joke. Tears welled in Laurel's eyes and spilled over her cheeks. She was still lying back against the couch cushions, but now her other arm was free, and she flipped off the safety and put both hands on the gun, aiming it just like she'd learned from all those videos she'd watched alone in the middle of the night while Dash slept soundly upstairs. But she'd never been able to prepare herself for Dash, for his strength and his rage like a vortex of energy hurtling toward her. And she couldn't make her thoughts go straight, especially not when the front door opened and Asher Finch entered the living room. Asher froze, locking eyes with Laurel as Dash leaped on top of her and tried to pull the gun from her hands. It went off, a single bullet that cracked through the still night air.

JADE

9:21 p.m.

Jade could barely see in the dimly lit parking lot outside the hospital. The tears that filled her eyes made everything blurry until the cars looked like ink smudges, the other visitors like phantoms.

They'd done it—both of them—*Sam and Jeremy*. It's what Cora had confirmed when she'd emerged from Sam's room, crying, asking Jade and Sarah to take the twins home. And now Jade couldn't escape the image of her husband manhandling Maggie's dead body like a rag doll.

"Let me drive," Sarah said. Jade's hands shook as she handed over the keys.

Sarah unlocked the car door and unstrapped George from the stroller. She lifted him and held him against her, rocking him gently with a shushing sound. Jade bent and tried the same thing with Lucy. Lucy's little body was so warm. She curled a tiny fist and put her thumb into her mouth, her eyes still closed. Her cheek felt so perfect against Jade's collarbone.

Jade followed Sarah's lead. Carefully they placed the twins into their car seats, still making that shushing sound that all mothers seemed to know how to do. For once, Jade didn't feel like a fake when she tried it. She climbed into the passenger seat as Sarah turned on the ignition. The parking lot was full, and Sarah maneuvered the SUV around an illegally parked Prius. Out on the main road, Jade said, "It's not just that he kept a secret, and it's not even that he lied." She went quiet again, not sure how much more she wanted to say because she was worried about upsetting Sarah. "It's that he moved her body and framed her." She turned to Sarah, who stared straight ahead at the road passing beneath them. "How could he have done that?" Jade asked. "Is he just a monster? An indescribably tragic accident happened, and what Jeremy thought about was how to let Maggie take the fall?"

"He wasn't the only one who lied," Sarah said as they passed a CVS with two teenagers smoking in the parking lot.

"I know. Sam, too," Jade said, and all she could think about was Sam and Jeremy switching Maggie's body from the passenger seat into the driver's seat. Or what if Maggie had been thrown from the car? Had Sam and Jeremy walked over to the wooded brush and dragged her back to the car? It was inconceivably disgusting.

"Sam killed Maggie," Sarah said, her voice cold. "He was the driver."

Jade looked out the window, watching the houses slowly increase in size and property as they left the town the hospital resided in and made their way toward Ravendale.

"What are you going to do?" Sarah asked, her voice careful.

"I'm going to leave him," Jade said, knowing her words were true the second they escaped her mouth.

"You know you can stay with me if you need to," Sarah said, and then she flinched as she made the left turn onto Crawford Farm Road.

"Are you okay?" Jade asked, sniffing back tears.

"My hand," Sarah said, taking it off the wheel. "It hurts again. I can't believe I . . . I can't believe I was just in Dash Madsen's office today, letting him take care of me. I enjoyed it, actually, how soothing he was. How sick is that?"

Jade shivered as they cruised down Cora's street. She was so distracted that she barely noticed the sound of an ambulance until Sarah asked, "Why would the cops still have their sirens on?"

Sarah picked up speed until Cora's house came into view, but the cops weren't there. They were next door at the Madsens', and so was an ambulance. A police officer stood on the lawn, gesticulating wildly to another group of officers. A pit formed in Jade's stomach when she saw Laurel's daughters sitting on the front porch, a blanket pulled around their shoulders, their faces white.

SARAH

9:31 p.m.

Sarah pulled into Cora's driveway. The night sky was black and spotted with stars, but police lights illuminated the activity crawling over the Madsens' property. Sarah surveyed the officers barricading a perimeter with yellow tape. Her eyes settled on a petite female officer saying something into a radio. "Let's carry the twins up to bed," Sarah said to Jade. "And then I'm going over there."

The weight of Lucy's warm body steadied Sarah as she maneuvered through Cora's first floor trailed by Jade and George. In Lucy's room, Sarah got her granddaughter easily into her crib, but she could hear George cry out in the room next door. Sarah moved toward George's room and found Jade rocking and shushing a whimpering George, who was snuggled against her, eyes closed. Sarah gestured toward the Madsens' house as Jade sang to George, her lips close to his smooth, pale skin.

Ring around the rosy, pocket full of posies, ashes,
ashes, we all fall down.

Sarah slipped from the room. Outside, she flew across the grass, forgetting about the creek until it was too late. She stood at the precipice, gazing into the black water, unsure if she could cross it. It was a few feet wide, dissecting the Madsens' property and Cora's, along with the property of that neighborhood boy Asher. The police lights were enough to help her find a rectangular rock that perched over the creek. Sarah inched forward on the rock, her feet uncertain in her kitten heels. At the edge, she pushed off and held her breath, and when her feet landed on soft grass, she started running. Red-and-blue lights scattered over the expanse of lawn between Sarah and the Madsens', and the police had already barricaded the driveway and perimeter of the property. Sarah headed toward the side of the house and slipped beneath the yellow tape. There were at least ten cops outside, but no one seemed to notice her. She kept her head down, and when she got to the front porch, she took in the faces of Laurel's children—Mira was shaking violently, and Anna had vomited all over herself. "Girls," Sarah said softy. She bent down and put a hand on Anna's knee. "Are you okay? What happened?"

Mira stared down at the blanket wrapped around her. There was blood on her hands, and on Anna's, too. Anna looked up first, but it was like she was staring straight through Sarah, her pupils dilated and her gaze fuzzy. Mira spoke, still staring down at the blanket. "I thought Asher should go check on my mom," Mira said, rocking back and forth. "I wanted to go, but my mom said Anna and me needed to stay put at Asher's, so we sent Asher, because we figured she'd be less mad . . ."

Mira's voice trailed off. Sarah pulled the blanket tighter around Mira's and Anna's shoulders, smoothing a lock of blood-tinged blond hair from Anna's face. She glanced over Anna's head to try to see inside the house, but it was filled with police officers. Through the doorway walked the same detective Sarah had seen in Cora's kitchen. He spotted her and asked, "Are you related to Cora O'Connell?"

Sarah nodded.

"It would be extremely helpful if you could get your daughter here," the detective said. "I'd like to question her in relation to what happened tonight."

"What happened? Are they all right?"

The detective shook his head. "If you could get your daughter here," he repeated, "I'd like to speak with her and anyone else who was close to the Madsens."

TEXT MESSAGE RETRIEVED BY THE RAVENDALE POLICE DEPARTMENT, SENT FROM CORA O'CONNELL TO ISABELLA GONZALEZ AT 9:33 P.M.

I'm sorry for the way I dismissed you at the coffee shop. I've reconsidered your accusation of Jeremy spreading lies about Terrence based on something I've recently learned. Let's talk again. I want to help you.

CORA

9:50 p.m.

Cora was speeding down 1-72 toward Ravendale. Something had happened at the Madsens', and she wasn't sure what because her mother had been so infuriatingly vague. And even though Cora presently despised her husband and his lies, she didn't want to leave him alone at the hospital. But if the detective wanted to speak with her, she couldn't well say no, not after what Sam had done to Mira. What if the detective wanted to investigate what had happened between them?

No. Police officers didn't investigate sexual advances. Mira wasn't a minor.

So what, then?

At the hospital, Sam had become so agitated that the doctor sedated him, and she told Cora he needed to sleep now and that it was completely fine for her to leave for a few hours, or even overnight, which was the exact opposite of what she'd told Cora earlier in the night before she realized her presence would be so upsetting.

Cora gripped the steering wheel tighter. She hated driving at night, always imagining her sister's fate when she saw the black forest edging up against the road. She navigated a sharp turn, and then she pictured Sam on the night of their engagement party, the way he'd wanted more booze, more food, *more, more, more*, and she imagined Maggie, laughing as Sam and Jeremy convinced her to go into town, too, like it was some great adventure.

Cora pressed the accelerator hard. She sped past Buzzed, The Sweat Box, The Bumble Bee, and then down Ward Hill toward her house. A light rain had started to fall, making the dirt road even harder to navigate. She avoided the potholes from memory and turned on Crawford Farm. How had all of this happened tonight? How was her husband lying in a hospital bed? How had he done that with the babysitter? How had he kept such a murderous secret about her sister? And what was next? Call the cops and turn him in? What was she supposed to do?

The car rounded a bend, and Cora saw police lights. She held her breath until the Madsens' house came into view. Blue-and-red flashing lights illuminated cop cars and dozens of officers, and Cora's heart pounded at the sight of crime scene tape. Her hands shook against the wheel as she parked next to the Madsens' mailbox. Up the driveway she ran, stopping at the yellow tape. She could just make out her mom sitting next to Anna and Mira on the front steps. "What happened?" Cora called out to them, but she was intercepted by a police officer with *Lisa Hoxie* emblazoned on a name tag. "I'm here to see Detective DeFosse," Cora said, and the woman lifted the tape for Cora to pass.

"Stay here," she barked. "Your name please?"

"Cora O'Connell."

The woman took off into the house. Cora tried to get her mother's attention, but she was so busy comforting Anna and Mira that she didn't see her. What the *hell* was going on inside that house?

Detective DeFosse emerged and came toward Cora. "Mrs. O'Connell," he said. "There's been an accident. Laurel Madsen was shot tonight."

Cora's hands flew to cover her face.

"She's at Westchester General as we speak. I'm not aware of her condition, but it wasn't promising when she left here. I'd like to speak to you about the relationship between Laurel and Dash Madsen."

The sound of blood filled Cora's ears. The detective kept talking, and Cora tried so hard to make out what he was saying, something about how he knew she was a friend of Laurel's and how he was *deeply sorry* to be the bearer of this news. So many people had said they were sorry to Cora over the past decade: her father when he ran off with Abby; the entirety of Ravendale when they learned of Maggie's death; and now her husband, for kissing their babysitter and killing her sister.

"What happened to her?" she asked, her voice robotic, unfamiliar.

"That's where I need your help, and the help of anyone you know who was close to Laurel."

Close to Laurel. Did Cora know anyone close to Laurel? She scanned her brain through the various mothers she'd seen with Laurel over the two years they'd lived in Ravendale. There was no one special, no one who jumped out as Laurel's close friend. Cora saw Laurel socializing at parties and functions, but wasn't that so different than deep friendship? Laurel was always so *on* at social gatherings that Cora had just assumed she had an army of friends. But other than the white car, there wasn't a mark of a friend who always stopped by to visit. How had Cora not noticed that before?

"There's a visitor Laurel entertains every month or two," Cora said, a damp breeze tossing her hair. "A tall brunette woman who drives a white sedan—an Audi, maybe? Connecticut plates."

The detective nodded. "Any idea who she is?"

Cora shook her head.

"And when did you see her last?"

"Yesterday evening at the end of the party. She pulled into the Madsens' driveway around five thirty."

"I'd like to bring you down to the station with Laurel's daughters," the detective said. "Asher Finch and Dash Madsen are already there, and I'd like statements from all of you about what happened in your home tonight, and anything you may know about the Madsens."

Anything you may know about the Madsens . . .

"Was it Dash who did it?" Cora asked, her voice incredulous. She remembered the fundraiser that morning, and the thumb-size imprint on Laurel's neck, the one she'd covered up so quickly. An image of Dash lunging across her kitchen to attack Sam played through her mind, and then she thought of Sam kissing Mira, and it nearly made her sick, until she reminded herself it wasn't even the worst of what Sam had done; he'd driven her sister fifty miles an hour into a dark line of trees, and then he and Jeremy had lifted Maggie's dead body and arranged it into a lie. Cora thought of her babies, and the way their father's secret covered all of them now, and then there was that feeling again, that sharpness she'd felt earlier that evening when the detective was questioning Sam, the dawning realization that she was so incredibly awake and alive.

"I think I do know things," Cora said softly, almost to herself, and a flicker of something unreadable passed over the detective's face. "And I'll help however I can."

The detective nodded. "Wait with Mira and Anna on the porch," he said, "and don't enter the house. I'll let you all know when it's time to depart." He led Cora to the spot on the porch where Sarah sat with Laurel's daughters. Mira's beautiful face was puffed and stained with tears.

"Girls," Cora said, exchanging a glance with Sarah as she knelt in front of them. "I'm so sorry about what happened to your mom. I'm sure she's in the best hands. I'm sure she'll be okay!"

The girls stared up at her. Cora cursed herself. Why was she lying? Laurel could be dead before morning or forever changed. Hadn't there been enough lies already between all of them?

Mira's eyes were steady as she met Cora's gaze. Cora would have expected her to look away, or bolt, even. After what had happened with Dash and Sam, Mira had to know that Cora knew everything. But instead, Mira looked Cora straight in the eye. Moonlight cut between the leaves of a large oak tree above their heads, giving Mira's skin a patchy glow. "I'm sorry, Mrs. O'Connell. I'm so sorry for what I did. I never, ever should have slept with your husband."

JADE

9:52 p.m.

Jade was downstairs in Cora's kitchen, staring out the French doors onto the scene unfolding at the Madsens'. The police lights still flashed, but Jade couldn't see clearly enough to make out what was happening. She'd texted Sarah and Cora for an update but hadn't heard back. And of course she wanted to go over there, but she knew Cora would have a heart attack if she left Lucy and George alone in the house, even sound asleep.

The doorbell rang, and Jade jumped. Who would ring a bell at this time of night? They could wake the babies!

Jade crept through the downstairs and stared through the peephole. *Jeremy.* Hours ago, she'd left him a voice mail about Sam being in the hospital, but she'd ignored his calls after learning what he'd done. Now she flung open the door, mostly because she was afraid he'd ring the bell again.

"Where the fuck have you been?" he demanded, but Jade didn't answer him right away. She stared at him with everything she now knew, expecting him to somehow look different. But he didn't. "I've been calling you all night, Jade," he said.

He seemed so big standing there, so entirely capable of hurting Maggie.

"Were you worried?" Jade finally asked, and then she smiled. She knew it was a bizarre reaction, but it was there; she could feel it: a smug smile had descended on her face, and she couldn't seem to wipe it off.

"Of course I was worried. What's wrong with you?"

Jade took a breath. "Maggie's dead. I think that's what's been wrong with me for the past six years."

Jeremy shook his head, staring at her like she'd lost her mind. Maybe she had. "Let me in," he said.

"I'm actually done doing anything you want," Jade said, feeling her feet against the floor, steadying herself.

"Jade—"

"I know what you did to Maggie," she said, her heart pounding. Jeremy's features folded, as though a string had pulled them down.

"What are you talking about?" he asked, his voice low.

"I know Sam was driving the car that night. And I know that after he crashed it, you both moved Maggie into the driver's seat."

"And who told you this?" Jeremy snarled, his face so dark it was nearly unrecognizable.

"*Sam.* He told all of us. Me, Cora, Sarah."

"You don't know what you're saying," Jeremy said, moving toward her.

"Really?" Jade asked. "You're a *liar.* You lied to all of us. And your lies hurt us, and they hurt Maggie. The truth is going to come out now, Jeremy, it has to, and it *should.*"

Jeremy came closer, but Jade blocked the doorway.

"The babies are sleeping. Please go home!" She was suddenly crying, her emotions entirely out of her control.

"Let me in," Jeremy said.

"Maggie was my girlfriend," Jade blurted, and she stopped crying. She wanted to shout it for the entire neighborhood to hear. "We were in love. Did you know that?"

Jeremy's entire disposition changed. "Really?" he asked, barking a sarcastic laugh. "You're *gay*?"

Gay. Bisexual. Straight. Jade didn't need a word to define a fluid feeling.

They stared at each other. When Jade didn't say anything, Jeremy let out a grunt that was maybe supposed to be another laugh. His features had transformed again, and Jade had never seen this particular look on his face.

"Why don't you enlighten me, Jeremy," Jade started, dizzy with the force of what she was saying. "Why don't you tell me exactly how and why you and Sam moved Maggie's dead body into the driver's seat so she could take the fall for her death?"

"Keep your voice down," Jeremy growled. "I don't need the neighborhood to hear Sam's deathbed confession, okay?"

"Sam's not dying," Jade said. "He's plenty capable of telling the whole world what happened with Maggie."

"And that's what we should talk about," Jeremy said coolly. "Now let me inside the house." His voice was controlled, but Jade heard the fear beneath his words. He pushed past her, and Jade saw a streak of mud across his otherwise-pristine sneakers. She shut the door behind them, and they stood face-to-face in the foyer. "Where are Sarah and Cora?" Jeremy asked.

"I don't know," Jade lied.

"You need to make them keep their mouths shut, and you need to convince them to make Sam do the same," he said.

"Why would I ever do that?" Jade asked.

"I didn't kill Maggie," Jeremy said. "Sam did." Jade swallowed, surprised. They usually had each other's backs. "My work is a business of *image*," Jeremy went on. "Do you understand that? If this gets out, Sam will be tried in court, and I'll be charged and tried, too, and our lives will be ruined. Is that what you want? Me in jail? Or if not in jail, the bad publicity and I lose all my clients? Are you going to pay for your lifestyle with your bullshit forty-thousand-dollars-a-year jewelry business?"

"Do you seriously think I'm worried about money right now?" Jade asked.

"You should be," Jeremy said. "You should be worried about your future, Jade—yours and mine."

"So many lies," Jade said, "and look where they've gotten us. Your sperm is probably fine, by the way. I've been taking birth control pills this whole time."

"What the *fuck*?" Jeremy spat, his jaw loosening, his mouth dropping an inch.

"You're not really one to judge right now, are you?" she asked.

Jeremy folded his broad arms over his chest. "You're a liar, too, then," he said.

"I am," Jade said, feeling the sting of words she already knew to be true. Emotion rose inside her chest, and she tried to channel Sarah's calm. *Grace under pressure,* wasn't that what she'd seen Sarah do, over and over again? Jade stared at her husband and asked herself what she really wanted. She was about to tell him they were over, if he hadn't already figured that out, and she didn't want him to beg for her to stay, because that would only make it worse; plus, she suspected he didn't have that in him. More likely, he'd give her anything she wanted to keep her mouth shut. She thought about her house, and how she'd ask for that, of course, and then, inexplicably, she thought of Terrence Washington on her porch today, holding that envelope and looking at her with pleading brown eyes.

"I want you to back off Terrence," Jade said. "I want you to stop telling people he had an accident because he was on drugs. I want you to find him a job, which we both know you can do."

"Why do you give a shit about Terrence?"

"Because he's a good person as far as I can tell. Or at least better than you and I have been lately."

Jeremy was smart enough to know she had the power to make all of this worse or better for him.

"I can't be your wife anymore, you must know that," Jade said, and even as she watched the muscles in Jeremy's body tighten, she felt sure of herself. "And I want to live in our house," she said. "I want you to sign it over to me." The mortgage was already paid off, and they could easily afford to purchase another home for him. "And you need to move out. And if Sam comes forward like you say he will, if there's a trial, I can't protect you."

Jeremy's hands curled into fists. "You can't *protect* me? You're my *wife*!" He looked at her, disbelieving. "I would do anything for you," he said, but he had to know that wasn't true. He cleared his throat and tried again. "I would lie for you in a second, Jade," he said, as if that were the ultimate declaration of love.

"I know you would," Jade said. "But this is Maggie we're talking about, and Sarah and Cora, too. They're my family."

"I'm your family," Jeremy said.

"Not anymore," Jade said, her voice choked.

Jeremy looked as though she'd slapped him. "So this is it? We're over, just like that?"

Jade nodded. "We're over," she said.

"You're cruel," Jeremy said.

"Maybe I am," Jade said, her voice coarse and tired. But what other choice had he left her? Any other decision would be a betrayal of Maggie, and of herself.

Jeremy stood blinking, and then he shook his head gently. He opened the door and moved onto the stone path, winding his way toward the car.

Jade's tears came faster as she watched him climb inside. They didn't have children; they shared only finances. Once those were squared away, could they uncouple seamlessly, as though the years together had been nothing more than a fleeting mistake?

Maybe.

The ignition roared to life, and Jade watched her husband back down the driveway. She wiped away her tears, praying to forget him and all the ways she'd loved him, and to start fresh, hoping she had the strength to do those things alone. She pushed a dark lock of hair from her face. She'd lost before, and she'd survived.

"Goodbye, Jeremy," she said, her voice a whisper.

CORA

9:59 p.m.

Mira," Cora said carefully, "what did you just say?"

Mira's eyes widened. She exchanged a glance with her sister, but it was too late. She'd said it: she'd told the truth. Cora saw it on her face. Mira's mom lay dying somewhere, and now wasn't exactly the time to spin a lie.

"I said I shouldn't have slept with him," Mira whispered.

Cora looked up at her mother. Sarah's face was stone still, her blue eyes hard. She gave Cora a small nod, but Cora wasn't sure what she meant by it. Should she go on asking Mira questions? Maybe about how many times she and Sam had slept together? Did it matter?

"When? When did it happen, Mira? And where?" Cora asked.

Mira held Cora's gaze. How was she even able to do that? Cora thought of herself at twenty-one, obsessing over her grades at Vanderbilt to be sure they were good enough for grad school. Not that she'd been perfect, but sleeping with a thirtysomething father of two?

The rage Cora felt for Sam was blinding. She needed to forget him—for now, forever—and she needed to know what had happened so she could do it. "How many times, Mira, start there," Cora said to Mira's bewildered gaze.

"Once," Mira said. "And then he said it was a mistake and that it couldn't happen ever again, and he made me promise I wouldn't tell anyone, and I didn't!"

The way Mira said it made Cora go cold. It was like Mira was still tied to him, like she was devoted to keeping his secret. How could he do this to her? She was so young!

"Where?" Cora asked carefully, catching sight of her mother, who still had a hand on Anna's shoulder. "Where did it happen?"

"In your house," Mira said.

"In our *bed*?"

"No!" Mira said. "On the stairs."

"On the *stairs*? The secret fucking staircase?" Cora thought she would lose it entirely, but then Mira burst into tears, and Cora got herself under control. What did it matter, anyway? "I don't get it, Mira. I'm always freaking home. How did this even happen?"

Mira swallowed. "You were at the grocery store and Sam texted me. He said he needed me to babysit. He said you were at Whole Foods and he needed to go somewhere. So I came over."

Cora's heart lurched with exactly what this meant. *"You did it while my kids were in the house?"*

"They were in their cribs!" Mira said, and this time Anna started crying.

Cora turned to Sarah, and the look she saw on her mother's face mirrored the one she had worn the year after Clark left. Cora recognized it for what it was then and now: *rage and despair.*

Cora let go of a long breath. She would take the kids to her mother's house. Jeremy could take care of Sam when he left the hospital and help him pack his things.

"I'm going to check on the twins," Sarah said, standing.

As Cora watched her mother duck beneath the yellow tape and cross the lawn, she felt the chill again, her skin prickling beneath a sweep of cold across her neck.

LAUREL

10:01 p.m.

Laurel's eyes fluttered open. Her vision doubled, the room stretching apart like taffy until she saw it evenly split. She turned to see an IV inside a vein in her arm, taped expertly against her skin. Her bare feet poked out at the end of the bed beneath the white sheets. A hospital . . . she was there because . . .

She wasn't sure why she was there. But she was okay. She thought she was okay. Where were the girls? Were they here, too?

She closed her eyes and slipped back into sleep, dreaming of the summer she and Dash had taken Mira to a beach in Westport. Mira had been a baby, and Laurel had been lathering her smooth skin with SPF 50 nearly every twenty minutes. Dash smiled at her and Mira, delighted by their company, but then the dream took a turn when Dash stood to his towering height and blocked out the sun. Everything in Laurel's world went dark, and everything that she had been meant to enjoy—the day, her daughter, her safety—was shadowed by this giant of a man raising his hand to strike.

RAVENDALE POLICE DEPARTMENT

INTERVIEW OF DASH MADSEN, CONDUCTED BY DETECTIVE MARK DEFOSSE

Detective Mark DeFosse: *Why don't you tell me how your wife was shot, in your own words.*

Dash Madsen: *What happened tonight was a tragedy.*

Detective Mark DeFosse: *I'm not asking you to give a eulogy. She's not dead, you realize that? And if she does die, I'm actually hoping to have you imprisoned by the day of the funeral. What I'm asking is that you recount exactly what led to the shooting of your wife.*

Dash Madsen: *It appears you're incredibly deluded about what happened tonight, Detective. I loved my wife, Laurel, very much. Unfortunately, she's always had dark moods. I took her to therapy years ago to try to fix her problems, but it didn't work. She refused to even try. After the trauma of tonight, after I did what I did to Sam O'Connell, something in Laurel snapped. She was screaming about how our family would be the talk of the town now. Laurel was very concerned what other people thought. She thought I'd ruined our life here in Ravendale, and I tried to console her that people would forgive us, but she was crazed. I had absolutely no idea she owned a gun before I saw it in the O'Connells' kitchen tonight, and that right there shows her state of mind—keeping a loaded gun in a house with children. When Laurel reached for the gun, I knew she was going to try to kill herself, and I did everything I could to stop it. I grabbed the gun just as she was trying to shoot herself, and it went off. You know what happened next. I called the police, but I had a hard time stopping the bleeding, and I imagine she sustained severe internal injuries.*

Detective Mark DeFosse: *Really? Is that your professional opinion?*

Dash Madsen: *Yes, actually, it is.*

Detective Mark DeFosse: *Neighbors say they saw a white sedan with Connecticut plates visit your house quite often. Mind telling me who the visitor is? I'd like to speak with her.*

Dash Madsen: *I have no idea who you're talking about. Laurel has plenty of friends she entertains whom I've never met.*

Detective Mark DeFosse: *I believe you were home when the woman visited, let's see, around five thirty p.m. last night.*

Dash Madsen: *I'd like to speak with a lawyer now.*

Detective Mark DeFosse: *I figured you'd say that. Did you know your wife and I were romantically involved?*

Dash Madsen: *Excuse me?*

Detective Mark DeFosse: *Yes, we were actually quite serious for a few years there in high school.*

Dash Madsen: *She didn't mention that.*

Detective Mark DeFosse: *Funny, I don't remember her ever having dark moods at all.*

RAVENDALE POLICE DEPARTMENT

INTERVIEW OF MIRA MADSEN, CONDUCTED BY DETECTIVE MARK DEFOSSE

Detective Mark DeFosse: *Mira, I'd like to start by saying I'm very sorry for what happened to your mother tonight.*

Mira Madsen: *I need to go to her. I need to get to the hospital.*

Detective Mark DeFosse: *You'll be taken there shortly. I'm just going to ask you to recount what happened tonight, but first I'd like to ask you something very important, something I think you'll be able to help me with. I'd like to ask if you have any reason to suspect your father would hurt your mother.*

Mira Madsen: *No. I don't. Of course not.*

Detective Mark DeFosse: *When your mother came to see me yesterday afternoon, when she thought you were missing, I noticed a bruise on her neck. She was trying to cover it up with a scarf. Did you ever see or suspect that your father hurt your mother?*

Mira Madsen: *No! God. You want to lock my dad up, do you? So I have no parents at all if my mom dies? Where would I go?*

Detective Mark DeFosse: *You and Anna are both over eighteen. You would go to college. So let me ask you this in a different way: Do you think your dad could have tried to shoot your mother tonight?*

Mira Madsen: *I absolutely do not.*

Detective Mark DeFosse: *Okay. Well, it's certainly interesting, because Asher Finch, in his recounting of what happened tonight, said that he heard an argument in progress when he opened the door. Your father's body was blocking his view of the gun, and all Asher can remember is it going off, not who was holding it. When you and Anna returned to your home to find your mother on the floor, Asher said that your father pulled you aside to talk with you privately, and that the ambulance came as you were huddled in a corner of the living room, crying as your father spoke with you. I have this funny sense that your dad was warning you not to tell me something. Am I right, Mira?*

Mira Madsen: *No, you're not.*

Detective Mark DeFosse: *Okay, so let me see here, then you must agree with your father's story, which is that your mother was trying to kill herself. Do you believe your mother would try to kill herself, Mira?*

Mira Madsen: *No, absolutely not! It must have been some kind of accident. She was our mother! She would never do anything that would take her away from us.*

RAVENDALE POLICE DEPARTMENT

INTERVIEW OF CORA O'CONNELL, CONDUCTED BY DETECTIVE MARK DEFOSSE

Detective Mark DeFosse: *I'd like to show you photographs of the victim taken on Crawford Farm Road nearly one hour ago, when our officers arrived on the scene after a nine-one-one call. These images are graphic, and you should brace yourself for what you are about to see.*

Cora O'Connell: *I understand.*

Detective Mark DeFosse: *Do you, Mrs. O'Connell? That's good, really good, actually, because all of us here at the department are very much hoping you can help us sort out what happened tonight.*

Cora O'Connell: *I'll try my best to help, of course I will.*

Detective Mark DeFosse: *Do you need a tissue, Mrs. O'Connell? Here, please take a tissue. I'm sure this must be very hard for you.*

Cora O'Connell: *These are, oh God, these are awful.*

Detective Mark DeFosse: *They are, indeed.*

Cora O'Connell: *And her girls? You didn't show them these pictures.*

Detective Mark DeFosse: *I didn't need to. They saw their mother. Now, Mrs. O'Connell, this part is very important. Dr. Madsen is claiming that Laurel was so incredibly upset by him hurting your husband, and that her concern was so great that news of the incident between Sam and Mira, and consequently Dash's attack of Sam, would spread through Ravendale, that she attempted to take her own life. Dr. Madsen also claims that he tried to stop her, and in doing so, a gun fired accidentally.*

Cora O'Connell: *No! That can't be right. Not over something like this. She wouldn't.*

Detective Mark DeFosse: *I can't charge Dash Madsen without motive. Do you have any reason to think Dash Madsen might have hurt his wife tonight? Because, you see, it looks like Laurel Madsen is going to survive. And that means it will be her word against his. Dr. Madsen is a respected doctor and a pillar of the Ravendale community. That doesn't usually play well for the victim. Now, if a friend of Laurel's—or, even better, two friends, or, say, a therapist and a friend, or any such combination—could corroborate what I imagine Laurel's story will be, that her husband had a pattern of violence . . .*

Cora O'Connell: *There was a bruise on her neck this morning, before all of this happened.*

Detective Mark DeFosse: *We have techs who can identify when Laurel received the bruise, if she's willing to be examined. But likely, in a situation like this one, Dr. Madsen will claim that Laurel sustained the injury elsewhere, either at her own hands or at the hands of an extramarital affair. Perpetrators of domestic violence rarely admit to what they've done. Did Laurel say anything about the bruise, where she got it?*

Cora O'Connell: *She told me she got it in a boxing class.*

Detective Mark DeFosse: *And did you believe her?*

Cora O'Connell: *No, I didn't, not at all. She acted very strangely when I asked her if she was okay, and she was very evasive about the bruise. She covered it up quickly, as though she didn't want me or anyone else to see it. She behaved like someone who'd been purposely hurt, and if I hadn't been so buried in everything that was going on with my family, between Mira and Sam, with everything I read in that notebook you've already seen, then I would have been a better friend. I would have pushed further, tried to get to the bottom of it. Because something absolutely wasn't right.*

Detective Mark DeFosse: *And are you willing to testify to this under oath?*

Cora O'Connell: *Yes. I'd do anything to clear the name of someone wrongly accused of attempting to cause her own death.*

Detective Mark DeFosse: *If there's anyone or anything else you can think of . . .*

Cora O'Connell: *Asher Finch, the Madsens' neighbor. Have you spoken to him?*

Detective Mark DeFosse: *Yes, I have.*

Cora O'Connell: *And has he been forthcoming?*

Detective Mark DeFosse: *He has not.*

Cora O'Connell: *Asher Finch has been watching Laurel and Dash—maybe all of us, actually—for a very long time. He gets away with it because he's lounging in his own yard, and he's young, and it seems harmless. But I know he has a view into the Madsens' bedroom windows, and I've often seen him staring into them. I'd bet my life he's seen something. If you press hard on him, I have a feeling he'll come clean.*

Detective Mark DeFosse: *Thank you, Mrs. O'Connell. You've been extremely helpful. You're free to go; I'm sure you're eager to get back to the hospital.*

SARAH

11:04 p.m.

Sarah drove to the hospital. It felt like being in a trance, as though the entire drive were a single breath drawn and held tight against her chest. When she arrived, she walked into the ER just as she'd done earlier that night, but this time, she didn't sit and wait. The time for waiting felt long gone. "I'm a visitor for Sam O'Connell," she said to the receptionist. "I'm family, and I know it's past visiting hours, but I have permission from the doctor to stay in his room until my daughter can return."

The receptionist scanned a computer. "He's been moved out of the ER. You'll need to take the west bank of elevators to the third floor, room 302."

Sarah followed the receptionist's instructions, tapping the button for the elevator. She thought about Clark, about the phone call she needed to make telling him about what had really happened to their daughter, and then she imagined Sam's face, and what he'd say when he saw her. She practiced everything she would say to him: *How could you do this to Cora? How could you do this to Maggie? How could you take my daughter from me, and then be complicit in framing her and keeping the truth from my family for so many years?* To Sarah, Jeremy was nearly a stranger, a person she tolerated but with whom she'd never grown close, or even trusted. Sam was her *family*. He was the father of George and Lucy. So how could he betray them like this?

The elevator doors opened and Sarah stepped inside. Images paraded through her mind as the elevator climbed: Maggie, four years old, holding out a bouquet of freshly planted daffodils, a mischievous look on her face as though she knew she wasn't supposed to pick flowers from her mother's carefully curated garden; and then again on the first day of kindergarten, Maggie wearing Cora's denim skirt, her wave tentative as she climbed the stairs to board the bus. Sarah felt the swell of emotion like it was yesterday, seeing in her mind's eye Maggie carefully navigating the school bus under Cora's protective care. Sarah had cried that morning when she'd returned to an empty house. And now, wasn't an empty house all she had?

No, not true: she had Cora, Lucy, and George, and she'd work harder at those relationships, making them count.

The elevator opened and Sarah stepped onto the third floor. She passed a nurses' station confidently, as though she were merely returning from a coffee break to sit vigil by her son-in-law's bedside. She pushed through swinging doors and moved toward Sam's room, opening the door and closing it carefully behind her until she heard a *click*. Sam lay on crisp white sheets, his eyes shut. Sarah hadn't imagined he'd be sleeping. Now what? Would he hear her?

She lowered herself until her lips were close to Sam's ear. "You killed my daughter," she said. She thought of Lucy and George running across the grass at their birthday party just yesterday, and it gave her pause. But then she thought of Maggie, the blood across her face, smeared over the party dress they'd picked out together: a beautiful white eyelet cocktail dress with lilac stripes. "And you disgraced her dead body." Sarah stared at Sam's placid face, overcome with fury and helplessness. "Wake up, Sam," she begged, tears rolling over her cheeks. What was *wrong* with him? How could he lie there like that, so peaceful, after everything he'd done to her? "Wake up!" she shouted, but he wouldn't, and Sarah began to feel every ounce of the control she'd maintained for six years start to slip away. "Someone, help me," she said beneath her breath, crying harder. "God, please." Sam stirred, and his eyes fluttered open and then closed again. Sarah tried to stand, but her legs felt too weak. She needed to get back to Cora. She needed to see someone real—someone who was true and loyal and alive and hers. Sam stirred again, and this time it seemed he was waking up; he mumbled and opened his eyes again, blinking at her.

"Sarah," he said, his voice rough and cracked. But then his eyes shut. Sarah tried again to stand, and when she was on her feet, the door swung open. She expected a nurse, but instead Jeremy emerged. He went still beneath her gaze.

"Sarah," Jeremy said, his voice heavy. The door shut, and he walked slowly toward her.

A shuffle sounded behind Sarah, and she turned to see Sam trying to sit up. Blood flecked the white bandages covering his head. *"Maggie,"* he said, and Jeremy's body went still.

Sarah swallowed, suddenly terrified.

"We did it to her," Sam said to Jeremy.

Jeremy arched forward like he was about to pounce, and Sarah watched them, seeing a hologram of what they'd done together.

"I killed her," Sam said to Sarah, working hard to push himself into a sitting position. Watching him fall back was like watching an infant flop back against pillows. "It's over," he said to Jeremy. "They know what we did. They know we framed her. Now we need to make it right, okay, man?" He sounded stoned, high on whatever medication they'd given him.

Jeremy turned to look at Sarah, his eyes flashing. "Sarah, you need to keep him quiet, you know that, right? It's the only way to protect George and Lucy." His voice was like butter, as though his number-one concern was truly the children. He stared at her, waiting for her to agree. But she couldn't. "Sarah," Jeremy said, even softer this time, "you need to keep quiet *for your family's sake*."

"You think I need to keep quiet about my dead daughter *for my family's sake*?" Red-hot anger burned through Sarah's limbs. Sam thrashed beneath the sheets and then went still again. He mumbled something indecipherable, but Sarah and Jeremy ignored him. "What about what *you* did?" Sarah asked Jeremy, backing up until her legs hit the hospital bed. "You moved my baby's dead body. You picked her up and curled her fingers around the steering wheel. You can't possibly think you should get away with what you've done."

"Sam's life would have been over if we didn't do what we did," Jeremy said. "Cora wouldn't have a husband, and you wouldn't have your grandchildren."

The air felt like it was full of knives. "You don't decide those things for me, no matter what you think I might have lost," Sarah spat.

"She was already *dead*," Jeremy said, and it was in that moment, hearing the words from a mouth unfit to speak about Maggie, that an even darker thought slipped into Sarah's splintering mind.

"Do you know that for sure?" she asked. "You could have killed her by moving her body!"

Jeremy blanched. Had he really never thought of that?

Sarah felt herself crack, and she flew at Jeremy. She raised her arms, her hands flailing wildly. She felt her nails connect with his cheek and then something wet—blood? "You bastard!" she screamed, and she fought to keep hitting him, but he easily caught her. Instead of fending her off, he pulled her close, tight against his chest. He squeezed so hard she could barely breathe. "Let me go!" she screamed into the dark fabric of his jacket. Was he trying to crush her, to scare her into not telling what he'd done? "I mean it!" she cried, her voice muffled. She squirmed and tried to pound against his chest. "Let me go!" she tried again, managing to turn her head. The call button was so close . . . she could almost reach it . . .

"I'm sorry," Jeremy said.

Was he going to kill her? It was so hard to breathe like this. The room felt like it was spinning, and then Jeremy rearranged his hold on her, and said, "I'm sorry for what I did to Maggie," and Sarah realized with a sinking sensation that his grip was meant to be an embrace. She went still against him, never expecting him to apologize.

"Get your hands off of me," Sarah growled.

Jeremy released her. Tears blurred Sarah's vision as she stumbled across the room and flung open the door. It clicked shut behind her, and she was determined to race from the hospital, to get as far away as possible from the two men who had hurt her daughter, when suddenly she couldn't move. She felt pulled toward Sam's hospital room like a magnet. She backed up against the wall just outside the door, her breathing shallow. She tried again to step forward, but she felt frozen, literally, as though a deep chill coursed through her limbs. She wanted to call for someone to help her, but there was no one around. It was nearly midnight. She'd never been inside a hospital at midnight except when she'd delivered the girls, and the hallways were far too quiet.

A low, urgent voice came from inside Sam's room. Sarah peered through the pane of glass and saw Jeremy's face contorted into a mask of rage.

Sam started shouting, but it was garbled, and Sarah couldn't make out what he was saying. Jeremy leaned in and furiously said something in reply, and then Sam, out of nowhere, slung his fist and tried to strike Jeremy, but his movements were far too clumsy and he didn't come close to landing a punch. Jeremy stepped back, and his face went still. Gone were the furrowed eyebrows and the drawn features, and in their place was an even more terrifying version of Jeremy. It was as though an eerie calm had descended upon him.

Sarah's hands went slowly to her face. She felt like she was burning up with a fever, and she tried to make her thoughts go straight. If Sam wasn't alive, there was no case against Jeremy; there was only conjecture:

three bereaved women blaming a man for Maggie's death six years after the fact, based on something they swore a dead man told them. Without Sam, it would be only Jade's, Cora's, and Sarah's word against Jeremy.

Jeremy was a smart man. He must have realized this, too.

Sam, seemingly exhausted by the effort of trying to hurt Jeremy, closed his eyes again.

Jeremy stepped forward and grabbed a pillow from Sam's bed.

Sam. Her son-in-law. Sarah imagined every hour she'd spent being civil—*friendly*, even—to her daughter's killer. How many thousands of moments had they spent carrying on like nothing evil had happened? She used to feel sorry for Sam for being one of Maggie's passengers! Truly, she felt almost *guilty* about it, like she owed him an apology for the tragedy Maggie had caused.

Sarah dug her nails into her palms as Jeremy brought the pillow closer to Sam's face and then covered his nose and mouth. Sam squirmed beneath the pillow, but his movements were so medicated and weak it was futile.

Sarah put her hand on the door handle. She should open it—she had to open it. And yet . . .

Her lungs needed to scream and cry, but she couldn't seem to make a sound. Is this what Jeremy thought he felt in the room with Sam now? Betrayed by the person he thought would keep his secret?

He couldn't know betrayal like Sarah did.

Sarah shook her head, mildly aware she was losing control. Jeremy thought he had everything to lose if Sam lived to open his mouth, but Sarah had already lost everything.

Jeremy kept the pillow pressed tightly against Sam's face.

George and Lucy.

The children floated through her mind. Sarah lifted her hand to pound on the door, to stop Jeremy—*George with Cora and Maggie's nose; Lucy with Maggie's dark, almond-shaped eyes*—but then Lucy's face quickly transformed into Maggie's, and Sarah saw Maggie as a baby, staring up at her with a peaceful expression, believing her mother would always keep her safe.

Come back to me, baby.

All the helplessness Sarah had felt after the accident flooded back, and her whole body shook as she found her phone in her pocket. She pulled up the camera. The most recent video—the one she'd sent herself of Maggie, age eleven months, just learning to walk across a soft carpet—was displayed in a tiny square at the bottom of the screen. She had the inane urge to watch it, but there wasn't time now. Maybe later—maybe tonight?

Yes. I'll watch you tonight, sweet girl. I'll be with you then.

Sarah lifted the phone and angled the lens through the pane of glass. She pressed record, and through the camera she watched Jeremy smother Sam with the bright-white pillow as Sam tried to struggle against him. She taped the rise and fall of Sam's chest for a few seconds until it started to stagger and slow. She could barely breathe, feeling as though her rational mind was slowly slipping away, feeling as though she could melt into the cracks of the hospital floor and go to sleep for a very long time, and then, if she were lucky, wake up in a world where Maggie was still alive.

"Mom?"

The voice sounded so far away. It sounded like Maggie's voice.

"Mom!"

It was one of Sarah's favorite words in the entire universe; it was the best thing she'd ever been called. Sarah turned slowly toward the sound and saw Cora coming down the hall toward her.

"What are you doing?" Cora asked, the words rising in pitch. "Why are you videotaping Sam's room?"

"Please forgive me, Cora, please, you have to forgive me," Sarah said, her words jumbling together. "I can't lose another daughter, please."

"What are you—is Sam okay?" Cora asked. She peered through the pane of glass into Sam's hospital room, and let out the loudest scream Sarah had ever heard from her.

Sarah put her head in her hands as Cora flung open the door. Cora's screams sounded from inside Sam's room, and a breath later, medical personnel came tearing down the hallway. Sarah shuddered at what she'd done, what she'd allowed to happen. She pressed her back against the wall and slid to the floor, her breath coming fast. A second later, the door flew open and Jeremy emerged, and he didn't look back at her as he raced from the room and took off down the hallway. Sarah watched his large, muscular form move through the swarm of nurses and doctors toward the elevators.

He thinks he's done it again. He thinks he's gotten away with another crime.

Not quite.

Sarah dialed 911. "My son-in-law was just assaulted inside Westchester General Hospital," she said. "Room 302. He's either dead or badly injured, please send the police!"

Cora was shouting Sam's name from inside the room as the doctors barked orders. Sarah needed to go help Cora, but first she had to make sure the video was crystal clear. Her wrist ached as she opened up her phone and pressed play. Tears streamed over her face, but as the video played on, she felt like she could take a full, deep breath for the first time in forever. It was evidence; she knew that much. Whether or not Sam died, Sarah had something concrete in her possession to prove Jeremy's propensity for evil, and it was likely the closest she'd ever get to redemption for Maggie. Now she just needed to pray Cora would forgive her for what she'd done.

Sarah watched Jeremy's muscles flex as he pressed the pillow harder against Sam's face, his perfect features easily identifiable: the gentle slope of his forehead; the tanned, flushed skin at his cheeks; the close-cut beard so in fashion these days. Truly, Jeremy should have been an actor. He looked even more handsome on film.

Sarah pressed stop and slid the phone into her pocket.

It was her favorite video yet.

EPILOGUE

CORA

One Year Later

Cora set a homemade cake covered with three blazing candles in front of George and Lucy on the patio table. They looked so big sitting in booster seats, their lips stained blue from the Popsicles Sarah had given them. It was hard to believe they were three years old today.

"Happy birthday to you!" Clark and Abby started them off, and then they were all singing. Lucy smiled shyly while George methodically removed a candy flower from the cake and popped it into his mouth.

Cora glanced at Sarah, spying the way she nervously checked her watch. *Any minute, Mom; he said he'd be here, and he will.*

"Happy birthday to you!"

It was overcast and only in the upper sixties—chilly for July. A breeze moved through the trees, and Cora locked on Sam's tired brown eyes. None of this was easy—they were officially separated—but it was certainly better than Lucy and George growing up without a father. Sam was sheepish as he returned Cora's stare. It was the look he often wore now, as though he were perpetually grateful to be alive and guilty for what he'd done. Cora's family decided not to press charges, but whisperings of the truth had filtered through Ravendale. How different things would have turned out if Cora had known what Sam had done, but every time her mind went there, she reminded herself that she wouldn't have her children if she'd known the truth all those years ago.

"Happy birthday, George and Lucy . . ."

Clark eyed Sam from his position at the opposite end of the table. Of all of them, Clark was the one who had the hardest time being in the same space as Sam. At least he wouldn't have to see Jeremy anytime soon. He was in prison for the next seven years, convicted of attempted murder. There was Sarah's video, of course, and then Terrence came forward with information on the illegal trade Jeremy had been working on, and even though it turned out Sam hadn't done anything criminal, he still knew what Jeremy had done, and Sam's lawyer argued that Jeremy's trying to keep him quiet had been premeditated.

George started scream-singing "Happy Birthday" along with his guests while Lucy watched the scene with a sly smile on her face. Jade laughed at George's antics as she bounced Natalie, the beautiful eight-month-old baby she'd adopted the month prior. Cora hadn't seen Jade so calm and happy since before Maggie died. Truly, Cora had never seen anyone take to motherhood the way Jade had, and Cora loved being around her and Natalie. George and Lucy adored Natalie, too; Lucy pretended she was her baby and dressed her up in doll clothes that barely fit. There were so many playdates now, and sometimes even Isabella joined them with her little seven-month-old daughter.

"Happy birthday to you!"

Laurel's voice rang out, and she was smiling. Cora realized how rarely she'd seen Laurel smile when she was still with Dash.

Sarah sidled up to George and Lucy and gave them gentle squeezes on their tiny shoulders. Lucy reached for Natalie, and Jade obliged by lowering her baby down for a kiss. "Is he still coming?" Jade asked Sarah.

"Any minute now," Sarah said, her voice a little higher-pitched than usual.

"Can you blow out your candles?" Cora asked her children. Lucy looked like she might cry—she'd been so sensitive lately. Really, ever since Sam had moved out, both George and Lucy were quicker to cry. Cora wished she could blame it on their age, but she knew why deep down. "Can I help you, Lucy?" she asked, and Sam came forward, too, and then all four of them were pursing their lips and blowing out the candles.

"Make a wish!" Laurel said, clapping. Her shimmery tank showed off the triceps she'd gained at the gym—sometimes she even convinced Cora to take her biweekly martial arts class. Mira didn't come to the party this year, of course. Cora barely saw her unless they ran into each other, and then she always seemed embarrassed and made excuses about why she had to hurry off somewhere. But Anna was there, standing close to her mother. She'd lost the pregnancy during her first trimester, and even though at first it seemed she might delay her start at NYU, she ended up going to New York City at the end of August, just as she'd planned. Dash was living in an apartment in Mount Pleasant, and so far Laurel seemed okay with how the divorce was proceeding. Ultimately Mira wasn't willing to testify against her father, and another therapist-type named Rachel, whom Laurel was very obscure about, wasn't able to testify against Dash due to client privilege. Asher Finch was the only one who came forward with information, but Laurel didn't want to put her girls and Asher through a trial. She cited the statistics to Cora, the ones that showed how shockingly low the conviction rates for domestic assault were. Laurel said her lawyer assured her there was still time to change her mind; if she wanted to ruin Dash's practice and name by charging him with assault, she could. But the problem for Laurel was that Dash was still her girls' father, and Laurel said she wanted to protect them above all else. So for now Dash was undergoing weekly therapy per a stipulation in their divorce proceedings, which didn't strike Cora as enough of a consequence, but she certainly wasn't about to judge her friend for her decisions. Their friendship had turned into something so much stronger than Cora ever could have imagined when they'd first become neighbors. She knew she'd be seeing a lot less of Laurel starting this fall, when Laurel returned to medical school, but they'd still have evenings and weekends to get together.

Cora sliced into the cake with a butter knife. "Who wants a piece?" she trilled. No matter what had happened last year, she somehow felt more settled. Maybe it was because the kids were a little older; maybe it was because her relationship with Sarah was closer than ever before; maybe it was because she finally knew the truth about her husband and her sister, as painful as it was.

Sarah helped Cora put the cake slices onto paper plates. The party was so much simpler this year. "Mom," Cora whispered, "he's here."

Sarah glanced up to see Grant Farridy striding across the grass, and Cora caught the smile on her mom's face. "Mr. Farridy!" Cora said, giving him a friendly wave. (She couldn't stop calling him Mr. Farridy, no matter how many times he told her to call him Grant.) He was wearing trousers and a light-blue polo shirt and holding a folder filled with papers.

Sarah quickly handed a piece of cake to Jade and then brushed off her hands on her white jeans. "I'd like you to meet someone," she said to Clark. Clark glanced up at Grant heading toward them.

"Everyone, this is Grant Farridy," Sarah said when he reached their group.

Cora furtively watched her father as she passed out plastic forks. She saw recognition flicker over her dad's face, and then he said, "Of course, Mr. Farridy."

Grant reached out his hand to shake Clark's. "Please call me Grant," he said warmly. "I'm not sure if you remember, but I taught Cora and Maggie English senior year of high school." He was clearly nervous, too. He and Sarah had met at physical therapy this year, and they'd been seeing each other, and he was so kind, and he made Sarah so happy, and Cora was thrilled that her mom was finally ready to bring him to a family event. Jade was watching Sarah, too, smiling as Natalie played with her rubber teething necklace. Cora and Jade both knew what this meant to Sarah.

Clark nodded. "I do remember," he said.

Grant gestured to the folder in his hands. "I hope you don't mind, but I've taken the liberty of printing out Maggie's essays and short stories from my class. She was a wonderful writer, as you know. And I thought you might like to read them."

Clark's eyes went glassy. He cleared his throat, and Abby put a hand on his arm. "Thank you, yes, I would. Very much," he said.

Grant passed the folder into Clark's hands. Clark gave him a grateful glance, and then Sarah blurted, "Who'd like some dessert?" and quickly resumed cutting the cake.

Cora smiled at Jade, who grinned back at her. "I miss Maggie," Jade whispered.

"Me, too," Cora said, reaching out to pat Natalie's sweet baby belly. She moved back to her mother's side to help. George and Lucy were happily eating icing with their fingers, grinning at each other like they couldn't believe their luck.

Cora and Sarah exchanged a glance. How different this year could be from the last one.

That night after what had happened in the hospital, Sarah had turned her recording of Jeremy over to the police right away, admitting exactly what she'd done—she said she wouldn't be a liar like Sam and Jeremy—but no law enforcement was willing to charge her for not entering a room where an assault was taking place. Sarah spent the following months profusely apologizing to Cora for not stopping Jeremy, but Cora assured her mom she understood perfectly. What would Cora do if it were Lucy who'd been hurt? She'd do anything to protect her, and would seek revenge if she couldn't.

She was a mother, too, after all.

ACKNOWLEDGMENTS

This book exists because my agent, Dan Mandel, encouraged me to write a suspense novel. After a decade of his steadfast guidance, words can't express how lucky I feel to work with someone I consider to be my family.

The awesome Carmen Johnson at Little A had a vision for *We Were Mothers* from our very first conversation, and her dedication never wavered. Thank you to Carmen for keen, no-nonsense editing that made this book much stronger. I am very excited to be working with someone so talented, and I can't wait to see what the future brings.

Thank you to everyone at Amazon who helped bring this book into the world: especially Michelle Hope Anderson, Merideth Mulroney, Daniel Byrne, and Lucy Silag. I feel very lucky to be one of your authors. Thank you to Elizabeth Shreve for her enthusiasm and publicity know-how.

Thank you to Kimberly Glyder for such a beautiful cover. Thank you to Jennifer Mullowney for an author photo shoot that came with so many laughs.

Thank you to every librarian and bookseller who has welcomed my family and me into your aisles. Thank you to Kristin Cacciapaglia, Roisin McGuire, Kirstin Zarras, Barbara Nasti, Elizabeth Fortune, Susan Ross, Lena Nurenberg, Patty Peterson, and Erin Joslyn for nurturing my sons' love of learning and reading.

Writing this book felt like an adventure, and the best part came when my mom-friends got involved. Thank you to my first reader, Sarah Webb, who made me think I really had something with this book. After her encouragement, I printed out more manuscripts, and suddenly my quiet town was rabidly reading handheld pages, calling me with all kinds of helpful feedback and enthusiasm that I will forever be grateful for. Thank you to early readers Sarah Mottl; Jesse Randol; Nina Levine; Chrissie Irwin; Michelle Kenny; Lindsay King; Alex White; Caroline Rodetis; Janine O'Dowd; Ali Tejtel; Brinn Daniels; Sarah Jenkins; Wendy Levey; Tracy Weiss; my sister, Meghan Sise; and my sister-in-law Ali Sise. And thank you to the awesome dads who read *We Were Mothers*, Davey Tejtel, Pete Kenny, and Roby Bhattacharyya (who read it *twice*!): you guys are rock stars.

So many thoughts on motherhood in this book are my own; so many are not. But I hope all of them felt authentic, and if they did, for that I have my friends to thank. I live in a community that supports mothers and children, where we feel safe to lean on each other and ask for help. This has made my family and me stronger, and I am forever grateful to every teacher, mother, and librarian in my town. I love being a mother here, and I have my community to thank for that.

Thank you to Liz Davis, counselor advocate at Women's Support Services in Sharon, Connecticut, who patiently answered my questions about sexual violence and about the varied nature of violence within relationships and marriages. She is reachable to any victim of violence at 860-634-1900.

Thank you to every woman who spoke with me about sexual violence she experienced during her lifetime. Those pages were very difficult to write, and any mistakes are mine. Thank you to Richard Sise for answering my questions about criminal law, and to Joan Miller for providing such helpful information about adoption agencies and the types of open house events like the one Jade attends in this book.

Over the past ten years, the following editors have shaped my writing, and I am very grateful: Alessandra Balzer, Kelsey Murphy, Brenda Bowen, Sara Sargent, Lanie Davis, and Jennifer Kasius. So many teachers encouraged my creative writing along the way, and I am thankful to Mrs. Harrison, Mr. Bedell, Mrs. Orr, Mrs. Kuthy, Mrs. Betro, and Dr. Danaher. Thank you to all of my teachers at the University of Notre Dame, especially Shannon Doyne, Siiri Scott, and Mark Pilkinton, who were strict with me—which I needed—and taught me the discipline necessary to pursue a creative life.

Thank you, thank you, *thank you* to every reader who purchased this book and spent time in its pages! Thank you to all the bloggers who helped spread the word about this book and my previous young adult novels. Thank you to good friends Linda Harrison, Bob Harrison, Caroline Moore, Jamie Greenberg, Erika Grevelding, Claire Noble, Megan Mazza, Kim Hoggatt, Tricia DeFosse, Jessica Bailey, Gabriela Hurtarte, Katelyn Butch, Stacia Cannon, Jenna Yankun, Dani Super, Yana Yelina, Kate Brochu, Maria Manger, Jen Singer, and to writers Fran Hauser, Noelle Hancock, Allison Yarrow, Anna Carey, Kimberly Rae Miller, Micol Ostow, Alecia Whitaker, Melissa Walker, Jen Calonita, and Kieran Scott. Thank you to Sydney Del Fico, Morgan Cartularo, Madison Cartularo, and Emily Bayuk: my family adores you.

I am very lucky to have parents and siblings who have supported my creativity ever since I first started writing stories as an eight-year-old. Thank you, Mom and Dad, for loving me and always reading every word I write, and thank you to my best friend and sister, Meghan, for making me laugh, and especially for her loyalty and friendship, and to my brother, Jack, who is a great support and sounding board, and whom I respect and love so much.

Thank you to the most incredible aunts, nieces, nephews, and in-laws anyone could ask for, especially Bill Sise, Angela Sise, Joan Miller, Posie Parker, Carole Sweeney, Ray Sweeney, Ali Sise, Christine Hawes, Tait Hawes, and to my partner in books and lengthy discussions about every topic we find interesting that no one else does: Roby Bhattacharyya.

My children are the absolute best thing that has ever happened to me. When I finished the first draft of *We Were Mothers*, I got the surprise of my life by becoming pregnant with twin girls. I can't wait to meet them. My sweet boys, Luke and William, and my husband, Brian, are the loves of my life. The biggest thank-you is for them.

ABOUT THE AUTHOR

Photo © 2018 Jennifer Mullowney

Katie Sise is a jewelry designer and television host. She is also the author of the young adult novels *The Academy*, *The Pretty App*, and *The Boyfriend App*, as well as the career guide *Creative Girl*. She lives with her family outside New York City. *We Were Mothers* is her first novel for adults. You can visit her online at www.katiesise.com.